IANTHE JE
THERE MAY BE

Ianthe Jerrold was born in 1898, the daughter of the well-known author and journalist Walter Jerrold, and granddaughter of the Victorian playwright Douglas Jerrold. She was the eldest of five sisters.

She published her first book, a work of verse, at the age of fifteen. This was the start of a long and prolific writing career characterized by numerous stylistic shifts. In 1929 she published the first of two classic and influential whodunits. *The Studio Crime* gained her immediate acceptance into the recently formed but highly prestigious Detection Club, and was followed a year later by *Dead Man's Quarry*.

Ianthe Jerrold subsequently moved on from pure whodunits to write novels ranging from romantic fiction to psychological thrillers. She continued writing and publishing her fiction into the 1970's. She died in 1977, twelve years after her husband George Menges. Their Elizabethan farmhouse Cwmmau was left to the National Trust.

Also by Ianthe Jerrold

IANTHE JERROLD

THERE MAY BE DANGER

With an introduction
by Curtis Evans

DEAN STREET PRESS

There May Be Danger, the second and final mystery novel that Ianthe Jerrold published under her Geraldine Bridgman pen name, appeared in 1948, eight years after the previous Bridgman mystery, *Let Him Lie*—a rather considerable fallow period for a working crime writer. *Let Him Lie* had been issued by William Heinemann, publisher of Margery Allingham and John Dickson Carr, but *There May Be Danger* was published by Aldus Publications, an intriguingly odd press owned by Francis Aldor (émigré Hungarian author Paul Tabori) that is best known for having produced an English translation of the purported diary of Eva Braun, mistress to Adolf Hitler, under the title *The Private Life of Adolf Hitler: The Intimate Notes and Diary of Eva Braun* (1949), which Charles Hamilton in *The Hitler Diaries: Fakes That Fooled the World* (1991) has described as "[o]ne of the most entertaining exercises in Führerian fiction."

Like Eva Braun's spurious diary, Ianthe Jerrold's *There May Be Danger* concerns dramatic events occurring during the Second World War. The novel takes place in the autumn of 1940, shortly after the Nazis commenced "the Blitz," their punishing strategic air bombing campaign, against England. Given that Jerrold's previous Geraldine Bridgman mystery was published in 1940 and set before the war, one is tempted to speculate that the author may have originally composed *There May Be Danger* later that year, drawing on current events, with every intention of publishing the novel with Heinemann in 1941 as a wartime follow-up to *Let Him Lie*. Could the novel have been turned down by Heinemann on the grounds that it was more a wartime thriller than a classic detective novel? Whether or not this is the case, by the time *There May Be Danger* appeared in 1948 the book was out-of-date compared with other contemporary British crime thrillers, such as Michael

Gilbert's *They Never Looked Inside* (1948) and *The Doors Open* (1949) and Andrew Garve's *Came the Dawn* (1949), all of which dealt with social circumstances in the postwar world. Yet today, in the twenty-first century, modern readers of vintage mystery should find much to enjoy in Ianthe Jerrold's *There May Be Danger*, a scrupulously observed depiction of British life during the earlier days of the Second World War that is also a beguiling tale of baffling mystery.

Like American crime writer Helen McCloy's 1945 detective novel *The One That Got Away*, which is set in Scotland during the waning days of the Second World War, *There May be Danger* revolves around the fate of an adolescent boy gone missing in the British hinterlands. In *There May Be Danger*, the vanished boy is twelve-year-old Sidney Brentwood, a London evacuee residing with a married couple in the village of Hastry in sparsely populated Radnorshire, Wales. Upon hearing of young Sidney's case and learning that for family he has only an eccentric great aunt more concerned with the fates of her absconding cats than any absent human relations, Kate Mayhew, a young woman "resting" from a West-end theater job with a friend working on a farm in Radnorshire as part of the Women's Land Army, quixotically decides that she will investigate the situation herself. Like Jeanie Halliday, the female protagonist of Jerrold's earlier Geraldine Bridgman detective novel, *Let Him Lie*, the intrepid Kate Mayhew finds herself investigating, at considerable personal danger, gravely suspicious circumstances in a mysterious rural world of old homes and ancient tumuli (burial mounds). This was a world that Ianthe Jerrold knew well, having with her husband in the 1930s acquired and renovated a rambling seventeenth-century black-and-white timbered farmhouse situated on a ridge overlooking the Wye Valley in the English borderland county of Herefordshire.

There May Be Danger and *Let Him Lie* share another point of similarity with Ianthe Jerrold's own life in that both novels detail the courageous actions of caring women concerned with the fates of displaced children. The plot of *There May Be Danger* revolves around Kate Mayhew's investigation into the fate of a missing twelve-year-old evacuee boy, whose only relative in England is his aforementioned distant and dotty great-aunt (the boy's mother is dead and his father is serving in the merchant navy), while in *Let Him Lie* Jeannie Halliday takes an interest in the future of the murdered Robert Molyneux's niece and ward, thirteen-year-old Sarah Molyneux, and hopes to keep the anxious girl out of the selfish clutches of her "queer, neurotic and unhappy mother," Myfanwy Peel. In real life Ianthe Jerrold, who though married was herself childless, around this time adopted a young girl, Pauline ("Polly") Jerrold; and clearly the author drew on personal circumstances in both of her Geraldine Bridgman novels, lending the books considerable dramatic heft. Admittedly *There May Be Danger* crosses over the borderline from the pure detective novel into thriller territory, but I suspect that few fans of vintage mystery will be able to lay down the novel until they have finished its thrilling final chapters, in which that most determined stage-struck amateur investigator, Kate Mayhew, finally plumbs the depths of a dark plot against Shakespeare's sceptered isle.

Curtis Evans

Chapter One

On a sunny October morning, the stucco-fronted houses of London are a symphony in off-white tones, the brick cliff-sides of the new blocks of flats discover charming shades of pink and apricot, and even in the smoke-grimed brick of mid-Victorian warehouses, the yellow under the encrusted black responds to the long soft rays of the low sun.

Even the Edgware Road, on such a day, looks charming.

Even Kate Mayhew, though she was out of a job and saw but small hope of getting into another one, felt the powerful charm of the autumn sun as she left her bus at the corner of Chapel Street and strolled along towards Maida Vale. The sky was blue, and almost cloudless. True, an arabesque pattern of thin white vapour trails hung, slowly dispersing, over the Metropolitan Music Hall. But this was not caused by a disturbance in the weather, but by a recent encounter high in the heavens between eight Dornier bombers and seven Spitfires.

Kate was returning, for the second time this week, from a hopeless round of the theatrical agents. Business in her suburban theatre had been pretty poor since the beginning of the war. And when the first bombs dropped on London, and the West-end theatre rocked to its financial foundations, even a little theatre in a northern suburb had felt the jar. There had been a great rushing about and making of adjustments, but it did not help matters for long. The West-end theatre shut down. And a few weeks later, after a brave struggle by a company which had waived first its salaries in favour of shares, and then its meals in favour of cups of coffee, the Northern Heights Repertory Theatre also closed its doors.

Kate had not at first been able to believe that the receding tide of theatre-going might well have swept stage-management out of her reach, until, some day, the tide came in again. But she believed it now. For the last month she had been trying to find herself a job, and it had been a grim business. She had determined, if she failed this morning to get on the track of a job, to abandon the vain struggle and wait for the tide to come in again.

What she would do instead, she was not yet quite sure. She had a friend, Aminta Hughes, working on a farm in Radnorshire, who was continually writing and exhorting her to join the Women's Land Army. There was, in fact, a letter from Aminta in Kate's handbag now, all about the threshing of oats, a cow with a sore udder, sunrise over the mountains, and foot-and-mouth disease. Skimming it over her toast and apple at breakfast, Kate had practically decided to go in for munitions.

She paused outside a modest café to reflect on her situation, and to consider whether she would have a sandwich first and go to the Labour Exchange afterwards, or the other way round, when a handbill pasted to the window of the small modiste's shop next door caught her eye. "PLEASE HELP! PLEASE HELP!" Below these words, which were in inch-high letters and stood out with a quite painful urgency at the top of the folio sheet, was the photograph of a boy.

"Missing," ran the smaller letterpress below, "since October 1st, from his billet in Hastry, Radnorshire, Sidney Brentwood, aged 12½, height five feet four inches, well-built, fair hair, blue eyes, fresh complexion. Wearing grey flannel shorts, brown corduroy wind-sheeter, green stockings and brown shoes. It is thought he may be trying to make his way to London. Anybody who is able to give any information, or to help IN ANY WAY to trace this boy, PLEASE communicate immediately with his aunt, Miss Brentwood, at 105 Tranchester Terrace, W.2."

"October the 1st!" thought Kate mournfully, studying the photograph. "Nearly three weeks ago! Some hopes, poor kid!"

She looked carefully at the boy's photograph, with the usual remote hope that she might recognise him as someone she had seen. It was a round, candid face, still infantile in shape, with eyes wider apart than they would appear later after the full development of the jaw, a good broad forehead, hair tending to curl, short, straight nose and easily smiling mouth. It was the face of a nice, candid, not very clever, adventurous boy, decided Kate. Whether he ever returned to his aunt or not, Kate hoped very much that his adventurous spirit had caused his disappearance, and not some miserable accident. Poor aunt, responsible for the boy, and now helpless, distracted, dependent upon the machine-like, slow, impersonal help of the police. She wondered whether he had been happy, or unhappy, in his billet in far-off Hastry, Radnorshire. Queer that it should be Radnorshire, where Aminta dwelt among the sunsets and udders. Perhaps Aminta knew Hastry?

Kate started to move on, but those urgent, touching words seemed to follow her, draw her back. Please Help! Please help! But how can one help? One could go and look for the child, I suppose... but the police will have been looking for him for three weeks.

A member of this force happened to pass at this moment, and on an impulse Kate asked him:

"Can you tell me where Tranchester Terrace is?"

"Tranchester Terrace?" He paused and cast about, for he was a reserve policeman, new to the beat, and not as yet an encyclopaedia of West London streets. "I think it runs between Westbourne Grove and Talbot Road—Notting Hill way. I should take a bus down Praed Street if I were you, and get out at Bradley's."

Above the sound of traffic stole a thin eerie streak of sound, mournful, uncertain, high-pitched, slowly gathering certainty and volume as new streaks of the same sound joined in from all round the sky over London.

"All clear," remarked the policeman cheerfully, moving his gas-mask, which he had been wearing as a chest-protector, round to his back.

"Oh, was the warning still on?" said Kate, as was said by many at one time and another that morning, for it was one of those mild, blue autumn days of 1940 when the warbling and the sustained notes of the air-raid sirens were heard so frequently and at such short intervals that people going in and out of buses and shops and about their business in the streets were often surprised to hear a sustained note when they did not know there had been a warble, and a warble when they were happily anticipating a sustained note.

Kate walked back, and soon found herself in Praed Street waiting for a bus. She had all the day before her, and she might as well go and look at Tranchester Terrace. Of course, she wasn't going to do more than just look at it. She might write and ask Aminta if Hastry was anywhere near her place, and whether she had heard about the disappearance of a boy billeted there. If she knew Hastry, Aminta might even know the people the boy had been billeted on. How terrible, to be responsible for someone else's child, and to lose him, to have to write to his parents and say, your child is lost! Sidney Brentwood seemed to have no parents, though, only an aunt. Please Help! Please Help!

The bus swung round a diversion into Norfolk Square, for a bomb which had fallen at the entrance to a little barber's shop opposite the Great Western Hotel had made empty shells of many little shops, piled the roadway with heaps of masonry, and turned that end of Praed Street into a one-way traffic alley.

Your Children Are Safer in the Country! ran an L.C.C. poster on one of the hoardings Kate's bus passed in its cautious journey into unfamiliar streets. All except Sidney Brentwood. What had happened to Sidney Brentwood? I shall probably never know, said Kate to herself philosophically. But not so philosophically as she intended, for almost in the moment of formulating the words, her vague stirrings of curiosity in pity crystallised into a firm determination to find out.

Chapter Two

Number 105 Tranchester Terrace was one of the neatest of a rather shabby and dejected street of three-storey houses with little ironwork balconies hung frivolously on their dingy stucco fronts, and small square front gardens, which were for the most part little wildernesses of flowering grass and sprawling shrubs. Number 105 possessed a polished door-bell and a whitened doorstep, upon which sat a very large tabby cat with a Narpac disc round its neck and its tongue slightly out in an insolent devil-may-care expression.

Kate rang the bell. There was no answer, and she was about to ring again, when a door in the area below opened, and a little elderly lady came a few inches outside it and peered up at Kate. She carried in her arms another large tabby cat, and seemed to be using her feet to prevent the emergence from the area of yet a third.

"Yes?" she inquired, a little shortly.

"Are you Miss Brentwood?" asked Kate, looking down over the hand-rail.

"Yes," said the little lady in the area, keeping her eye upon the cat bent on escape and obstructing it neatly with her foot. "Go back. Pixie! Naughty cat!"

The thwarted cat swore loudly, and the large torpid animal in Miss Brentwood's arms looked on with a complacent expression, as if he thought Pixie deserved all he got.

"I saw your advertisement," began Kate.

"Oh, yes! Well, it's on the second floor, I'm afraid, but there's the use of an Anderson shelter," replied Miss Brentwood, in a slightly more friendly tone. "*Will* you behave, Pixie? Bad, bad puss! I expect you'd like to see over the flat, wouldn't you? Would you mind coming in this way? I'm short-handed just at present, and Pixie—"

"Oh, but I didn't come about a flat!" said Kate, descending the area steps. The large tabby cat who had been sitting on the front doorstep put its head through the railings and looked down as if to see what all the commotion was about. "I saw your advertisement in Edgware Road, and—"

"Oh, poor little Sidney!" exclaimed Miss Brentwood, with an air at once harassed and enlightened. "Have you any news of him? Do come in! Bobbie!" she cried suddenly, catching sight of the cat on the front steps, and speaking with deep reproach: "You naughty, naughty, naughty—Oh, catch him, *please*! I can't come, Pixie will escape if I do!"

Kate scurried up the area steps again, and was in time to see Bobbie remove himself in a leisurely and sinuous manner through the railings into the next-door garden, where he turned, tongue still out, to see what she would do now. She went quickly out of the gate of 105 and in at the gate of 103 in time to watch Bobbie's further exit through the railings into the garden of 101, where he turned again and gave her an interested look. She glared at him over the railings and repeated the performance. When he reached 99, however, he became bored with the game, and suddenly accelerating shot away from her, leapt on to a shed in the garden of number 95, which was the end house of the terrace, and disappeared, the devil-knew-where. Kate had to return empty-handed and apologising to the area of number 105, where Bobbie's owner still anxiously awaited him.

"Oh dear, he is a naughty, naughty cat! And there's cat-flu about, too! Do come in! You came about poor little Sidney, you said. *No*, Pixie, you *shan't* follow Bobbie's bad example! Look at Ki-Ki, what a good cat he is! *He* doesn't want to run out into the naughty dangerous streets!"

She led the way into a very dark basement passage about which hung a curious stuffy aroma that reminded Kate of the Zoo, and opened the door into a sunny, but also very stuffy, little room in which were at least four saucers containing milk or meat-remains perched about on various articles of furniture, besides three on the floor.

"Do sit down, Miss—"

"Mayhew."

"Not there, that's Pixie's chair and he *does* leave his hairs about so! So you've come about poor little Sidney, Miss Mayhew. I'm so terribly anxious about him. Have you any news?"

"I'm afraid not," said Kate, sitting down on a sofa whose broken springs protested loudly. "I—I saw your advertisement and I just came to see if I could help."

"Oh, I see," said Miss Brentwood a little vaguely. "Well, of course the police are doing all they can. But it's three weeks since we had news of him, and I'm afraid in a case like this no news is bad news!"

She put the cat she was carrying down in front of a saucer of sardine-bits, at which he sniffed with a replete and disgusted air, before stalking out of the room.

"Hasn't anybody seen or heard anything of your nephew since he disappeared?" asked Kate.

"Oh, there've been a lot of people who've thought they'd seen him in all sorts of places, but when the police come to investigate, it always seems to come to nothing."

Now that all her cats were out of the room, Miss Brentwood seemed a little more able to concentrate on the comparatively unimportant matter of her nephew's disappearance. She was a very thin, stooping little lady with an aquiline profile that had been pretty and now was rather too bird-like, and a quantity of untidy, fluffy grey hair.

"Of course," she pursued, "one mustn't give up hope. But I'm dreading the day when his poor father gets home to England—his only child, you know, that makes it so much worse, doesn't it? And of course, for my own sake—well, you can't help getting fond of a child when you've looked after him for over a year, can you? Not that Sidney wasn't a dear little boy, he *was*, but of course like all boys he was a handful and I must admit I was glad of the rest when he was evacuated! Children keep you on the go so! And of course with the cats, I really had my hands full already when his father left him here. Still I was very glad to do what I could for him. It's his father that's my nephew really—in the Merchant Navy, he is. Little Sidney's my great-nephew. His mother died when he was a baby."

Poor little Sidney! thought Kate: no mother, a father on the high seas, and only a great-aunt who prefers cats to care whether you live or die!

"Are you a friend of his father's?" asked Miss Brentwood curiously.

"No," replied Kate. "I didn't know anything about it until this morning. But I've got nothing to do just at present..." She paused, but only for a second, to listen to the voice of reason telling her not to be a fool, then took the plunge. "I thought I'd go and look for him."

"Oh, my dear!" stammered his great-aunt. "But—! The police *are* looking for him, you know—and it's three weeks since he disappeared!" She looked sidelong at Kate, as if doubtful of her sanity. "Of course, I should be very, very grateful, but I'm afraid-—well, how would you set about it? I mean, I'm beginning to think—"

"That he's dead?" asked Kate baldly.

Miss Brentwood looked pained.

"Well, three weeks without sight or sound of him! And that wild, mountainous country! What I can't help thinking is, that he must have gone off by himself into the hills—some boy's adventure, you know—and broken his leg or something, and—oh, poor little Sidney! Too awful to think of!"

"But surely the hills have been searched?"

"Oh yes, of course, but still people *do* get lost in such places— very wild, I believe, though I've never been there. I should have liked to go and see Sidney in his billet, but I find it so difficult to get away! My cats tie me so, you see! Is that Bobbie outside the window?"

But luckily for the continuity of their conversation the cat who was busily scratching a hole in her front garden was not Bobbie, but a low stranger. She made a few indignant shooing sounds at him, and returned to her chair.

"Sidney's billet was in a village in the hills. From their letters, they seemed nice people. The village postman, the man was, and his wife keeps a little shop."

"What happened exactly?" inquired Kate.

"Well, my dear," said Miss Brentwood unhappily, "it seems the child got up in the middle of the night, dressed, went off on his bicycle, without saying a word to anybody, and simply never came back! Disappeared! For no reason at all—I mean, there hadn't been any trouble, either at school or at his billet. And since that day—October the 1st, it was, a Tuesday—nobody's seen a trace of him. His bicycle's not been found, either. What can one think, except that he must have gone off and got lost in those wild, treacherous mountains?" said Miss Brentwood helplessly. "Any other kind of accident, you see—well, he'd have been found, wouldn't he, by now? Even if he was *drowned*, poor little Sidney, surely his bicycle would have been found by now! But with those miles and miles of wild, uninhabited country," said Miss Brentwood, who seemed, Kate thought, to regard Radnorshire as first cousin to the Arizona desert, "almost at his door, all rocks and forests and—"

"Could I have the name and address of the people he was living with?" asked Kate, taking an envelope and pencil from her handbag.

"Certainly, but do you *really* intend then—? It's very, very good of you, Miss Mayhew, but—"

Miss Brentwood gazed doubtfully at Kate with her faded blue eyes.

"I want to go to Radnorshire, anyhow. I've got a friend there," said Kate briskly, since it seemed necessary to rationalise her impulse for the benefit of the old lady.

Miss Brentwood brightened immediately at what she took for a sign of normality, and it did not seem to occur to her that Radnorshire was rather a large place. Searching behind a hideous black marble clock on the mantelpiece, she sorted out a collection of old letters and handed the address to Kate.

> Mrs. Cornelius Howells
> Sunnybank
> Hastry
> nr. Llanfyn, Radnorshire.

Kate copied it carefully.

"I *shall* be glad to hear from you, Miss Mayhew," said old Miss Brentwood, "even if you don't find anything out at once. I'm naturally very anxious. Of course, nobody can hold *me* responsible, but still, Sidney was in my care, in a way, and— oh dear! If *only* he'd gone to High Wycombe, where some of the other children went! Radnorshire is so far away, actually in *Wales*, isn't it? Acres of mountain country, I believe, worse than Cumberland, and we know what a lot of poor people lose their lives on those hills!"

Putting the address away, Kate asked:

"Is there anything you can tell me about Sidney that might help? I mean, the kind of boy he is?"

It was evident from Sidney's great-aunt's puzzled and vague expression that this question would get no useful answer. She looked as if she had never really noticed what kind of boy Sidney was.

"Well, I don't know, my dear. He was a nice, good- tempered boy, rather disobedient sometimes. I don't think he was specially clever at school, just average, you know. He was better at doing things with his hands than book-work," said Miss Brentwood rather helplessly.

Kate thought it would be useless with this unobservant aunt to pursue the subject further, and got up to go, narrowly avoiding treading in a saucer containing a little stale and dusty milk.

"I'll write to you, Miss Brentwood."

"Do, do! I am *sorry* I can't come with you!" said the old lady regretfully. "But of course it's impossible! My cats *tie* me so!"

Kate did not share her regrets. At the area door Pixie, who seemed to be a cat of one idea, was sitting with his nose against the crack waiting the opportunity to bolt from his loving owner into the wide world. To his furious indignation, Miss Brentwood picked him up before she opened the door for Kate.

"*If* you see Bobbie, *do* tell him to come home!" said Miss Brentwood. "I don't like the cats to be out in front, with all this traffic about, and now I hear there's cat-flu. *Good*-bye!"

They clasped hands, awkwardly, for the irate Pixie was lolloping, a dead weight, under his mistress's right arm.

"You know," said Miss Brentwood, "if I don't seem to express my gratitude to you very well, it's partly because I am so very much surprised!"

Her old blue eyes once again studied Kate's face half-doubtfully, half-admiringly, as if for the signs of insanity that did not appear on the surface. "Take care of yourself, Miss Mayhew! Don't *you* go doing anything rash and risking *your* life!"

"Not I!" said Kate, smiling at what seemed to her, then, a very absurd idea.

At the corner of the road she saw Bobbie sitting on the pavement watching the traffic, his pink tongue hanging out to catch any microbes of cat-flu that might be flying around in the dust.

"Go home, Bobbie," said Kate reprovingly.

He leered at her.

Chapter Three

The rest of Kate's day was occupied with preparations for departure, which included the purchase of a canvas knapsack and a pair of rubber wellingtons, for Miss Brentwood had conveyed to her a picture of unlimited wild forest, and herself tramping through it, though common-sense told her that a boy could not be lost in such country for three weeks, and still survive, and that it was at least equally possible that Sidney had never gone near the hills at all, but had headed back for London. At the same time, though of course she could not answer for Sidney, Kate felt that she herself would have had to be wretched indeed in her country billet before *she* would have headed back towards Bobbie, Pixie and Ki-Ki!

"Going hiking, dear?" inquired her landlady, bringing her a nice cup of tea, and some stockings and a brassiere she had kindly washed out for her.

"Yes, Mrs. Mander, I'm going to wild Wales."

"My sister-in-law's daughter, she's gone to Wales with 'er kiddies!" said Mrs. Mander. "You might see'er. It's wild where she is, all right. Gives 'er the willies properly. Not many bombs in Wales, that's one thing. There was a bomb on a farm, though, near where my sister-in-law's daughter's staying—killed nine sheep, it did. Bombing sheep, what next. Well, dear, I mustn't hinder you. If you *do* see Edna—I'll give you her address, in case—you tell her from me not to be a fool, and to stay where she is!"

Purchasing, packing, letter-writing and tidying up her room, left Kate no time to reflect in cold blood upon what she was doing. But in the small hours of the night, when even the most impulsive blood runs somewhat tepid, she awoke and contemplated her project without enthusiasm, and even began to wonder whether there was insanity in her family, and her mother and father had kept it from her.

She consoled herself by recalling other small-hour watches, before first-nights, when the most careful preparations would look like muddles, brilliant plays like hog-wash, and the rosy prospects of a run tinged all over with the grey hues of the bird. As usual, these vapours were dispelled by the sunrise.

They returned to her in some measure, however, when she found herself on the last stage of her long journey, in a little train-coach with its seats arranged sideways, like a tube-train, puffing slowly out on the single line from Llanfyn to Hastry. The day, which had started with sunshine, was closing in with a thin, driving rain. The wooded hills on either side of the long valley looked flattened against the grey sky. Kate looked at those grey, wet hills, and thought of Sidney Brentwood, unseen for three weeks, and her folly in supposing there was anything she could do to find him almost overcame her.

There were only two passengers in the coach beside herself, and both were sitting facing her. One was a small, round-faced woman in glasses, with a knitted wool cap on her head, who sat up in the corner nursing a shopping-basket on her knees, and looking at Kate and Kate's haversack whenever Kate was looking elsewhere. The other was a tall, large-featured, rather good-looking young woman in the brown uniform of a children's nurse, who sat with her elbow resting on the small suitcase on the seat beside her, looking in a rather melancholy fashion out of the window. Kate surmised that she was on her way to a new job in strange country, and that the sight of the wet, wild hills made her apprehensive for her comfort.

"Wild country, isn't it?" said Kate, happening to catch her pensive eye. Kate had scarcely spoken a word all day, except to an elderly evacuee who had not been able to decide whether her destination was Malvern Link or Great Malvern until it was too late to get out at either of them, and she had had to descend at Malvern Wells.

"I'll say it is," replied the children's nurse feelingly. "I've never been in this part before."

"Nor have I," said Kate. They both glanced at the little woman in the corner, who had the look of a native. But she was looking straight in front of her, with an untouchable, wooden expression on her prim round face.

"Going to a new job?" inquired Kate.

"Yes. Place called the Vault. At least, I suppose that's how you pronounce it. It's spelt V-e-a-u-l-t."

Again they glanced at the little woman in the corner, but she did not enlighten them.

"Yes, isn't it? It's a nursery-school for evacuated babies, or going to be. I don't like nursery-school work much, it's all running about and no thanks for it, but private work's all over the place nowadays. And I suppose one ought to pull one's weight when there's a war on. And at any rate," added the young nurse frankly, "I shall be away from the bombs. I'm not keen on bombs, are you?"

Kate was about to agree that bombs did not attract her, when the little woman in the corner suddenly spoke in one of the clearest, sharpest, most incisive voices Kate had ever heard, on the stage or off it.

"Indeed, and you have come to the wrong shop, then! There was a bomb over in a field to Aberwent last Tuesday fortnight."

The young nurse, with some facial skill, expressed polite interest to the speaker and extreme amusement to Kate.

"And Aberwent is not so far from the Veault, not more than eight miles, whatever!" pursued the woman with the market basket. She pronounced it Vote.

"Oh dear, my blood fairly curdles, doesn't yours?" said the nurse to Kate, gathering her belongings together as the train began to slow down. "Well, I'm glad it isn't a vault I'm going to, anyway. Good Lord, it's raining horribly! If they haven't sent a car to meet me, I shall go straight back to London by the next train!"

Kate struggled into her oilskin coat and picked up the one large knapsack in which she had packed all her luggage, and the three of them descended and straggled out into the yard, where stood a shabby old horse and trap, and a very expensive-looking little black car with a pretty girl in the driver's seat. A man carrying a quantity of dead rabbits slung on sticks was standing and conversing with the elderly driver of the trap.

The pretty girl swung open the door of the car, the children's nurse got in, and they drove off. Kate felt envious. A chilly wind was blowing the rain aslant, it would soon be dark, and she did not know where she was going to sleep the night. The road curved away up-hill to the left, past the gaunt shoulder of a hill, and to the right ran along the valley beside the railway line. There was no village in sight.

"Can you tell me which is the way to Hastry village?" asked Kate of the little round-faced woman who was settling her basket on the seat of the trap preparatory to climbing in herself.

"Hastry village?" echoed the man with the rabbits, before the woman had time to answer the question. "It would depend what part of Hastry village you wass wanting!"

Kate, who had not been so far west as the border before, had never heard such a melodious fall and rise of tone except on the stage, in the plays of Emlyn Williams. The man's bright brown eyes were fixed in a sort of foxy curiosity on her face, as also were the eyes of the middle-aged woman, and those of the elderly driver, who sat, collar turned up and cap well pulled down, with rain dripping off the reddened nose between his straggling grey brows and straggling grey moustache.

"It would depend, now, who you wass wanting in Hastry village," said the man with the rabbits zestfully.

"Mrs. Howells."

"Howells the farm, or Howells the post, would that be, I wonder?"

"Mrs. Cornelius Howells, Sunnybank—"

"Ah, that iss Howells the post! Well, now, Mr. Davis he iss going up by Sunnybank. He would let you ride in his tub, I shouldn't wonder!"

"Oh, ah!" said the driver of the vehicle affirmatively.

"Please to get in," said the little woman, as the tub, which was a sort of governess-cart, moved forward slightly, and the horse shifted his hooves under her own advent. "Well, goodnight, Mr. Morgan."

"Good-night, Mrs. Davis. Good-night, Mr. Davis. I shall be getting the rabbits from you on Monday?"

"Oh, ah!" agreed the man in the tub. "I will be bringing them down myself, early. There will be some good ones I shouldn't wonder."

His leathery cheek curved in a grin, and a peculiar look of humorous, secret understanding crossed Mr. Morgan's foxy face. It still lingered as he turned to Kate, who wondered passingly what there was about rabbits to cause this sub-humorous understanding.

"Good-night, young lady! Mrs. Howells will be expecting you, I expect?"

The grating of wheels, clattering of hooves and squeaking of springs made a reply impossible, so Mr. Morgan had to go for the present with his curiosity unsatisfied.

"I'm afraid she isn't," said Kate to the little woman, drawing her oilskin over her vulnerable knees. "I only decided to come yesterday. Is there anywhere in Hastry where I'll be able to get a room? An inn?"

"Mrs. Howells the post has a room empty, now the boy she had there is gone," replied Mrs. Davis, studying Kate with sharp grey eyes behind her round steel-rimmed spectacles. "Perhaps you are a relation of the boy—Sidney Brentwood his name was?"

"Not a relation. Just a—friend."

"Oh, indeed!" cried Mrs. Davis, her voice sharper than ever, and even the taciturn Mr. Davis turned his head about one degree towards Kate as if to lend an ear to what was going on. The trap was climbing the long uphill road, and over the brow of the hill Kate could see farther hills standing high against the sky.

These were certainly not the rocky and hazardous mountains of Miss Brentwood's urban imaginings: but seen in this evening light, their tops in cloud, the grey rain driving round their feet, they looked formidable enough, unfriendly enough, secretive enough, to daunt even Kate.

"There has been a lot of search-parties on the hills," said Mrs. Davis, noticing Kate's glance. "There was people from the villages making parties and helping the police, but nothing was found.

Mr. Davis, with an eye upon the hills, said something which the unfamiliar intonation of his quick speech made unintelligible to Kate. His wife turned to Kate and said half-apologetically:

"He is saying that the bracken-cutting has started, and perhaps something will be found now. The bracken is very high at this time of year."

"Did you know Sidney Brentwood?" Kate might as well waste no time in her inquiries.

"Yes, indeed, he came to Pentrewer on his bicycle to see the tump where Gwyn Lupton found the old piece of money!"

This had the elements of drama in it, and Kate seized on it.

"An old piece of money?"

"Very old, indeed, perhaps from when the Romans was here, Gwyn Lupton says."

"Where do you say it was found?"

"On the tump at Pentrewer, which is where we lives."

Kate was not enlightened.

"The tump?"

"Yes, there is a tump on Pentrewer bank, not far from where we lives. There is a lot of them on the hills. A gentleman who came from the Government in London was saying they are places where people was buried in history times, more than two hundred years ago, I shouldn't wonder!"

"Oh, a tumulus! And Sidney Brentwood came to see it?"

"He heard about the piece of old money Gwyn Lupton found, and he came over wanting to dig for treasure. But we told him he must not do that, because we had a paper from London to say we must not interfere with the tump, although it is on our land. The Government wants it, because it is in history!"

Kate made a mental note of the name, Pentrewer Tump. She knew a little about tumuli, for she had once been persuaded by an archaeologist friend, Colin Kemp, to spend a week assisting, in a very minor capacity, at the excavations at Maiden Castle. In Colin's company she had visited every place marked on the map in black-letter for miles around, and obediently got off her bicycle whenever a round-barrow came in sight, which happened more frequently than Kate would have believed possible. It had been an educative experience in more ways than one, for it had brought home to Kate what, before that week, she had been in danger of overlooking, the fact that earthworks and the theatre cannot live together. She had pointed this out to the young man, who had not at all agreed with her, but had been forced to submit to her conclusion, and had gone to South America to console himself among the remains of Incas. Kate still occasionally had letters from him, though she had not had one for a long time now, and still, more than occasionally, found herself thinking about him.

A new and gruesome thought struck her.

"I suppose," she hesitated, "there aren't any chambered barrows in this part of the world? I mean," she explained as Mrs. Davis looked at a loss, "big tumps, long-shaped, with entrances and stone passages inside where people can just crawl along?"

"I never heard of any tumps with passages! They are just round tumps, with grass over them, and some has trees growing on them. Some is flatter than others, and some has a ditch and a bank round the bottom of them. Perhaps that iss what you are thinking of?"

"No, but stone tunnels through them, that you can crawl into," said Kate, who had been suddenly afflicted with a horrible vision of an adventurous small boy, miles away from human kind, on the wild stretches of the hills, finding the bramble-hidden entrance to a great long-barrow, crawling down the dank earthy passage, trapped by a falling stone. The stone might not have been touched by human hand since the builder's had first placed it there in days before Julius Caesar was born, and the centuries in which rabbits had burrowed and foxes dug their earths might have undermined that builder's work, to make the stone fall at the first renewal of a human touch. The child would shout, and cry, but not for long. And the larks would sing, and the wild honey bees hum over the blackberries and nobody, nobody would ever know.

Perhaps the tenor of Kate's dark imaginings showed in her face, for Mrs. Davis subdued her high decisive voice into a lower key when she answered:

"No, there's no tunnels that I ever heard of. There iss a tunnel at Mr. Atkin's farm, they say, but there iss no tump there. There iss a lot of old ruins that visitors goes to see, and people say there was once an old tunnel in the cellar that ran under the hill towards an old castle that used to be there in history times, but nobody hass ever seen this tunnel that I know of. Mr. Atkins iss a queer man, he does not like visitors at Llanhalo."

"Llanhalo!" cried Kate, in joyful surprise. "Not Llanhalo Abbey Farm?"

"Yess, that iss the place."

"Oh, good! Is it far from Hastry? A Land-Army friend of mine works there!"

Mrs. Davis poked her husband sharply in the back.

"How far away iss Llanhalo from Hastry, George? The Land-Army young lady that works for Gideon Atkins is a friend of this young lady here!"

"Oh, ah, about five-and-a-half mile, I shouldn't wonder. Yes, five or six mile, pretty near."

Mr. Davis turned his head and looked at Kate with a sort of foxy humour.

"And how does the young lady like working for Gideon Atkins, Miss? Oh ah?"

He spoke with real curiosity, and Kate, glancing at his wife, saw that she was waiting, brightly intent behind her round child-like spectacles, for Kate's answer. Kate could not remember that Aminta had ever expressed any sentiments with regard to her employer. Aminta was not interested in human beings, only in cows and horses and other inarticulate animals. Mr. and Mrs. Davis, when she explained this, seemed both disappointed and sceptical.

"And how long's her been at Llanhalo, Missie?"

"Nearly a year."

"Well, well her must be a stout girl! Does her get enough to eat, oh ah?" inquired Mr. Davis with jocularity. "Reckon that's why Atkins picked a land-girl, missus, her wouldn't eat as much as a man!"

"Llanhalo's a draughty old melancholy house, though Miss Atkins is for ever scrubbing her fingers away on the floors," said Mrs. Davis, who seemed loth to believe that Kate had no second-hand titbits of gossip to pass on about Mr. Atkin's domestic life. "I wonder as that young lady likes to stay on there. No company, either. Gideon Atkins does not like visitors. There iss only the summer visitors from Llanfyn that comes to see the old Abbey ruins, and there iss not so many of them as there used to be, now that Gideon Atkins makes them pay sixpence each! Sixpence each they hass to pay, to go and look inside his farmyard at a lot of old stones!"

'Ah, Gideon Atkins would ask sixpence admission to his own funeral," remarked Mr. Davis, clucking to his horse as if to share the joke with it. "And there's plenty would pay it, whatever!"

"And he'll have 'Trespassers Will Be Prosecuted' written on his tomb-stone, too!" added Mrs. Davis with bright enjoyment.

Kate was certainly a little surprised that Aminta had made no comments on this individual. All Aminta had said about her employer was that he was a transplanted Yorkshire man. Yet Mr. Gideon Atkins was evidently a character of the countryside, and, to judge by this harping on his future obsequies, not a popular one.

They had descended the hill now, and were clopping quickly along a little road that led through the valley. Kate, who was tired, stiff, cold, hungry and getting wetter every minute around the wrists and ankles, longed for a lamp and a fire.

"It'll be black-out time soon now, I expect," said Mrs. Davis. "Reckon them'll be very strict with the black-out in London, Missie?"

"Yes, very strict."

"Them's pretty strict here. Oh, ah. Pretty strict them is."

"And so they ought to be!" said his wife vigorously. "We have aeroplanes flying over here often at night. The Berminster water works is quite close the other side of Rhosbach, which is this hill ahead of you, Miss. Well, here is Hastry. And that is Howells the post, up the bank beyond the school."

They were plodding uphill again, and had entered a pleasant little village that seemed to cling to the side of the great rain-hidden hill. The houses lay mostly to one side of the hillside road and looked across the little valley. Here and there along the street a lit window looked a welcome. One or two little slate-roofed cottages lay higher up the slope, like look-outs keeping a watch upon the valley for the whole village. They passed the humped church behind its great yew-trees, and the neat, but regrettably red-brick, elementary school; and a little farther up Mr. Davis drew rein before a row of cottages, the character of whose walls was hidden under many coats of whitewash, but whose pleasant wide-angled gables and stone roofs vouched for their antiquity. They lay above the road, with steep little front gardens still cheerful with set and drooping asters, marigolds and dahlias, and one of them, the end one, had a Post Office sign, and a little window filled with jars of sweets and faded cardboard packets of groceries.

"Here you be!" said Mr. Davis. "Us'll wait and see you in."

"Mrs. Howells will give you a room, I am sure," said Mrs. Davis, handing Kate's knapsack down to her. "But if Mrs. Howells cannot take you, you are welcome to Pentrewer for the night."

"Oh, how kind of you!" said Kate gratefully, hoping all the same that she was not doomed to a further journey in the trap in the rain, which was now setting in with a bleak determination to soak everything thoroughly before the morning. "Thank you a thousand times for giving me a lift! I *should* have got wet if I'd walked!"

She would not really have got much wetter, and she would certainly not have got so cold, reflected Kate, as she hurried quickly up the steps of the steep little garden so as not to keep her kind friends sitting in the rain: but she would have missed quite a lot of interesting and possibly fruitful information. The first thing she must do when she found herself alone, and when she was warm and dry again, must be to look at her Ordnance Survey map.

With cold wet fingers she knocked at the door, which was round the side of the cottage. Steps sounded on stone in a moment, and the door was opened by a fat middle-aged woman in an apron, with red cheeks, slightly tousled hair, rolled-up sleeves and the floury hands that tell of kitchen, stove and food. A door was open behind her, and from it came the smell of baking, and that most welcome of all sounds to the cold traveller, the swish and hiss of flames rushing up round logs in the grate. To Kate at that moment the thought of a kitchen was like the thought of Paradise. Her sense of adventure was ebbing low. She asked for nothing of the gods but to be allowed to go into a kitchen, and listen to that noise, and smell that smell.

A moment later she was waving farewell to her friends the Davises and following Mrs. Cornelius Howells into a kitchen, low-raftered, lamp-lit, close-curtained, with fantastic flames rushing up around great cleft logs thrust endwise in the grate, and a huge iron kettle swinging on a chimney crane. An enamel teapot stood on the hob, and a meal was laid on the square table. There was a gleam of oak furniture and a glitter of black-lead and polished brass. There was an old high-backed settle with a red cushion on it drawn up close to that fire. A side of bacon hung on the wall, and a ham swung from the ceiling. It was a cottage kitchen of the kind that the stage often tries, and always fails, to reproduce; the kitchen of the weary traveller's dreams.

Chapter Four

A couple of hours later, Kate was sitting on that curved-backed settle in front of the fire, hot-faced and replete with a large meal of fried green bacon, potatoes, bread-and-butter, strong tea and hot cake, and fortified in her resolve to find Sidney Brentwood by the simple approbation with which Mr. and Mrs. Cornelius Howells accepted her intention.

"We was real upset to think of Sidney's relations coming here, and yet when they didn't come, we was more upset," said Mrs. Cornelius, who, in contrast to Mrs. Davis of Pentrewer, had a very gentle voice, soft and deliberate, yet full of colour, with the clear consonants and rising inflections that Kate had noticed in the Davises. She was a stout, black-haired woman of about fifty, with large rosy cheeks and a pleasant untidiness of person, in contrast with the glittering orderliness of her kitchen. Her husband, who sat upright in a wooden chair opposite Kate, was a little man, grey-bearded and wrinkled, with a shrewd eye and a clipped, jovial tone of voice that Kate found rather difficult to follow. He had come in, in his oilskin cape, shortly after Kate's arrival, from some remote outpost of the G.P.O. which he visited daily to sell stamps and receive letters and, incidentally news. Kate was just getting used to the almost shockingly human look of a hatless postman, when, having finished his tea, Mr. Howells retired into the bakehouse and came out in an old tweed jacket, with only the red pipings up the seams of his trousers to remind Kate that she was talking to a Government official.

"Well, you see, his father's in the Merchant Navy, and the great-aunt he lives with is a very old lady," said Kate.

Mr. and Mrs. Howells exchanged a stolid, and yet, Kate, felt, subtly ironical glance.

"We had a letter from Miss Brentwood saying she couldn't leave her cats," stated Mrs. Howells simply, folding up the cloth and putting it away in a drawer. "We was surprised about that, Cornelius and me."

"Her's an old maid, I reckon," said Cornelius tolerantly, "and they be mostly cankerish... So Davis Pentrewer drove you out from the station! He be a rough kind of man, I reckon!"

The tone, as well as the words, was disparaging, and Kate perceived that the Post Office looked down upon Pentrewer.

"Is Pentrewer a farm?"

Mr. Howells exchanged a bright, humorous glance with Mrs. Howells.

"You could call it a farm, I reckon, if you could see the land for bracken," he opined. "Them've got a bit of hill land there and a few ship. But them turns a hand to anything for a living, mostly."

The contemplation of Mr. and Mrs. Davis and their manner of livelihood seemed to cause Mr. Howells some secret amusement, as though he knew more about them than it would be neighbourly to say.

"Sidney Brentwood went over to see them one day, or so Mrs. Davis told me."

"Boys get in all kinds of company," said Mrs. Howells apologetically. "You can't stop them going where they likes. I wasn't too pleased when I heard as Sidney had stopped to tea along of Davis Pentrewer. But young people has to learn there's all sorts of folk in the world, hasn't they, and we can't keep them all the time tied to the right sort. I asked him not to go there again."

Kate, puzzled by this social ostracism, protested:

"I thought Mr. and Mrs. Davis seemed rather nice people."

"Well—I'm not saying they isn't, but—" Mrs. Howells looked at her husband, who helped her out.

"Reckon they've got too much gipsy blood in them for us kind of folk to take to, Missie. They be harmless folk in their way, I expect. But over Pentrewer way people mostly isn't as particular as us Hastry people. A tidy lot of them be a roughish sort, I reckon."

"I see," said Kate, still a little puzzled. Those who lived Pentrewer way, she must take it, then, including her kind Samaritans, were a lesser breed dwelling without the pale of civilised Hastry life. She was about to pigeon-hole the information under the heading of Distinctions (Social) when Mr. Howells added:

"They isn't as particular what they turns a hand to as us is, you sees, Miss. Not particular enough, us thinks."

He seemed disinclined to say more on the subject, and Kate docketed his remarks temporarily under the label of Prejudice (Moral).

What she wondered, did Hastry village think of Gideon Atkins, whom even the Davises appeared to despise? But Gideon Atkins, it appeared when she mentioned his name, was a farmer in a biggish way, a warm man, and although Mr. Howells readily admitted that he was not popular in the district, he seemed to entertain a certain respect for him.

"He be a bit close-fisted, Missie, that's how it be, and not only that, but he ben't a friendly man. He be not long from Yorkshire, and it *do seem* as if farmers round here can't get on with him and doesn't want to. But he be a goodish farmer, I reckon. People here is inclined to be jealous of strangers, unless they makes theirselves agreeable. Now, there's strangers at the Veault hasn't been there above six months and is more liked than Gideon Atkins after two years! But then they be free with their talk and their money, and he be tight with both, and that's the difference, I reckon!"

"The Veault!" exclaimed Kate. "I travelled in the train from Llanfyn with a children's nurse who said she was going to the Veault!"

"Ah, it's to be a home for London children, that's what they say. George Hufton the builder is working there, putting in plumbing enough for a hotel and baths I don't know how many!"

Mrs. Howells reckoned in an aside that they'd be needed, if the London children were like some that had come to Hastry village!

"They say it's an American lady is doing it," continued Mr. Howells. "Her and her niece. There's to be room for forty children there, they says, with five nurses to them. Well the Veault's a big old rambling place, but 'twill be a puzzle to fit them in, I reckon! When you go to see your friend at Llanhalo, you can take a look at the Veault at the same time, Missie. It stands on the same bank, not above a quarter mile from Llanhalo, and that's six miles from Hastry, pretty near."

"I wonder whether I can hire a bicycle," said Kate, who had foolishly not anticipated these distances, nor a bus service that ran only twice a week.

Mrs. Howells said that she thought her daughter, who lived in the village, would be pleased to lend hers, as now that she had a baby to push about she didn't use a bicycle any more.

"You needs a bike to get about in this country," she agreed.

"Sidney was for ever running around on his bike, poor boy. He was a real country kind of boy, not like some of them that's evacuated here and can't find anything to do with themselves. He was a real nice boy, and I can't bear to think what has happened to him! Our children is all grown up and married, it was like being young again to have him in the house!"

Tears sparkled in her kind eyes, and Mr. Howells, looking very grave said: "Ah, that was so, indeed!"

A little later, after a perilous walk down the garden path in the black-out and the rain, Kate was shown up the box-stairs to her bedroom.

As Mrs. Howells put the candle down on the chest-of-drawers and made sure the window-curtain over the little window was fast, Kate looked about her. This had been Sidney Brentwood's room. His little collection of books was still on the mantelpiece. His football boots were still under the washstand. A photograph of his father in a frame of Woolworth tortoise-shell stood on the pillar-like commode behind the big, puffed bed.

"Excuse me, I never can come in this room without feeling bad," said Mrs. Howells, plumping down Kate's knapsack, which she had insisted on carrying as well as the candle, and wiping her eyes on the back of her broad hand. "I cannot bear to think what has happened to that poor boy!"

Kate patted her shoulder and made consoling noises, adding, for it was her business to investigate every possibility as quickly as possible:

"What do you *think* has happened to him, Mrs. Howells?"

Mrs. Howells could not, or would not, say. She could, and would, say what had not happened to him, however.

"The police thinks as he went back to London," she said with some indignation. "They thinks that if a boy's home is in London, that will be sure to be where he's gone, too! But me and Corney knows as Sidney would never have wanted to go back to London! He was always saying that even when the war was over, he would never want to go back! We used to be surprised that he did not care more for his home and relations, but when we had the letter from his aunt after he went away, then we was not so surprised!"

Kate nodded. She was looking thoughtfully at the little row of books on the mantelpiece. "The Boy's Own Annual," an ancient bound volume of "Children's Encyclopaedia," "Wild Life in Streams and Ditches," and a book called "Things For a Boy to Do," shared the space with a collection of well-battered schoolbooks. She picked up the latter volume, which had the yellow label of the County libraries, and ran her eye through it.

"Had Sidney any special hobbies? I suppose he didn't say why he took this book out of the library?"

Mrs. Howells smiled sadly.

"Sidney was a boy that was always wanting to do things," she sighed, and nervously rubbing her hands over the big knob at the bed-foot, she said hurriedly, as if she could hardly bear to utter the words, but had better get them out: "I am afraid he is dead, or he would have come back."

"But to have disappeared so completely, Mrs. Howells, bicycle and all!"

"I knows, but—the bracken is very high on the hills at this time of year, and the hills is very wild," said Mrs. Howells in a low voice, repeating almost what Mr. Davis had said.

"Why do you think he went out at all, in the middle of the night, like that, without telling anyone?"

Mrs. Howells shook her head.

"Boys is like that, isn't they? They never talks about the thing they're thinking most about doing. But I knows, whatever he was trying to do, he was not going back to London. Well, I hopes you'll be comfortable, young lady!"

She withdrew, and Kate heard her going down the little wooden staircase, and the murmur of voices below, and the raking out of the fire, and later, as she sat up in bed studying her Ordnance Survey map by the light of a candle, the quick padding steps of Mr. Howells' stockinged feet and the slower, noisier step of Mrs. Howells' shoes, coming up again to the next bedroom, and the rattling of a chest-of-drawers on an uneven floor and the creaking of a loose wire-mattress, and then silence.

Kate sat up on an extremely buxom feather bed on top of two or three other varieties of mattress and two creaking straw palliasses, feeling like a princess in a fairy-story, and examined the map spread out on the Marcella counterpane. Cartography was not Kate's strong subject, but she supposed that she could master the elements of it with a little determination.

Radnorshire, according to the map, seemed to be mostly of a brown, warty nature, shading to narrow strips of delicate green, and gemmed here and there with little spots of blue. Hastry was on a pale brown strip, Hastry Station on a pale-green. There was the main road she had come along in Mr. Davis's tub, crossing the little stream in the valley and forking just this side of it. Here was Pentrewer, in slightly better baked biscuit colour than Hastry, and an inch or so north of it, and here was the black-letter word MOUND, with which Kate had become so familiar in Dorsetshire two years ago. On the other side of the large brown wart Kate took to be Rhosbach, there was a big blue spot and a few black dots marked "Control Station"—doubtless the Berminster waterworks referred to by Mrs. Davis. This was a half-inch map, and Kate, guessing at a radius of five inches, searched everywhere for Llanhalo and Aminta. She found them at last, on a pale brown strip due north of Pentrewer. And there was the Veault, a quarter-of-an-inch farther on.

Childishly pleased with herself, Kate folded the map up and blew out the candle. The room was so small, and the bed so big, that the little window was within reach, and she leant and drew back the black-out curtain. But she looked into a blackness almost as dense as that within the room. She could not tell whether she were looking on to the pale green valley or the dark brown hill. There was a gusty, noisy wind tearing across the sky. But, at least, the rain had stopped.

Chapter Five

The next morning, waking disgracefully late, with a slightly suffocated feeling induced by the feather bed, and a mild rheumatic affliction of the hip-joints induced by the straw palliasses underneath, Kate decided that the first thing she must do must be to acquire a bicycle.

Mr. Howells had gone forth on the business of His Majesty's Government, and Mrs. Howells was attending to customers in the tiny stone-flagged shop. The tearing wind had torn blue spaces in the clouds for the sun to shine through, and was still at the attack. Kate could see in the distance, down the valley, the slanting lines of rain, but here the wind had blown the hillside dry, tindery leaves rolled along the road, and Monday's belated washing flapped above the cabbages and battered asters.

When Kate returned from the cottage of Mrs. Howells' daughter, Mrs. Evans, it was on a bicycle, with pockets full of pears which Mrs. Evans, foiled in her hospitality by Kate's refusal to drink another lot of tea or eat another lot of bread-and-butter, had pressed upon her. The straggling village, bathing coldly in the autumn sunlight, looked a very different place from the rain-enwrapped, silent huddle under the lowering hill which Kate had approached last night in Mr. Davis's trap. There were people about, and a grocery-van at the kerb, and a man with a flock of sheep and a collie dog. And in the playground of the red-brick school a large number of small children in shirts and dresses as variegated as a flower garden were performing toes rise and double knee-bend under the tuition of a stout elderly teacher who was struggling bravely to get an untrained voice across the wind— Kate made a mental note that she ought to go and see Sidney's schoolmaster. He might give Kate another angle on Sidney's character and habits.

So far, the impression of Sidney Brentwood that she had derived from Mrs. Howells tallied pretty closely with the sketchier portrait supplied by his great-aunt in Bayswater. It was, Kate surmised, the portrait of a boy who might well go off on his own and get lost; but it was not the portrait of a boy who would have any dark or abstruse reason for doing so.

Sidney Brentwood's character seemed singularly free from psychological complications. The reason for his absence, Kate, toiling up the village street on a bicycle far too low for her, decided, was probably simple. Had he intended to go for good?

On the face of it, the answer appeared to be no. For to go off and send no word for three weeks to Mr. and Mrs. Howells seemed too heartless an action for a "real nice boy." But, Kate reminded herself, many real nice boys were of that adventurous temperament which neither worries nor considers worry in other people, which looks always ahead and never backward, and to whom to be out of sight is to be out of mind. Kate reflected that Sidney's father was a sailor, and that there was something traditionally sailor-like about such a character.

However, if there was no psychological improbability about Sidney's trying to disappear, there was a strong practical improbability of his succeeding, in these days of ration-books and registration-cards. One could discount the possibility, Kate thought, of a successful voluntary disappearance. What remained?

Accident. The obvious answer, and one Kate had already received not only from Miss Brentwood and Mrs. Howells and

Mrs. Davis, but from Mrs. Evans and the nice woman in the County Library as well. Sidney had left Hastry for a boy's simple reason, a night's adventure, and had met with an accident, and had not come back.

But what accident could completely remove every trace of a boy and his bicycle? The answer to that question was not so obvious, and nobody, so far, had been able to provide it.

Perhaps, then, the adventure upon which Sidney had gone that night was not so simple as it had seemed to him: perhaps there had been other people, not happy-go-lucky boys, involved in the adventure: perhaps he had been prevented from coming back. That would explain his complete disappearance better than any easy, sorrowful talk of "accident" could do. But what kind of adventure could such have been? Kate had to admit that the possibilities that flitted through her mind were vague, wild, and improbable: but then, she reminded herself, the complete disappearance of a boy and his bicycle is itself an improbable thing, yet it has happened.

She propped her new bicycle up against the woodshed wall in Mrs. Howells' garden, and stood frowning at a small troop of purple asters in a box-encircled camp. Suppose the adventure Sidney had set forth upon that night had been dangerous, more dangerous than he knew? Unlawful, more unlawful than he knew?

If only all Sidney's words and actions for, say, a week before his disappearance could be recalled, so that Kate could pore over the record for any hint of what had been occupying his mind! But nobody noticed, nobody remembered, the things children chattered about, the questions they asked! Only from the librarian in the County Library had Kate received a hint of one subject which had recently interested Sidney, and that was an unexpected and an innocent one enough. He had wished, it seemed, some weeks ago, for a book on net-making.

Turning aside from her review of the trooped asters, Kate went in at the front door, which opened, in fact was already open, straight into the shop.

Kate had taken for normal Welsh expressiveness the high-pitched vocal noise that had been going on in the shop while she had been reviewing the asters. But as she set foot on the worn doorstep, she saw that there was a grand row going on. Kind Mrs. Howells, her hand resting on a biscuit tin as though she might at any moment hurl it like a hand-grenade, stood crimson-faced behind her counter. And on the strip of jute matting that protected her well-whitened floor, stood a spare little elderly woman with a large basket over her arm, clutching an umbrella as if it were a rifle. Between them on the counter stood an old-fashioned pair of brass scales, one or two loaves of bread and several tall glass sweet-jars, mostly empty. Leaning unobtrusively against the window sill, listening to the duel going on between the two women, stood a gaunt, elderly man of strange, poetic and wild appearance.

"It iss no wonder the poor boy ran away!" the customer was saying all but at the top of her voice. "He ran away because he wass neglected and I do not blame him!"

"Please not to say another word, Ann Gilliam!" said Mrs. Howells. Her voice was lower, but vibrated more.

This was, it seemed, a public row, so Kate, seeing no reason why she should retire, remained in the doorway.

"Please to get out of my shop, Ann Gilliam!"

The customer, who was no match in size for Mrs. Howells, stood with a back like a poker and two rather large feet in black gum-boots well turned out at the toes, and replied, without moderating her tone at all:

"I will have my half-pound of sultanas, if you please, before I go, Mary Howells!"

Mrs. Howells seized up her hand-grenade and banged it on to a shelf behind her.

"Oh, indeed, and you will not!"

"You cannot refuse to serve a customer!"

"Indeed, then, I can and I do! And if you do not like it, Ann Gilliam, you can go to the police!"

"Well, I wonder you would be talking about the police, Mary Howells, in that free way! The police has been here often enough, hassn't they, asking questions you wass not able to answer!"

The bard-like being by the window here intervened, in a melodious, rather melancholy voice:

"There is plenty questions none of us can't answer, Miss Gilliam, but there is also plenty more as us could answer if us was willing, but as us doesn't answer because us is not willing, and that is more of a different matter, Miss Gilliam, whether the police is aware of it or not!"

What there was in this speech, which was delivered not at all in a threatening, but rather in a pensively jocular, fashion, to damp Miss Gilliam's fires, Kate could not see. But damped they obviously were.

"Nobody wass asking you for your opinion, Gwyn Lupton!" she said, with a somewhat half-hearted sharpness.

"If I was always waiting to be asked for my opinion," said the bard imperturbably. "I should not have said many words in my long life. And yet there has been some times when I has not said so many words as I might have said, and people has been grateful to me because I has not said them."

So fascinating did Kate find the melodious and dignified delivery of these remarks that she scarcely realised that she was listening to a kind of poetic blackmail, until she saw the effect of them on little Miss Gilliam. Miss Gilliam clasped her umbrella slantwise in her arms, as if it were a lily and she a saint, tucked her elbows well into her sides, and backed a few steps towards the door.

"I shall change my registration, Mary Howells, and I shall be a customer at the International where they knows how to be civil!"

"It is all the same to me so long as you do not come here asking for your pound of sultanas when there is not enough to go round!"

"And as for you, Gwyn Lupton, I am surprised you have not got something better to do in a war than poke about in the ground after old pieces of money and stand about in shops poking your nose into other people's affairs!"

But the powder was damp, and even this squib did not go off properly. Its utterer paused in an angry and discomfited fashion, as if she were trying to set light to a new one, and then, giving it up, made a right-about-turn and departed, her umbrella still clasped rigidly in front of her, her empty basket on her arm, and her comical oilskin pixie-hood giving her the look, from behind, of a very inflexible and alarming little girl. She stumped down the garden steps and disappeared.

"Well!" exclaimed Mrs. Howells, still very red in the face. "I never did expect to be insulted in my own shop over half-a-pound of sultanas!" Catching Kate's eye, she moderated her wrath, and half-smiled. "That was all because I could not sell Ann Gilliam more than half-a-pound of sultanas this week, Miss Mayhew! Does she think I would not rather sell her a pound, or two pounds, if I could?"

"Who is she?" inquired Kate, taking off her oilskin coat.

"She lives up on Rhosbach at the Cefn," said Mrs. Howells. "She has a little smallholding there that her auntie had before her. She is a great gossip. I don't know will Cornelius like it when I tell him I have quarrelled with her. She will say all sorts of things about me in the village now, I shouldn't wonder!"

The gaunt elderly person by the window-sill collected his loose limbs together and crossed over to the counter.

"I would not be worrying your head about that, Mrs. Howells. There is women that gives forth venom like the snake does because it is in their nature, and Miss Gilliam is one of them, and her auntie was the same, and her great-auntie, who had the Cefn before that, was worst of any!"

Kate thought that the speaker, scarcely looked old enough to have been acquainted with so many of this curious dynasty of Gilliam, which seemed to dispense with parents and consist entirely of aunts and nieces. He appeared to be a well-preserved fifty-five, a gaunt, loose-hung man with an eagle-like cut of profile, a ruddy complexion somewhat dimmed by a grey stubble, a dark, piercing and observant eye, and long iron-black hair that fell in a lock across his lined forehead and curled over the collar of his ancient, green-black, homespun coat. A handkerchief knotted round his scrawny throat gave the last touch of the poet, rather than of the labourer, to his distinguished looks. But his hands, large, stiff and glazed, were those of a labourer rather than a poet, as they fumbled with an old purse he had taken from his pocket. Kate wondered whether he had in that purse the Roman coin he had found on Pentrewer Tump.

Evidently the opening of the purse brought the same subject to Mr. Gwyn Lupton's mind, for having asked for two-pennyworth of cloves for his wife's tooth-ache, he went on with melodious melancholy:

"Miss Gilliam has no business to speak as if I was for ever delving in the ground for treasure as the pigs does after roots. It was setting rabbit snares in the evening after my work that I walked upon the tump, and it was in the rabbit-hole, there at my feet, I saw the piece of money."

Could I see it?" ventured Kate.

Gwyn Lupton turned his dark, majestic gaze upon her and shook his head.

I have not got it any longer, young lady. The gentleman at the Veault, where I am working, is an antiquary gentleman and very interested in the old remnants of our forefathers. He has bought it off me for his collection. I was not anxious to sell it," said Gwyn Lupton grandly, "but since he wished to buy it I obliged him. Five pounds he gave me—it may have been worth more, I cannot tell."

"Five pounds! It must have been something unusual. Not many old silver coins are worth that."

"I made a mould in putty of the piece of money, to keep as a curiosity, and one day when you are passing my place at Pentrewer, I will show it you if you will please to step in. But the piece of money is at the Veault. If you are ever in that direction, call at the Veault, young lady, and ask Mr. Morrison to show you the piece of money. Say Gwyn Lupton sent you. Mr. Morrison is a very obliging gentleman, and if you likes old houses, young lady— and most London ladies does, I have noticed—you will like to see the Veault. It is a very ancient old timber house. They say as King Charles hid there when he was running away off to France one time."

Kate could not help smiling at poor King Charles, that peripatetic monarch, under the patronage of whose shade so many inns, old manors and oak trees flourish!

"I have been working on the Veault for Mr. Hufton the builder, getting it ready for the London children that is coming there, so I knows what I am telling you about, young lady. There is some grand old panelled rooms there, if you likes panelled rooms, and most London ladies does, I has noticed. There is a spit, too, in the kitchen, and some of the ceilings has their beams and joists showing, and there is a front staircase that has carved newel-posts and a back staircase that is like a corkscrew," said Gwyn Lupton, who was evidently a pretty good judge of the taste of lady fanciers of house property. He added: "And now there is four baths, no less, and lavatories galorum."

"When will the children be coming, Mr. Lupton, have you heard?" asked Mrs. Howells, shaking the cloves out of a large tin on to the scales.

"Pretty soon, I expect, Mrs. Howells. The young lady from the Abbey Farm was at the Veault the day before yesterday to fix up with Mrs. Morrison about supplying the milk for the children."

"That will be your Land Army friend, Miss Mayhew!"

"Oh, indeed, young lady, so the young lady from the Abbey Farm is a friend of yours?" said Gwyn Lupton with melodious interest. "Well, Llanhalo Abbey is an old ancient place, too, but there is not so much to see there as there is at the Veault, and what you see you has to pay sixpence for." Mr. Lupton seemed firmly convinced that old houses were Kate's chief interest in life. As a carpenter, reflected Kate, he probably had to listen to a good deal of feminine gush about oak beams and such objects. He pocketed the screw of cloves and picked two pennies out of his little black purse.

"Gideon Atkins isn't popular, is he?" commented Kate, amused.

The bard, planking down his two pennies, flashed his remote and haughty glance at her.

"Good opinions cannot be bought with gold, it is true, but bad opinions is the reward of the miser," he observed. "There is men in this world thinks so much of money they doesn't know the value of anything, and Gideon Atkins is such a man. He is a man who would die to save a doctor's bill, if it were not for the funeral expenses that would follow."

Kate wondered whether Aminta, who was a detached and somewhat unobservant girl, was aware that her employer's funeral formed one of the more frequent, and more cheerful, topics of local conversation. Gwyn Lupton's haughty and poetic features wore quite a rapt expression.

"Well, Mrs. Howells, well, young lady, I must take my leave of you, for my wife is suffering great agonies, poor woman, and I must not be lingering on my way to her more than is reasonable. Do not forget, young lady, when you are at Llanhalo, seeing your friend, to go to the Veault and ask Mr. Morrison to show you Gwyn Lupton's piece of money. Good-day to you, Mrs. Howells, I would not be worrying if I was you about Miss Gilliam's tongue. There is other people has tongues besides Miss Gilliam, and could use them if they liked."

And with this dark observation Gwyn Lupton departed, bumping out with his fist and sticking on the back of his head an ancient felt hat that he had been carrying flattened under his arm.

"If words could charm away the tooth-ache, Gwyn Lupton's wife would not be sending for cloves!" observed Mrs. Howells with a smile.

"What did he mean by that last bit?" Kate inquired, taking a seat by the counter and studying the selection of cigarettes that shared a little glass case with some dummy packets of chocolate.

"Well, I dare say as being a carpenter and working a lot in people s houses, Gwyn Lupton gets to know things about the people he works for as they wouldn't always like to have spread about," explained Mrs. Howells.

Kate smiled. No doubt a village carpenter did possess grand opportunities for inspecting the skeletons in his neighbour's cupboards before putting the doors right!

"That was what he meant, I expect. There isn't many houses about here as Gwyn Lupton hasn't done repairs in, one time and another. Well, I must be getting on with my polishing."

"Can you remember, Mrs. Howells, Sidney ever saying anything about making a net?"

"A net!" echoed Mrs. Howells, pausing with the flap of the counter held up in her hand. "No, I don't remember ever he said anything about such a thing. What kind of net?"

"I don't know. But I've just been to the County Library. And I asked the woman there if she could remember anything Sidney Brentwood did or said when he went to the library to take that book out—you know, the one you showed me in his bedroom. And she said that he had asked her whether there was a book in the library about making nets."

"Net!"

"Yes. Apparently he didn't go into any details, and she didn't ask for them. She just said that 'Things for a Boy to Do' would be the only book in the library that might have a chapter on net-making, and he at once took it out and went off with it."

"Nets!" echoed Mr Howells again, letting her counter fall and shaking her head in a mystified manner. "No, I cannot recollect that Sidney ever said anything at all about nets. Would it be nets for rabbiting, I wonder, or—"

"I don't know. It seems he just wanted to know how to make a net. It's queer, isn't it, Mrs. Howells? What could he have wanted a net for? What are nets used for?"

"Well, for snaring—they uses them sometimes rabbiting, and for keeping haystacks down. And for putting over fruit. But if Sidney had wanted to go rabbit-snaring he could have borrowed a net, there's plenty about!"

"He may not have wanted a net, I suppose. He may have just wanted for some reason to know how to make one," said Kate, though from what she had heard of Sidney Brentwood his interests were more likely to be practical than theoretical.

A little quiver passed over Mrs. Howells' broad rosy face. "If that was all he wanted, Corney could have showed him how to do netting! But boys is funny, they will not say what is mostly in their hearts, they gives themselves and everyone else a lot of trouble sooner than speak out, they is like that, boys!"

Mrs. Howells departed to her polishing in the already brightly polished kitchen, and Kate sat a moment or two in the shop, reflecting on these last remarks. If Sidney had wanted to learn netting sufficiently to look for a book on the subject in the library, and yet had not mentioned his desire to Mr. and Mrs. Howells, it seemed probable that his net-making was connected with something that he wanted to keep a secret. Nets! thought Kate, bird-nets, fish-nets, butterfly-nets, camouflage-nets, nets for rabbiting, nets for snares—

There was an echo here of what Kate had been thinking as she toiled home on her bicycle. Snares were dangerous—for the snared creature. And sometimes a hunter was caught with his own snare, and the danger was his. Was there a connection between Sidney's interest in nets and his departure? Had he already made his net secretly before he went? Kate picked up her oilskin coat and went upstairs to her bedroom. Taking up "Things for a Boy to Do," she was about to turn to the index when she found it was unnecessary. The book fell open at page 105, Netting. The page had that peculiarly fingered and dingy appearance reading matter acquires when the young idea has been poring over it.

"For Netting," read Kate, "a netting needle and a spool are needed—"

And, Kate supposed, quite a lot of string. If Sidney had been secretly practising net-making during the month before he went—perhaps during those fight evenings when Mrs. Howells had thought him touring the countryside on his bicycle—he must have acquired his materials from somewhere. No doubt it was possible to buy twine and netting needles at Llanfyn, which was the nearest market-town. But, if Sidney had bought his materials there, the police would surely have discovered it and questioned Mrs. Howells about the transaction?

Or Sidney might have got his materials privately, as a gift, or loan. But if so, why had the giver kept the matter so quiet that Mrs. Howells had not heard of it? Was the giver involved in whatever danger had overtaken Sidney? Did he even know —too well, perhaps—what had happened to the boy?

Kate, standing there in the little bedroom with the boy's book in her hands, became aware that she was casting her own nets a bit wide. They were catching at all kinds of distant, sinister possibilities which she was quite unable to draw in and examine. For the present, she had better attend to collecting facts, rather than to casting about for possibilities. She thought a bicycle-ride would clear her head, and went downstairs to raise the saddle of Mrs. Evan's bicycle a couple of inches, and to tell Mrs. Howells that she was going over to Llanhalo and would not be back till evening.

Chapter Six

Kate's cycle-ride took her downhill and up again on a road that skirted along the lower slopes of Rhosbach, on whose far upper slopes the distant sheep seemed to crawl like lice. Below her, to her left, when she could glimpse the landscape through the tall hedges and the woods that clung here and there around the base of the hills, lay wide, rolling tracts of farmland and handsome old magpie houses showing tantalisingly here and there behind the yew trees which protected them from the winds.

Occasionally a farmer's battered motor car, or a flock of sheep with drover and collie, passed her on the road. And once a gipsy's caravan went by, with two rough ponies tied on behind the vans, and a couple of half-grown boys walking alongside.

As they passed her, Kate thought of Sidney, and even turned her head, as if hoping to see, sitting in the back doorway of the lumbering vehicle, a fair-skinned, fair-haired boy. But the person who sat on the step nursing a baby and smoking a cigarette was an old wrinkled woman, anything but fair-skinned.

The afternoon was fine, with a tattered blue and white sky and a lovely shifting light upon gold-turning trees and gleaming, browning grasses. The road crossed the valley, and then went uphill once more, and then down and up again along the lower slopes of the spurred hills until she caught sight, on the bank below her, of a rather ruinous-looking small church or chapel, a square stone house and a great many barns huddled round it, and decided that she had better get off and take a look at her map.

However, there was a man engaged in slashing at the hedge with a long-handled sharp-edged tool not unlike a Cromwellian halberd, and since Kate always preferred making verbal inquiries to reading a map, she pedalled on a few yards and stopped beside him.

"Please can you tell me if Llanhalo Abbey is far from here?"

The man, who was a small, tubby, elderly man with a prevailing sandy-greyness of hue about him, paused in his onslaught on the brambles long enough to shake his head. In so doing he shook crooked his steel-rimmed spectacles, and had to waste another valuable second in adjusting them. While he did this with one hand, he made a motion with his pruning hook straight down the track to the ruined church on the bank below.

"Down there?" asked Kate.

The man nodded. Kate was surprised at his taciturnity, and as is usual with humanity when it comes across true economy in words, she proceeded to redress the balance by wasting a good many words herself.

"Mr. Atkin's Farm, I mean—Llanhalo Abbey Farm?"

The man nodded silently, and laying hold of a great snake of blackberry with his thickly gloved hand began to haul it relentlessly on to the road, which was already littered with thorny clippings enough to puncture a fleet of bicycles.

"Perhaps you work there," suggested Kate, "and if so, perhaps you can tell me whereabouts I'll be likely to find Miss Hughes?"

Jerking his long whip of bramble free, the man paused as if he were considering whether it were possible to answer this question without articulating. He looked at Kate thoughtfully from the sharp little grey eyes behind his still somewhat crooked spectacles. He had shaved more recently than Gwyn Lupton, but not very recently, and this chiefly accounted, Kate saw, for the greyish bloom that overlay the uniform brown of his roundish, heavy-chinned face. He transferred his pruning-hook from his right hand to his left, and lifted his ancient tweed hat with his right to scratch his head, as if he might thus become inspired with a method of answering Kate's question in silence. It was no use. He had to open the tight-closed trap of his lips and let some precious words out.

"In byre yonder."

"Straight down this track?"

"Aye."

"Is Mr. Atkins about anywhere?" pursued Kate, for she did not intend to miss a chance of seeing this celebrity while she was on the spot.

"Aye."

"I suppose that's the farmhouse, that square stone place beyond the chapel?"

"Aye."

"Thank you so much. It's a grand afternoon, isn't it?"

"Aye."

"I suppose you know that half the bicycles that come along here will get their tyres punctured on these bits and pieces of yours?" said Kate, with amiable remonstrance, as she wheeled her machine aside on to the farm road.

"Aye."

A little piqued, Kate said:

"It's all the same to you if they do, I suppose, eh?"

"Aye."

"Oh, do say something different!" cried Kate, half amused, half exasperated, and waited a second to see if he would. But he became a sphinx again, and she cycled cautiously down the rutty lane, smiling to herself, to look for the byre which contained Aminta.

She felt extraordinarily pleased to be going to see old Aminta again. Before the war, Aminta had worked as secretary to a firm of photographers, an occupation which she had arranged to desert for the Women's Land Army almost before the Women's Land Army had come into being. Aminta was never happier than when in the company of dumb animals of one kind or another, the larger the better. And now, Kate imagined, nothing would ever lure her from her work among the cows—or nothing but the chance of a job in a circus, with elephants, or in a Zoo, with camels.

The chapel Kate was approaching was a curious neglected building, and Kate scarcely thought it could still be in use for religious services. A great pile of faggots stood just outside it, and a harrow was lying close up to the lee of its ancient wall. There was no glass in the fine traceries of the window at the gable-end, and the delicate stonework was weatherbeaten and damaged. Obviously, the walls were of great antiquity. But the roof, or most of it, was of corrugated iron, like any little non-conformist chapel newly put up to house a remote, poor congregation. The track ran round it, a very secular-looking approach, scratched up by hens and waddled across by ducks, and the farmyard pond lay near. A large square stone-built house of a strictly utilitarian Victorian type stood farther along the trackway behind a little orchard of scraggy apple trees. A perfect huddle of lean-to roofs and ancient lichen-covered barns and sheds sprawled around the house and cuddled intimately up against it, so that it preserved its smug square look of nineteenth century respectability with some difficulty, seeming to apologise, with raised stone eyebrows under its penthouse roof, for the odd company it kept.

Which of these manifold buildings was the byre which contained Aminta, Kate could not guess. She got off her bicycle. A wall-eyed collie came suspiciously up to her, his hackles rising. She propped her bicycle against the orchard fence, and was contemplating going up to the house's very prim front door when there came to her ears, from a long low stone roofed building beyond a very muddy yard that lay behind the chapel, the peculiar low-toned musical sound which even a town-bred ear ran recognise as the sound of milk spurting into a pail.

Kate skirted the yard and looked in at the open door. She was rewarded by the sight of Aminta, sitting precariously on a three-legged stool, the top of her head buried in the soft part of a bony roan cow, making great play with the muscles of her brown forearms.

"Aminta!" cried Kate joyfully, and realised the next instant, from the cautious manner in which Aminta, who had started violently, recovered herself, moved her tipped bucket to a safe position and herself to an upright one before looking round, that she ought to have approached with more circumspection. The cow, however, evidently a quiet lady, looked mildly round and went on eating hay.

"Hullo Kate!" said Aminta with pleasure, but without undue surprise for the actions of her fellow-creatures rarely surprised her. She added "Lucky Tulip's a quiet cow, or she might have kicked half my milking over, being bounced at like that."

"I'm sorry. I say, I *am* pleased to see you, Aminta! You do look grand and rugged, too. Like a piece of mountain scenery."

Aminta, clapping Kate on the shoulder, replied genially:

"I thought somehow you'd come along."

"You did? You must be psychic if you thought that, because I didn't think it myself till the day before yesterday."

"I thought my last letter'd fetch you. Have you joined up yet, or are you waiting to join up at the county headquarters?"

Kate looked at Aminta, marvelling not for the first time at the strange misconceptions which add zest to friendship.

"Your letter didn't fetch me, darling. No."

"Didn't it?" said Aminta without offence. "Look, Kate, I've just got to finish Tulip, if you don't mind waiting a moment. Whups, my beauty!"

Taking her stool in her left hand and her milk-pail in her right, Aminta inserted herself with great skill and precision between them and groped about under the cow, inquiring in a rather cow-muffled voice as she did so:

"What *did* you come for, then?"

But the spurting of milk drowned Kate's attempt at a reply. In the year since Kate had last seen her, Aminta, who had always been pale and inclined to run to fat, had become comparatively slender, nut-brown in colour, and to judge from her forearms up which at the moment terrifying ripples of muscle were passing, as hard as iron. There was evidently a great deal to be said for the Land Army as a beautifying agent.

Kate stood in the doorway and looked across the yard at the picturesque collection of roofs which lay at the back of the farmhouse, and at the first building she had seen, which she now perceived was an ecclesiastical ruin patched up to serve as a barn. Behind it, a graceful melancholy shell of stone, holding nothing but sky in its empty windows, was, she supposed, one of the relics of antiquity to inspect which visitors paid Mr Gideon Atkins their sixpences. What looked like the remains of a cloister joined the two buildings. Kate thought that Mr. Gideon Atkins might really use some of his sixpences in clearing away the brambles which were doing their best to drag these ancient stones back into the earth from which they had come.

Aminta stopped making soothing noises to her cow and rose to her feet.

"That's the lot, I think," she said, putting the frothing pail down on the cobbles and removing the ancient man's cap she had been wearing. "Tulip's a nuisance just at present. She's got twins and she tries to save up milk for them."

Hooking her two buckets on to an iron hoop, she stepped into the middle of it, lifted it, and with this simple safeguard against splashed milk, led the way across the yard to the dairy.

The house itself might have a prim Victorian look, but the cavernous dairy, when they entered it out of the sunlight of the yard, reminded Kate of a mediaeval dungeon. They had to descend a few steps into it, for its stone-flagged floor was below ground-level, and the vaulted, rather low stone ceiling, gave the impression of a place quite sunk below the earth, although the walls were whitewashed to reflect what light there was. The scrubbed wide shelves that ran around the stone walls, carrying flat bowls of milk, dishes with remnants of cooked food, cheeses and other such harmless and even attractive objects, looked out of place.

Aminta put down her milk-pails with a sound like the clanking of prisoners' chains.

"I always thought," said Kate, looking around her, "that a dairy was a light, sunny place where pink-cheeked maidens, mostly called Chloe or Amaryllis, sang songs about their swains while they swung the churns."

"You try singing a song while you swing the churn, my child! And if the dairy was sunny, everything would go off in the hot weather. Still, I admit most of the dairies I've been into are a bit more cheerful than this," said Aminta, taking a strainer and a couple of milk-cans down from nails on the wall.

At the darker side of the room, the vaulted ceiling broke in a low stone archway, with a short barrel-roofed passage beyond, which ended in a heavily-nailed door. A variety of things, including oil-drums, old brooms, mole-traps, wooden trestles, beer-barrels, and what might have been the original butt of Malmsey that drowned the Duke of Clarence, stood in this doorway.

"Where does the door at the end of that passage lead to?" asked Kate.

Aminta glanced up.

"To a cellar."

Kate's interest, already roused by these ancient quarters and the menacing and dungeon-like aspect of the old door, sharpened.

"What, the one where there's a secret passage?"

Aminta laughed.

"Who's been pulling your leg about a secret passage?"

"The Davises of Pentrewer, who drove me up from the station, said there was supposed to be—"

"Yes, there *is* supposed to be the beginning of some tunnel or other, miles long, that pops up goodness knows where—Wigmore Castle or Aberystwyth or the Garden of Eden—you know the kind of thing! Most old houses with cellars are supposed to have secret passages, aren't they?" said Aminta, busy over her milk-strainer.

"You mean there isn't the vestige of such a thing here?"

"I don't know, I'm sure," said Aminta indifferently. "Old Gid says there isn't, and he should know. I've never been in the cellar."

Such incuriousness seemed to Kate excessive, even for Aminta.

"You've been a whole year in a house that's supposed to have a secret passage leading out of the cellar, and you've never even looked in the cellar to see if there's a trap door or anything?"

"Well, I'm generally rather busy doing other things. And as a matter of fact, the cellar door's always kept locked, so I wouldn't be able to look around there, even if I wanted to."

"Kept locked! Why?"

"Oh, well, sightseers used to come sometimes and want to look round it. It's part of the old foundations of the Abbey, you see. And Gid hates sightseers, and small blame to him. It's bad enough to have them crawling round the yard in the summer, without letting them into the house. And when the Morrisons first came to the Veault, Mr. Morrison annoyed old Gid rather by coming and enthusing about this imaginary secret passage and wanting permission to search for it—he's an American, awfully nice, but rather enthusiastic—and Gid got very cross about it. And one day he found Mr. Morrison in the cellar looking round, and suspected him of having designs on some old rusted-in grating that Gid says leads to an old drain, if it leads to anything at all. And there was a great row, and Gid's kept the door locked ever since. He threatened to have the cellar filled in, but he hasn't done it yet, and I should think he'd had too much sense to waste money on such a thing. But gosh he was cross! Old Gid's home is his castle, and nobody's allowed to forget it!"

"Sounds a bit of a dog-in-the-manger to me."

"Oh, I don't know, Katy! A historic ruin is a trial to its owner, you know. Anybody that wants to come and gape at old stones seems to think it's your duty to leave off work and show them round. Mr. Atkins makes them pay sixpence each to come in the yard and walk round the refectory and cloister ruins, and won't have them in the house at any price. That keeps them off a bit," said Aminta, with satisfaction.

But Kate's sympathies were with Mr. Morrison, locked out from the promising beginning of an adventure with a secret passage. Secret passages, were, she imagined, mostly figments of the popular imagination: but even the flimsiest rumour of a secret passage must invest an ancient cellar with a peculiar fascination, and she thought it very uncivilised of Aminta's employer to deny a harmless amateur archaeologist his bit of fun.

"I've heard a lot about your Mr. Atkins in Hastry," said she. "What's he like, Aminta?"

"Oh, all right," replied Aminta. It was her invariable reply to inquiries of this sort.

"Shall I see him?"

"I wonder you didn't see him as you came in. He was hedging up by the gate half-an-hour ago."

"What? Do you mean to say *that* was him?"

"I expect so."

"That tubby quiet little man? With eye-glasses?"

"Yes, I believe so," said Ami looking a bit vague, as though a year were hardly long enough for her to have noticed whether her employer wore eye-glasses or not.

"Well, I'm blowed!" muttered Kate, trying to reconcile the reality of Mr. Gideon Atkins' unobtrusive and rotund personality with what she had heard of him.

"Why?"

"So meek and mild! I thought he was a much more terrifying kind of chap."

"He can be, when he likes," said Aminta, on a slightly defensive note, as though she felt it her duty to protect her employer's reputation from the charge of meekness. "You ought to have heard him an hour ago ordering the gipsies off the farm!"

"I wish I had! I like people to live up to their reputations."

"Didn't know old Gid had got one," said Aminta, straining some milk out of her bucket into a couple of tall milk-cans.

"You ought to hear Mr. Gwyn Lupton rhapsodising about him, then."

Aminta muttered:

"Oh, him!"

"Why 'Oh, him'? I fell for Gwyn Lupton, personally."

"I daresay, but then it's your part of job to listen to people talking," said Aminta, acutely for her. "You wouldn't fall if you had him working for you. Nobody gets any work done when Gwyn Lupton's about. He was here a couple of days last week putting up a gate, and nobody could get past him in less than twenty minutes. In the end, I just took to pretending he wasn't there and walking straight through without even saying 'Hullo', leaving him talking to his mallet, if he liked. Even old Gid doesn't know how to shut him up. And most people are like you, and don't even want to."

"I wonder anybody employs him, then!"

"Oh, he gets through quite a lot of work himself. It's other people's work he lays a blight on. At the Veault, Mr. Morrison used to think out most carefully how he could keep Lupton and the other men doing jobs in quite different parts of the house. But it turned out just as bad as letting them work together, because the other men kept finding excuses to visit him to borrow tools or take him cans of tea. People round here like listening to other people talk, I believe."

"I travelled up in the train from Llanfyn with a children's nurse who said she was going to the Veault."

"Oh yes, Rosaleen told me they were expecting one."

"Rosaleen?"

"Rosaleen Morrison. She's awfully nice. I'm going over to the Veault now with this milk. You can come if you like. When the children arrive there, I shall have to take a pony and cart over with the milk and stuff, I suppose. They'll be wanting about five gallons a day."

"When are the children coming?"

"As soon as the house is ready for them, you know what builders are. I think Mrs. Morrison expected the creche'd be in full swing long before this, but now they seem to think it'll be another three weeks at least."

"Isn't it rather odd to engage a nurse such a long time before the children come?"

But speculations upon the oddities of her friends' behaviour did not interest Aminta, who merely replied:

"We'll go through the fields, it's quicker than by road. You'll like Rosaleen, Kate. She's an awfully decent sort."

"I suppose they'd engaged her already, and didn't like to put her off," said Kate, answering her own question.

It was like dear old Aminta, reflected Kate, to be strolling through a field in Radnorshire with a friend she had supposed, until half-an-hour ago, to be in Highgate, without evincing the slightest curiosity as to what had brought her here. Kate was introduced to the calves, who tossed their heads and their tails and cavorted away, to the flock of ewes, who promptly turned their backs and see-sawed off down the hill as one ewe, and to a couple of enormous and far too affectionate carthorses who inspired Kate with a strong hidden desire to imitate the ewes and flee. As they took the footpath through the woods, Kate inquired:

"Have you ever heard of Sidney Brentwood, Aminta?"

"The evacuee boy who disappeared? Yes, of course I heard of him. Why?"

"I came to look for him."

"Oh, did you? Well, you're a bit late off the mark, aren't you, Katy? That was weeks ago. Rosaleen and I joined the search-parties several evenings."

"What happened?"

"Oh, it was dismal, really. Such enormous hills, such a lot of bracken, it gave you a hopeless kind of feeling before you started. And also you couldn't help knowing the kid would probably be dead, if you did find him, which made it seem more dismal still. At least, it did me. Rosaleen was marvellous. She never says die about anything. You'll like her, Kate," said Aminta with enthusiasm.

"Shall I? What do you think happened to Sidney Brentwood, then?"

"Accident," said Aminta briefly.

"If he had an accident, still, he must be somewhere."

"Yes, somewhere nobody's been yet," said Aminta. "Sooner or later somebody'll go there, and then he'll be found—poor kid! Radnorshire's the thinnest-populated county in England and Wales, did you know that?"

"I didn't, but I can well believe it. What's all this barbed wire for?" asked Kate, as Aminta removed a hurdle and they dived under an unsightly wire barricade out of the wood into an open field.

"Fox-hunters," said Aminta, picking up her cans. "Old Gid hates them worse than poachers, and that's saying a lot."

Kate was a little startled at a view of fox-hunters which classed them with poachers. Her own sentiments about foxhunting were the usual urban mixture of pleasure in a picturesque procession combined with an uneasy dislike of blood-sports.

"Mr. Atkins wrote and told them what he'd done, so it's up to them to keep away," said Aminta. "Why should we put up with people trespassing about the place, leaving gates open and breaking hedges down, looking for foxes and ruins and so on?"

"Well, you don't get many people looking for ruins nowadays, I should imagine! Most of us are beginning to get sick of them!"

"No. Though there was a man around here yesterday, wanting permission to make plans of the ruins, who seemed to think we ought to put him up for the week while he did it. Old Gid said he wasn't going to give house-room to ruin-fanciers, but the young man could go and stay somewhere else and come and draw the ruins at sixpence a time, if he liked. So off he went. He was here doing some drawings this morning. Miss Atkins wanted to let him have a room—she's always complaining she doesn't get enough company, poor old thing."

"What's Miss Atkins like?"

"All right," said Aminta, as usual. Miss Atkins, however, had evidently made some impression on her genial indifference, for she added: "She mothers me rather a lot, which I hate."

They passed through a gate into a sloping field, and Kate saw beyond the dip a cluster of old stone roofs under a protecting huddle of great trees.

"There's the Veault," said Aminta. "It's about a thousand times better worth looking at than Llanhalo, but nobody ever comes gaping round here, I suppose because it's not a ruin. I hope Rosaleen's in, Kate. You'll like her."

Chapter Seven

The Veault certainly bore little resemblance to Llanhalo, and was infinitely more picturesque. It was a Tudor period timber-built house, looking across the valley, sheltered at its back by the slope of the land, its farm-buildings, and big trees. In contrast with Llanhalo's curious mixture of Victorian primness and mediaeval gloom, it bore a sunny, tranquil and benevolent look, with the sun gleaming on its ridge-tiles and twinkling on its square-paned casements, and blue smoke rising from a great stone chimney-stack that terminated in shafts of the most delicate brickwork.

There was scaffolding around the chimney-stack in the cobbled back court across which Aminta and Kate were clattering, and a heap of builder's sand, planks and buckets testified to repairs still being carried out. The house had evidently recently been re-tarred and re-lime-washed, for the magpie effect for which west country houses are famous, was positively startling in its contrasts of black and white.

"I say," exclaimed Kate, as they crossed the yard towards a door which stood open on a cool stone passage. "What a stage-setting, Aminta!"

"Nice place for kids, anyway," said Aminta, who was not interested in stage-settings. She knocked casually on the open door, and led the way into a large stone-flagged kitchen, where the sunlight fell picturesquely through a large window over a girl in a yellow jumper and green cord slacks who was setting out cups and saucers on a silver tray.

"Ah, here's the milk!" cried the girl joyfully, looking up. She had a very fresh and attractive voice, with a slight American accent. "I was never more delighted to see anyone in my life, Aminta! Aunt Ellida gave the last drop of yesterday's to the builders for their morning tea, and we're quite out."

"Whatever time of the day I come here, you're making tea, it seems to me," observed Aminta, putting her cans down on the table.

"Maud!" called the girl, raising her pretty voice and directing it towards a narrow stone passage that seemed to lead towards the scullery. "Bring two more cups, will you?" She smiled delightfully at Kate. "Aminta, I suppose it's a secret who your friend is?"

Aminta in her leisurely way introduced Kate to Rosaleen Morrison. Maud, who at that moment appeared in the doorway with a tea-canister and two cups-and-saucers in her hands, Kate recognised as the tall children's nurse who had been her travelling companion. They exchanged genial greetings.

"Shall I take the tray, into the hall, dear?" said Maud.

"I expect that's where you'll find Aunt Ellida," replied Rosaleen. "I'm afraid you'll find Major Everyman there, too."

"Major Everyman?" inquired Aminta. "Who's he?"

"Major Humphries. We call him that because he never utters an original thought. He won't stay long, though. He's got to go and say a few clichés to the Home Guard at five o'clock. You'll stay for a cup, won't you, Aminta?"

"Sorry, I'm afraid I can't. I've got the cows to feed. In fact, Rosaleen, I must be off, if you'll just tip out your milk and let me take the cans."

"Oh come, Aminta honey, don't be so darned virtuous!

"Can't help it, Rosa, I was made that way. You can give Kate a cup of tea, if you don't mind. She wants to see the house. Mind she doesn't cut you out with Gwyn Lupton, though, she s fallen for him. See you later, Kate," said Aminta casually, and left.

"*Isn't* she lovely, your Aminta?" asked Rosaleen. "I think I'd have just *died* of *ennui* here, if it hadn't been for her!

"Have you been here long?"

"Seven long weary weeks. I had a wire from Auntie saying 'Children coming next week,' so I packed my grip and caught the first train for the west. And here we are, seven weeks later, kicking the builder's pants for all we're worth, and still we've only just got the baths fitted. Aren't your builders in England just dilatory, Miss Mayhew? It's quite fascinating the way they go on! What an English builder doesn't know about shattering folks' hope of a home to live in, is just nobody's business!"

Rosaleen smiled straight up into Kate's eyes. Our sympathies do not always respond obediently to the recommendations of our friends. But Kate was quite disposed in this case to oblige Aminta, and like Rosaleen Morrison. She had a free and friendly manner that reminded Kate of the young actresses she was so used to. And, now that Kate came to look at her, there was something about her appearance, too—the well-fitting but exotically-coloured slacks, the small soft hands, the sleek, careless wave of brown hair drooping like a child's lock down her cheek, the grand incongruousness, in these country surroundings, of the blue eye-shadow upon her upper lids— which made Kate feel quite at home with her. Nurse Maud, Kate had noticed, also indulged in much more make-up than was usual in children's nurses, but her make-up was a simple and heavy-handed affair of lipstick, rouge and face-cream. Rosaleen's was that of an expert in beauty.

As if she read Kate's thoughts—she was a good deal more reflective, Kate surmised, than most of the young actresses she resembled—Rosaleen said confidentially, leading the way out of the kitchen down a short stone-flagged passage:

"Don't tell anyone, will you, Miss Mayhew, but I am not *really* a country lover! I'd like to have stayed on in dear old London, bombs and all. But I'd promised my expectant aunt to give her a hand with her overdoo family when it arrived, and I couldn't go back on her. I like little kiddies, anyway, so it won't be too bad when the creche gets going, I'll put up with the mud and the other romantic elements of the English countryside for their sweet sake."

In the high, spacious hall into which Kate followed Rosaleen, the nurse in her neat brown uniform and muslin coif was pouring out the tea from a trestle-table against the wall, and a stout elderly lady, whom Rosaleen introduced as her Aunt Ellida was sitting in an easy-chair, conversing with a stocky, red-faced man in tweeds, who was just not standing in front of the log fire.

"Major Humphries has been explaining, dear, how it is that we shouldn't really let the gipsies camp out in our field, picturesque though they may be."

"Can't understand how anybody can find rags picturesque," said the stocky man bluffly.

"But most of us weak mortals find good looks and brown skins picturesque, Major Humphries!" said Rosaleen. "And I'm afraid that we benighted Americans are also attracted by pleasant manners!"

"Their brown skins are just dirt, if you ask me. And as for their manners, that gipsy effusiveness is all put on, you know Miss Morrison. They'd rob you as soon as look at you."

The Major spoke in a slightly softened voice, fixing Rosaleen with a prominent, inexpressive, but somehow humble eye. It was obvious to Kate that his own preferences were for pink-and-white skins and teasing, ironic manners. Rosaleen came and stood beside him with her cup of tea. Never was a greater contrast, in intention and effect, between two trousered human figures.

"Oh, sooner, surely!" she said in her fresh drawling voice. "What kind of a kick would they get out of just looking at me?"

"Oh, but I say, Miss Morrison!" protested Major Humphries, blinking and averting his bluish, boiled-looking eyes from the inquiring gaze of her long-lashed grey ones. "Surely, if you knew what thieving rogues they are, you won't—"

"We only knew by hearsay, not experience, up till to-day. We thought it would be interesting to see how they lived up to their reputations. And Auntie, too, fell in love with a cute baby in earrings a young woman had in a shawl. She won't fall so easily next time, though," said Rosaleen, removing her limpid gaze from the Major's face to her aunt's. "I've been taking a kind of inventory of what isn't here, and I'm afraid, Auntie— prepare yourself for a blow—your new clothes-line's gone."

"Oh, not my new clothes-line!" cried Mrs. Morrison, sitting up as straight as her easy chair would let her. She was a chic dowager with a head of grey curls, a pearly-powdered skin, and a general billowiness of those parts of her dress and figure which were not strictly moulded by her excellent corsets. "Not my new, lovely clothes-line!"

"Yes, Auntie dear, and all the new, lovely pegs, too."

"Oh, if that isn't too bad! Well, we expected them to take rabbits, and firewood, didn't we? But my clothes-line!"

"I just can't bear to break it to you, Auntie, but your clothesline was functioning at the time, too," said Rosaleen gently. "It had your blue knitted jumper on it, and the frilled pillow-cases out of the red room, and your eau-de-nil satin slip."

Mrs. Morrison, who had uttered a groan at each of these items, clenched her plump be-ringed fists on the arms of her chair, and exclaimed:

"If that doesn't beat everything for black ingratitude! When I think how I gave that baby my last orange, I could just wring its little neck!"

Major Humphries did his best to disguise his obvious delight at this fulfilment of his warnings, in a veil of insincere condolence.

"Well, there you are, Mrs. Morrison, I'm afraid! It's what I was saying, I mean to say. These people shouldn't be encouraged. Human vermin. Like Germans."

"Like *Germans*!" echoed the nurse. "I should have thought there never were two kinds of human beings less alike than a German and a gipsy!"

Major Humphries bristled an eyebrow at her and said shortly:

"Both vermin, both want exterminating, that's what I meant! Never known any Germans, I'm glad to say!"

"I was in Berlin once for a year with a German family," said the nurse.

He looked at her as if he thought she might at least keep this disreputable episode to herself.

"*They* weren't vermin," pursued the nurse cheerfully, apparently oblivious of his bristling disgust. "Most orderly and law-abiding lot of people I ever came across, they were. The children were so obedient it made me feel quite worried. You'd have just loved to have them in the Home Guard, Major Humphries."

"I should *not*!" said Major Humphries with suppressed explosiveness, picking up his hat. "If it's to be gipsies or German, give me gipsies!"

And Rosaleen interposed quickly and sympathetically:

"Of course! How's the Home Guard, Major Humphries?"

Kate thought that Rosaleen shot a narrowed, rather angry look at the nurse. Evidently, she did not want her admirer baited by anyone but herself.

"Fine," replied Major Humphries, turning to Rosaleen with a rather touching alacritous response to the sympathy in her voice. "I only hope we *do* get some Germans over here, that's all I can say! Well, good-bye, Mrs. Morrison. Glad you've seen the light about the gipsies. You let the policeman know double sharp next time they come squatting in your field, that's my advice!"

"You don't tell me that after helping themselves to my eau-de-nil slip they'll have the nerve to come *back* here?" said Mrs. Morrison in horror.

Major Humphries laughed, genuinely amused.

"Sure to! Why, they'll have marked this place as good hunting-ground."

"Well! And where've they got to now, do you suppose?"

Kate remarked:

"Mr. Atkins was ordering them off Llanhalo Farm a couple of hours ago."

Major Humphries was, Kate surmised, a fox-hunter, and even their common hatred of gipsies could not endear Mr. Gideon Atkins to him, for he muttered:

"Oh, *that* fellow!" in a tone scarcely more friendly than that in which he had spoken of his country's enemies.

"Don't you like him, Major?" inquired Rosaleen innocently. Innocence suited her large grey eyes, and Major Humphries blinked once or twice before opining firmly that Atkins was a frightful fellow.

"I wonder you go there as often as you do, if that's how you feel about him!"

Major Humphries snorted slightly!

"I don't go over there for the pleasure of it, I can tell you! I've been trying to come to some arrangement with Atkins about hunting over his land. It stuck in my throat to do the polite to him, but Llanhalo's some of the best hunting ground in the county. Used to hunt over it regularly till this feller turned up."

"Oh dear, I hope you got some good result from your visits, Major Humphries! Too sad to think of all those li'l foxes wondering what can have happened to the horses and hounds!"

"Result! He's wired Llanhalo Coppice all round, I hear—that's the *result* I've got! No good trying to reason with the fellow, evidently, and no good trying to soft-soap him! All we can do now's wait for his funeral, it seems to me," said Major Humphries, gloomily lining up, to Kate's amusement, with the popular pre-occupation.

Rosaleen, still half quizzically condoling, saw him off the premises.

Chapter Eight

"Well," observed Mrs. Morrison sententiously, "the English or rather Welsh, countryside has many interesting cross currents."

"If you mean Major Humphries," said Nurse Maud, collecting the cups together, "I should say he's more like a stagnant pool than a cross current."

Nurse Maud—Kate had not yet heard her surname—seemed to be on terms of surprising intimacy with her employers after only twenty-four hours. But perhaps, reflected Kate, she was an old friend as well as an employee. In which case it was rather strange, however, that she should be wearing her starched uniform and white muslin coif when she was not yet, and, it seemed, would not be for weeks, on duty.

"You must stay and meet my husband. Miss Mayhew," said Mrs. Morrison. "He's upstairs, trying to persuade the builder's foreman to put a little ginger into his plasterers. Your builders, Miss Mayhew, are certainly a highly individualistic lot of men."

"You haven't had dealings with them before, then?" inquired Kate, wondering how long it was since the Morrisons had crossed the Atlantic.

"I certainly have not. Up till this summer, my experience of your lovely country was mostly taken from hotels and furnished apartments. We only came over in the summer of last year. My husband wanted a rest, and thought he'd like to pursue his antiquarian hobbies in old England. We meant to make a long trip, and when the war found us still over here, we decided to make it longer still, and settle down here and see if we couldn't help you folk in your fight for freedom. So, as Rosaleen and I are both very, very fond of little kiddies, we thought we'd make looking after some of them our war-work. And that's how you find us here, Miss Mayhew. It isn't my fault if this old house isn't ringing with children's voices this minute. I'd never have believed that putting in a bit of plumbing and making a house weather-proof could take this long! But I strongly feel, Miss Mayhew, that where there's kiddies, there must be plumbing. Don't you think so, Nurse?"

"I'll say I do!" replied Nurse Maud feelingly, picking up the tray and carrying it out. "And the more of it the better."

"Of course, we really need electric light, too," pursued Mrs. Morrison. "But that's impossible at present. What do you think of our lounge-hall, Miss Mayhew?"

Kate thought that it might be a trifle draughty in the winter. Four doors opened out of it, one of them the wide, heavy front door of the house, and an old staircase with an oak handrail and twisted banisters led down into it beside the fireplace. As Kate made admiring comments on the dignified design of its wide treads and turned newel-posts, there appeared at the turn of it, and came leisurely down, an elderly gentleman in a blue suit and white canvas shoes.

"Why, Douglas, you *have* been a long time! This is Miss Mayhew, who's a friend of that charming Miss Hughes."

Mr. Morrison shook hands. The dark, humorous, small eyes in his broad sallow face looked at Kate both kindly and quizzically, as if he could easily, if he liked, have thought of a great many elaborate and charming things to say, but thought that on the whole he would just stick to "Pleased to meet you." Having said which, he pushed a thick lock of grey hair away from his right eyebrow, and remarked:

"I went upstairs to ask Lupton what to do about the damp in the buttery wall, and I've come away knowing all about his wife's toothache and how his grandfather once cured a rupture by crawling through a hollow ash tree.

"Well, you've missed Major Humphries, dear."

"Good," said Mr. Morrison dispassionately.

"I was just telling Miss Mayhew what an antiquary you are, and how you bought this place because of its quaint beams and brackets, and because you thought there ought surely to be a priest's hole in it, without a thought of whether priest's holes and beams were what my infants would chiefly want."

"And has it got a priest's hole?" asked Kate.

Mr. Morrison replied gravely:

"Well, there are a few small recesses in the bedroom walls here and there, but more of a size to hold candle-sticks than priests. So far, I haven't been able to find any romantic hidey-holes at all, but I have not given up hope that one day a stair may give way beneath my foot and reveal a secret chamber, preferably, of course, containing a skeleton. I am beginning sadly to think, though, that in the days of Good Queen Bess, folks must have been strictly Protestant in these parts."

"Very likely," agreed Kate. "But there's still Jacobites, you know, and smugglers."

"Smugglers! Now who, my dear lady, would smuggle what, in this romantic but scarcely commercial spot? No such worldly and profitable occupation as smuggling has ever sullied the pristine innocence of these country dwellers communing with the deeps of Mother Nature: they live too far inland. If you were to mention *poaching*, now, a blot or two might be discovered on that pristine innocence. Mother, there are two pheasants in the larder."

"Two pheasants! Where did they come from, Doug?"

"That is exactly what I asked the gentleman who brought them here, and he replied, with a wooden look, that he couldn't say. So all *I* can tell you is, they came out of this gentleman's pockets. I think perhaps he was a magician, needing a little practice, and materialised these birds just to show what he could do. You never saw a neater illusion, Miss Mayhew. There he was, one minute empty-handed, a little thin old fellow with a very sad moustache. And then he slipped his hand into his jacket pocket as if to get out his pipe, and out came a cock pheasant with a tail half-a-yard long! You couldn't see any bulges, either, in this gentleman's slender figure. It was a quite fascinating little exhibition."

"Oh, Doug dear, Major Humphries says we ought not to encourage the gipsies!"

"This gentleman was not a gipsy. He was a respectable farmer with a taste for conjuring-tricks."

"Mr. Davis?" ventured Kate.

"Yes, according to Mr. Gwyn Lupton, that is the conjuror's name. He stung me good and hard for the privilege of watching his illusion. I believe the local inhabitants have the idea that 'American' is a synonym for 'millionaire'. *Radnorsheer, poor*

Radnorsheer, never a park and never a deer—I presoom you know the old rhyme, Miss Mayhew? *And never a Squire of five hundred a year, but Richard Fowler of Abbey Cwm Hir*. Gosh, what a centre of interest to the local population that unique Mr. Fowler must have been!"

"Well, if he was alive now, I'd be making tracks this minute for Abbey Cwm what-is-it," said Rosaleen disconsolately from the doorway, and came in and flopped with an air of exhaustion upon the settee. "Show me a man that's unique, after half-an-hour of the millionth edition of England's Glory out there, and I'll just fall straight on his neck."

"So you say," said her uncle, offering Kate his cigarette case. "But there was a very interesting young man, that archaeologist who was here yesterday on a walking tour and then, when we had a chance of his company under our roof for a week, and you could have fallen on his neck all you wanted—always supposing he had no objection—you and your aunt turned him out into the snow."

"Heck, Uncle, where do you think Auntie and I could have put him, when there isn't a bedroom in the house apart from our own that isn't just crawling with painters and white-washers?" demanded Rosaleen. And Mrs. Morrison even more vigorously repudiated the implication of inhospitality.

"I was never so ashamed in my life as when I had to say we hadn't room for him, after the way you invited him, Douglas, but where there's a guest there surely has to be a bed! He *was* an outstandingly nice young man, though. I wonder where he got to in the end. He said he was going to try Llanhalo down the road."

"You can bet your life, Ellida, that if he tried Llanhalo, he tried in vain," said Mr. Morrison sadly. "I cannot see Gideon Atkins warming an archaeologist, however youthful and agreeable, in his bosom. He made it quite clear to me some time ago that he regards us antiquaries as little higher in the scale of creation than the caterpillar."

"Well, I hope that nice young specimen hasn't crawled on too far," said Rosaleen regretfully. "He said he'd come over one afternoon to tea. I'd be real heartbroken to think I wasn't going to see him again!"

"Your heartbreak at his having eluded you, Rosaleen, would be nothing to my heartbreak at missing a talk with him about the antiquities of this interesting district. I don't often get a chance of a chat with a brother antiquarian, and this young man Kemp, though still in the bud, indubitably knew his subject."

Kate dropped her cigarette. It went first on her lap and then on to the stone flags, from which Mr. Morrison retrieved it and insisted on throwing it away and giving her another.

"Did you say his name was Kemp?" asked Kate.

"That *was* his patronymic. Christian name, Colin."

The absurd Kate, although this time prepared for the name she heard, nearly dropped her second cigarette at the sound of it, and was much annoyed with herself for doing so.

"I know him. Or rather, I used to," she said. "I wonder what he's doing in this part of the world. I thought he was in South America."

This time it was Rosaleen who dropped, not her cigarette, but her petrol lighter. She laughed merrily as she picked it up.

"This dropping things seems to be infectious, doesn't it? Fancy that nice young archaeologist being a friend of your, Miss Mayhew! If we'd known, we'd have found a corner for him somewhere, if he had to sleep on the table! And fancy him having been in South America, Uncle Doug! Did he tell you that?"

"I don't remember that he did, Rosa. Owing to your aunt's preoccupation with the bed-famine, our period of conversation was strictly limited. Well, it's too bad to think we drove away a friend of Miss Mayhew's. But maybe he hasn't gone far. Did he know you were going to be in these parts?"

"Oh, no! I haven't heard from him for more than a year," said Kate, still feeling slightly flustered and extremely annoyed with herself: What was there about Colin Kemp to make anybody's heart give that absurd little jump which had caused her to drop her cigarette and, she feared, become the colour of the vulgarest kind of pink carnation? Kate did not often blush, but when she did, she blushed thoroughly. And I haven't *seen* him," she added brightly, "for over two years."

"Well, absence makes the heart grow fonder, doesn't it," said Mr. Morrison, fitting a cigarette into his long ivory holder. The perfect matter-of-factness with which he spoke convinced Kate that she was indeed carnation to the eyebrows. She was not, however, going to be daunted by foolish behaviour of her heart into changing the subject.

"Colin must have enjoyed seeing this house," she said with composure. "But, of course, what he *really* likes is a good tumulus. Gwyn Lupton tells me that you've got an old coin he found on the tumulus at Pentrewer, Mr. Morrison. He seemed to think you wouldn't mind showing it to me, and I'd love to see it."

"My dear Miss Mayhew, I should be just delighted!"

"I don't know much about old coins—just a bit, through spending a good many hours in Dorchester Museum with Colin. It must be something unusual, from what Gwyn Lupton says.

"It's a silver penny of Ceowulf, 874, as far as I can tell," said Mr. Morrison, looking quizzically at her as if to test her knowledge.

"Really? That's rather exciting, isn't it?"

"Ceowulf a friend of yours?"

Kate laughed.

"A friend of Colin's. Slight acquaintance of mine. King of Mercia, wasn't he?"

Mr. Morrison's quizzical look became tinged with a humorous respect.

"Why, you're quite a numismatist! It isn't in very good state, this coin, but I thought I'd risk a little on its purchase, as Mr. Lupton seemed to prefer a more modern coinage."

"I'd love to see it."

Rosaleen jumped up.

"You'd like to see the house, too, wouldn't you? I expect you've seen a great many lovely old English houses, but you know it's still new and exciting to us."

It was new and exciting to Kate, too. The Veault was much larger than it had appeared from the backyard approach. On the first storey there was a delightful long gallery which was, Rosaleen said, to be the main night nursery. Besides this gallery, there seemed to be innumerable bedrooms, both large and tiny, and mostly leading out of one another, so that by the time Kate and Rosaleen were back on the staircase landing, they seemed to have made a kind of circular tour without once retracing their steps. The second floor repeated the first floor, with three little bedrooms over the gallery, and above the second floor were the attics, dark, rambling, with swallow nests in the bare rafters, web-smeared windows and an elaborate arrangement of queen-posts and tie-beams. A brick panel in the back wall had been taken out for repairs. Kate looked out through it upon the great stone chimney-stack with the scaffolding round it that she had seen from the yard. A good many of the wide old floorboards, ingrained with the grey dust of centuries, were up, exposing the cobwebbed joists below.

"Uncle Doug doesn't let the men re-lay so much as a board without investigating among the joists for hidden treasure," said Rosaleen. "So far he's found enough husks to keep a family in breakfast-cereals for a year, innumerable spiders, a metal staybone of the Edwardian period, a broken celluloid comb and a mummified rat. But hope springs eternal in the hooman breast.

He still thinks he'll be rewarded one of these days with a sliding panel and a skeleton."

Kate lingered on the narrow stairs.

"I don't know anything about old houses, but I feel this staircase is *very* old."

Rosaleen patted her lightly on the back.

"But you really are quite an antiquarian!" she said. "You're quite right, honey. This part of the house and the hall and kitchen are remains of an older mediaeval manor that the Veault, as you see it, got built on to some time in Good Queen Bess's day. The way you tell, is chiefly something to do with the timber framing, so Gwyn Lupton was telling me. You see these long upright timbers in the wall here, set so close together without any cross-pieces? Well, that's mediaeval, it seems. Where the timbers are set out square, with lots of space for bricks or wattle in between, that's later. And the bigger the spaces and the thinner the timbers, the later you can bet your boots it is. They were real lavish with oak in mediaeval days. Well, here we are in the kitchen again. Let's creep through to the hall very, very quietly, or Gwyn Lupton in the scullery will hear us and come out and fix us with his eye and start telling us a piece as long as the Ancient Mariner. I'm like you, I just adore that man, but I prefer to choose my own times for sitting at his feet."

To Kate's disappointment, Mr. Morrison was not able, after all, to show her the silver penny of Ceowulf. He had recollected he said, that a friend he had shown it to on his recent visit to London had asked to be allowed to keep it a short while and show it to a numismatist, and that he had agreed.

"Perhaps it was a trifle rash of me," he admitted, "in view of the nocturnal proceedings over London at this disturbed period of history. But, as I was cheerfully leaving my friend in London, I felt that to refuse to leave my coin would scarcely be preserving the

doo proportion of things. I hope he'll mail it on to me soon. Are
you staying long in Hastry, Miss Mayhew?"

"Well—I don't know," replied Kate, and explained as well as
she could what had brought her here.

She was getting into the habit of watching people's reactions to
the information that she was searching for a lost boy who was
nothing to her but a photograph on a poster and an appeal for
help. Miss Brentwood had obviously thought her amiably insane.
Mr. and Mrs. Howells had taken her mission as the most natural
thing in the world. The woman in charge of the County Library
had simply not accepted the idea, and had continually referred to
Sidney, in all good faith, as "your little nephew". Aminta in
Aminta-like fashion, had shown no curiosity and very little
interest.

The Morrisons looked at her, and at one another, in silence for
a moment.

"Say, I think your real name must be Donna Quixote de la
Mancha," said Mr. Morrison then, admiringly. And Mrs. Morrison
said gently:

"My dear! But that poor li'l boy's been searched
for *everywhere*!"

"Not everywhere, Auntie," said Rosaleen, looking thoughtfully
at Kate, "because he hasn't been found. And he can scarcely have
been de-materialised."

"De-materialised!" echoed Mr. Morrison. "Well, now, for any
observations on the possibility or otherwise of de-materialisation,
consult the gentleman who called on me this afternoon. He was, as
I have intimated, an expert."

"Davis Pentrewer, as they call him," said Rosaleen
thoughtfully. "Well—maybe you've spoken wisdom in jest, Uncle
Doug. Davis Pentrewer is hand-in-glove with the gipsies, they tell
me. But there, I suppose that old idea of the child that gets stolen

by the gipsies is just a li'l bit out of date nowadays, isn't it? I suppose this kid Sidney couldn't be being held to ransom by toughs?"

"Nobody could pay a ransom worth the risk. His father's a captain in the Merchant Navy, and his great-aunt lets rooms in a house in Bayswater."

"Well, I must say I think you're real magnificent, Miss Mayhew."

"Oh no, I haven't anything to do just now."

"No, but when you don't *have* to look for the kid at all, to be so *grandly* hopeful!" said Rosaleen, half-sadly, getting up as Kate shook hands with Mrs. Morrison and bade her good-bye. "Most of us weaker mortals like our ventures to be just a li'l less forlorn!"

The word struck a tiny knell in Kate's heart. Rosaleen was a shrewd, sensible girl. Was she herself truly as hopelessly lacking in realism as, lying awake in the small hours, she had feared? No. Sidney Brentwood, or his body, was *somewhere* under the autumn sun. And the question of whether Kate *had* to look for him, had been settled all in a flash in the Edgware Road the day before yesterday.

Rosaleen and Nurse Maud, who emerged from the kitchen damp-handed, turning down her neat cuffs, both accompanied Kate up to the field-gate.

"If I can ever help you in your search, command me, honey! Anyway, we'll be seeing you again—and again, I hope!"

Rosaleen and Maud leant against the gate as Kate went off across the field-path, The high wind which was still tearing joyfully across the sky, carrying a chill with it now that evening was approaching, blew their voices after Kate so strongly that she half-thought for a second that Rosaleen was calling her back. But it was to Maud that Rosaleen was speaking.

"What did you want to go pulling Humphries' leg like that for?"

"Well, I was irritated, Rosa! I don't like the way the man looks at you!" replied the nurse.

Rosaleen's fresh laughter followed Kate up the slope.

"Anybody hearing you might think you were jealous on old Major Everyman's account! Or at least, anybody *looking* at you might!"

Kate could not help turning her head to look at Maud in the distance and see what it was that so manifested jealousy in her looks. But she looked just as usual, her white coif fluttering in the wind, and as Kate looked back she raised her hand and waved in a friendly manner. Had Nurse Maud, then, a secret tenderness for Major Everyman? If so, it certainly showed itself oddly!

But a secret tenderness was apt to show itself oddly, and who should know it better than Kate, who, with the utmost manifestation of lightheartedness, had let Colin Kemp go to South America without her? Kate forgot Maud, and Rosaleen, and Major Everyman, and thought about Colin all the way home.

The track at Pentrewer looked very dark and secret when she passed it, with the high darkling hills between it and the sun. Two rough ponies were grazing a little way up the track, and beyond a hedge Kate caught sight as she passed of the gipsy caravan, and a blue drift of woodsmoke. The gipsies were evidently spending the night near their relations at Pentrewer.

Chapter Nine

Kate, having ascertained that the school break was at half-past-eleven, decided the next morning to go and see Sidney Brentwood's schoolmaster, and, while she was about it, some of Sidney's contemporaries and friends.

"Mrs. Howells, I suppose it's no use asking if you've got any sweets in the shop?"

"Well, I think you are lucky, there was a few pounds of toffee come in this morning, and if it's for the schoolchildren you can have half-a-pound if you wish!" Mrs. Howells added, when she had weighed out the half-pound: "Now the boys and girls will be all swarming over my shop in the dinner-hour like ants when they smells honey, but never mind—I would rather it was them than Miss Gilliam and some others I knows as is always in here after sweets."

She tipped the little waxed-paper and bright tinfoil-wrapped cubes into a paper bag, and handing it to Kate, added pensively: "It was toffees like these that Sidney had in his pocket when he went off that night."

This was news to Kate.

"Yes, indeed," sighed Mrs. Howells. "It was finding one of the papers up the road made us think he had turned towards the hills when he left here that night, not towards the village."

"Whereabouts was this paper found, then, Mrs. Howells?"

"Oh, in the road about fifty yards up. The police didn't think a great deal of it, because of course there was plenty others bought toffee that day, and children mostly drops the papers about, whatever their teachers tells them! The reason Corney and me thought it was Sidney dropped this paper up the road, was, it was a green shiny paper like is on the peppermint flavours. And Sidney liked the peppermint flavours the best, and I picked out an extra lot of the green-covered ones to please him. Still, because plenty of other people like peppermint flavour, too, I did not give them all to Sidney," said Mrs. Howells replacing the lid on the tin, and the tin below the counter. "The police did not think so much of the toffee-paper because they believed he had gone back to London, as children mostly does that doesn't like the country, and London is the opposite direction from the hills. But I knows, and Corney knows, Sidney never had a thought of going to London."

"Did Sidney take any other food with him when he went out that night?"

"Not from here. Sidney was a very good boy, he never went to the larder like some boys as is billeted about here."

The extraordinary wavelike high pitched hullabaloo of young humans at play smote on her ears as she approached the school and when she went in at the entrance a football came hurtling through the air, missed her head by about three inches, and went hurtling back over the heads of innumerable shouting boys. In the tremendous noise, the interrogative upward inflections of the Marches mingled with the affirmative burr of the North, and was punctuated by the glottal stop of the Cockney kid. It occurred to Kate that the break probably only lasted a quarter of an hour, and that she had better get hold of Sidney's friend before seeking an interview with his teacher. She stopped in her tracks and looked about her for a Cockney. At once half-a-dozen boys, who had a second ago seemed oblivious of her presence, gathered round her inquiringly, with the touching helpfulness of the helpless young. The first to speak was a London child.

"Miss, do you want Mr. Pilgrim, Miss?"

"I'm looking for a friend of Sidney Brentwood's—his best friend, if possible."

There was a noisy and sibilant consultation, and in a very short time Kate was confronted with a wiry, freckled boy in a corduroy wind-sheeter and manly blue serge trousers. Half-a-dozen boys, interested in the possibilities of unfolding drama, introduced him zestfully as Ronnie Turner. Kate thought it best to say at once, that she had no news of Sidney Brentwood, but on the contrary, wanted Ronnie to tell her something about him. Ronnie looked rather reserved, but led her to the comparative privacy of a roofed shelter where one or two smaller boys were hopping about on the benches, offered her a seat with some self-consciousness, and stood in front of her with his hands in his pockets and one leg twisted behind the other, in silence. The other boys kept a respectful but interested distance of about three yards.

When Kate explained that she had come from London to search for Sidney until she found him, Ronnie's apprehensive frown cleared, but to all Kate's inquiries as to what his own surmises were, he answered only:

"Dunno, Miss." Kate was beginning to feel desperate when it occurred to her to break the charm by asking Ronnie a few questions about himself. His home, it seemed, was in Westbourne Grove, and he had been evacuated at the same time as Sidney. They were old friends and had hoped to be billeted together, but Sidney had gone to the Howells while Ronnie was billeted on Miss Gilliam at the Cefn up the hill.

"Do you like it there?"

The boy made the underlip grimace which is the Londoner's shrug.

"Not much, Miss."

"What's the matter with it?"

"Dunno, Miss," said Ronnie, reverting to his formula. This time, however, he added, with a sudden charming half-grin:

"I'd like to be billeted on the gipsies!"

Kate laughed.

"That's an idea! Have you ever spoken to the gipsies?"

"Sidney did, Miss. He had supper with them."

"Oh, did he? When?"

"When he went to Pentrewer, Miss." Kicking the asphalt with a child's grand disregard for boot-leather, Ronnie suddenly found his tongue and added mournfully: "*I* was going with Sidney, on'y I sprained me ankle."

"Was that the day Sidney went to see the tump where the piece of old money was found?"

Ronnie looked up, as if both surprised and pleased to find that Kate really did know something about Sidney and was not merely exercising the grown-up's boring prerogative of asking unexplained questions.

"Yes, Miss. Me and Sid were going over there together on our bikes to look for things. On'y I sprained me ankle so Sid went by himself. And the gipsies was camping there, and he had supper with them and all."

"I thought he had tea with Mr. and Mrs. Davis that day?"

"So he did, and supper with the gipsies, what they cooked out of doors. The gipsies is friends with Mr. Davis, see."

"Yes, I know. Sidney didn't tell Mrs. Howells he'd been with the gipsies, did he?"

Ronnie looked a trifle uneasy.

"Well, Miss, he would have told, on'y she didn't seem to like it when he said he'd been with Mr. Davis, so he didn't like to say he'd been with the gipsies as well, see. The people round here don't like the gipsies much, Miss. They say they pinch things. Miss, do you think Sid might've gone off with the gipsies?"

"I'm afraid not, Ronnie. I think he'd have been found long ago, if he had."

Ronnie looked dubious. He was a good-looking child, rather narrow-faced, with the clear skin and clear grey eyes that often accompany freckles in dark-haired people. He gazed at Kate a moment, and suddenly blurted half-interrogatively:

"Miss Gilliam says he's dead, Miss?"

"We mustn't say that yet. We're going to find him, Ronnie."

Ronnie looked at Kate as if he had suddenly had a glimpse of Eldorado.

"Oh, Miss!" he breathed, flushing brightly. "When shall we start?"

Kate, whose "we" had been the reassuring "we" of the grown-up tribe, perceived that Ronnie had taken it to include himself. She could hardly bear to dash the joyful and adventurous spirit that had suddenly swept all dubiety out of the child's bright eyes. She temporised.

"Well—of course school takes up a lot of *your* time, Ronnie."

"There's the evenings, Miss! There's Saturdays and Sundays! There's the nights!" breathed Ronnie, uncurling his legs and standing as lightly in his stubbed boots as though ready to spring off that minute into the unknown.

"The nights? What would Miss Gilliam say to that?"

"She wouldn't know," answered Ronnie earnestly. "Miss, it was the night when Sid went. Well, then, we ought to look for him at night, didn't we? The night's different from the day. Different things happen."

"How do you know that, Ronnie?" asked Kate, charmed by this sudden burst of enthusiasm, and putting off the moment when she would have to damp it down again.

Ronnie hesitated, and evidently decided to trust her.

"I know, I've been out at night, Miss," he said in a lowered tone, as if shelters might grow pedagogic ears, even in this din. "Searching for Sid. I went on my bike, lots of nights, when he was first gone. It's different to the day. Nobody about. The hills look ever so different. I saw a badger and a hedgehog. And there's noises... only when you get to where they are, you can't hear anything."

Kate suppressed a smile.

"You didn't ever see anything else, Ronnie, though? I mean, it's lovely to see badgers and hedgehogs, but they don't tell us anything about Sidney. And the noises at night are generally only horses and things moving in the fields, or birds, you know."

Ronnie came closer to her and said earnestly:

"One night I saw a man going up the track at Pentrewer."

"But, Ronnie! Probably he lived there! I mean—"

"No, it was further up than where Mr. Davis lives. There's nothing up there, I know, on'y an empty house. The track gets all narrow and is all trees after that."

"But still—farmers are often out at night. He might have been going to see some animal or—" But Ronnie's intense expression did not alter, and, influenced a little by it in spite of common-sense, Kate asked: "What kind of man? A gipsy?"

"No. More like a toff," said Ronnie. "It wasn't Mr. Davis, nor yet Mr. Lupton, nor anyone as I'd ever seen."

"And what happened?"

Ronnie looked a little embarrassed.

"Well, Miss, I—I lost track of him. I kept the other side of the hedge, and went up alongside of him. On'y I came to another hedge across the field, and by the time I'd got through it and out in the lane, I couldn't see him any more."

"What did you do?"

Ronnie looked distinctly unhappy.

"Well, Miss. I—I went back. There's an empty house up there that they says is haunted, and—and the valley gets awful narrow and crowded together up there, and it seemed so dark. And I heard funny noises—"

"Owls?"

"Yes, them, and rustling noises, too, Miss, and sort of clicking noises—"

"Pheasants, I expect."

"So I come back." He swallowed and admitted: "I got a bit frightened, see, all by meself, like. But I shouldn't be frightened if I was with you, Miss. When shall we start?"

"Well, Ronnie, I think we'd better talk it over when we've got a bit more time," said Kate rather evasively, though she was beginning to feel that Ronnie, in spite of, or perhaps because of, his youth, would make the best kind of partner in a forlorn enterprise, single-minded, candid, imaginative, and not too brave. "You live at the Cefn, you say, so I'll know where to find you."

Ronnie's face fell a little. Procrastination was an only too well-known grown-up habit.

"When, Miss?"

Kate hesitated, and rashly promised, as she had not intended to:

"To-morrow, or the day after. Will you take me to the headmaster now?"

Ronnie looked a little surprised and more dubious, as if he had thought better of Kate than that she should be hobnobbing with headmasters.

"*He* won't be much help, Miss. He thinks Sidney's dead, too. I heard him say so to the copper."

"Ronnie."

"Yes, Miss?"

"Sidney *may* be dead, you know. We mustn't absolutely refuse to face the possibility."

"Oh, I know that, Miss. On'y—you can't look for a person properly if you think he's dead, Miss, can you?" said Ronnie. He added simply: "*I* don't think he's dead, because I don't want him to be."

With this deplorable piece of reasoning but excellent piece of practical philosophy, he led the way into the schoolhouse.

Mr. Pilgrim was, as Ronnie Turner had prophesied, not much help. His estimate of his boys' characters and capacities was clear-cut and probably, so far as it went, correct, but a trifle rough-and-ready, as was but natural in a man under whose eyes the youth of the nation had been streaming in hordes for about forty years. Sidney Brentwood, of whom he spoke in a melancholy tone which

Kate tried not to find exasperating, had been a boy of sound character: a little scatter-brained, perhaps: not clever, oh, no! just normal ability: a nice boy: a superior family: the father a fine type: no mother: motherless boys were liable to cause trouble. Ronnie Turner? Oh, Ronald was a sound boy, too. Good stuff there, good brains. Not so enterprising as Sidney, but perhaps more reliable. A more thoughtful type. Had been rather difficult and unlike himself since Sidney's disappearance. Had played truant from school on two or three occasions. His billet wasn't very satisfactory. An old maid, and Mr. Pilgrim doubted if she gave the boy enough to eat. He was intending to see the billeting-officer about it. The job of a schoolmaster in wartime, as Miss Mayhew would no doubt observe, comprised that of a nurse. As well, said Mr. Pilgrim resignedly, with a sigh, bidding Kate farewell, as that of an office-boy. And he sat down to fill in forms about milk.

Walking back to the shop, when the school-bell had gone and break in the playground had ended in a clattering and shoving and chattering back in the school-building, Kate thought over her conversation with Ronnie Turner. She liked Ronnie, and thought it would be not only pleasant but useful to see him again, for, of all the people she had met, he seemed to be the nearest link with the missing boy. But he was, after all, only about twelve years old, an age which possesses all the virtues except discretion. He had certainly, though, shown a modicum of that elderly quality in his hedge-side tracking of the gentleman at Pentrewer and his withdrawal from the trail when he realised his loneliness before the empty house. If he had followed the trail, he would probably have only found it led to a sick cow sheltered in some tumbledown barn, or, at the most exciting, to a collection of rabbit snares; but with a boy like Ronnie, no doubt the dark, the mysterious lulls, the reputation of a haunted house and the sight, in the lonely night-time, of a fellow-creature walking up the valley, combined with the mission on which he was engaged, would put all such commonplace activities out of mind. Sidney had gone off into the night, and disappeared. The night was different from the day.

It was a sound idea, reflected Kate. The night was different from the day, and different in just the way that Ronnie's eyes and tone, rather than his halting words, had implied. It put different thoughts into one's head. It made one accept ideas which, in the day, one would reject. The sight of dark, huddling hills and gaunt black tree shapes suggested ideas which would never come from looking at brackeny, heathery slopes and autumn-hued oaks and ashes in the sunlight. To follow Sidney at night was not such a childish notion as might appear. The influences which had fallen upon Sidney would fall upon one, and who knew what queer inspiration might emerge that the day kept hidden under its commonplaces?

"I'll do it!" said Kate to herself. "I'll cycle out to the hills to-night!" For Ronnie, as well as Mrs. Howells, had seemed convinced that Sidney had gone towards the hills, though he had not been able to explain why. No doubt many childish conversations and fancy-spun yarns and romantic surmises between the two boys during their stay in Hastry had contributed to Ronnie's conviction, and Kate felt inclined to build on that conviction even more strongly than on the clue of the green toffee-paper which had been mentioned by Mrs. Howells.

Kate studied her map earnestly that afternoon, for the moon would scarcely be bright enough to read by to-night, bright as it might be. She memorised the lie of the hill road and the farm-tracks that ran into it and the woods below it and the streams that crossed it from the high hills. Alongside the words "Pentrewer Farm," "Mound" was printed in archaic characters, and up the next fork of the road two small black dots no doubt represented Ronnie's haunted, empty house and its outbuildings. Straining her eyes over the map and wishing she had brought a reading-glass, Kate saw that these dots were named: Hymns Bank.

Chapter Ten

It was a wonderful night, with the moon flooding the hill-slopes with a theatrical radiance. By its light Kate could almost have identified the few late flowers that still hung about the October ditches. Under the clumps of silver-topped, scraggy trees, deep darkness stood like a presence. A white drifting mist, floating a foot above ground, lay in the valley below the sloping fields to her left, and mist blotted the far hills.

There was no wind, but the night was cold, and Kate was glad of her leather jacket and the wool hood she had tied under her chin. When Sidney had gone, it had been nearly a month nearer to summer. He had not taken his overcoat nor sweater. You must be cold now, Sidney, wherever you are.

Ahead of her was the little stone bridge that crossed the stream at Pentrewer. The gipsies' encampment in the moonlight gained in dignity what it lost in colour. The tents and two caravans looked as if they might have been there since primeval times, as if they housed, not the eccentric wanderers of a mechanical age, but the owners of the earth they slept on, the craftsmen-inheritors of the Stone Age, the metal-workers, the sword-makers of the new expanding world of iron.

But then, Kate thought, remembering talks with Colin, the landscape would not have looked like this. The valley would have been full of trees, only the hills bare, with scrub climbing their lower slopes. She would not have been able to stand here and look across a gentle, agricultural valley.

She had stopped on the bridge, and as she glanced down the valley she saw something which put the Iron Age and its forests quite out of her head. Below her was a small sloping pasture, and below that, separated from it by a light wire fence, was a larger field. Across this field she could plainly see a man moving.

He moved in a queer, crouched, and purposeful way, holding up his arm stiffly and strangely, across the field. Then an overgrown hedge that met the wire fence hid him from her view. But there was still, it seemed to Kate, a sort of movement in that field, a sort of dark disturbance, as though a wave were passing over the grass. But there was no wind. Kate strained her eyes, but the moon will never yield up her secrets, as the sun does, to the straining eye. The field was quiet now, so quiet that Kate might have thought she had dreamt that queer effect of movement flowing over it in the wake of the vanished man.

She hid her bicycle in the ditch, and got over a gate into the pasture below. A footpath ran from the gate diagonally across the field towards the tree behind which the man had disappeared, but Kate shirked the moonlight and kept close to the hedge on her right hand. Her footsteps made no noise on the soft ground but the brush of wet grasses around her ankles. A few sheep lying in the lee of the hedge got up and trotted off at her approach, and she stood still a moment, up close to the hedge, afraid that whoever it was in the field below might see that scared movement of the flock in the moonlight and take some warning from it.

Her woollen hood caught against the thorny twigs of a blackthorn tree and she stopped to disentangle herself. Re-tying her hood, she glanced down and saw something lying at the foot of the blackthorns in the dry hedge bank. A heap, a small dark mass, a piece of sacking.

She stooped, rather nervously, and lifted the sacking. Under it lay a hank of some dark soft material. Before she picked it up, she knew what it was. It was a hank of dark net, silk net, strong but supple, hanging heavy and limp on her hand.

Her thoughts sprang to Sidney, as if she might almost expect to hear him breathing beside her in the hedgerow, she held her own breath and peered into the dark spaces between the stems.

Sidney had been learning to make nets when he had vanished at midnight. Now, at midnight, with a net in her hand, surely Kate must be at least upon his trail!

She stretched her fingers through the silk mesh. It was a mesh of about an inch-and-a-half, dark brown as far as she could tell in this light, made of a thread of supple but tough quality. Kate stood there a moment, weighing the net in her hand, trying to see the connection between this net lying at night at the foot of a blackthorn tree, and the disappearance of Sidney Brentwood into the dark. Suddenly she thought she heard a movement in the field below, and dropped the net back where she had found it, for no doubt it belonged to the crouched man she had seen from the road creeping across the lower field, and it might be that he would be keeping an eye upon his cache and see the moonlight on her face or on the metal zip of her leather jerkin, which now seemed to her to shine alarmingly.

She replaced the sacking, and as she stooped thought she heard a horse trotting up behind her. But it was her own heart. She crept along under the hedge to where a clump of brambles masked the beginning of the wire fence, and behind this clump she hid and looked through its spraying whips into the lower field. The lower field was of stubble, irregular and faintly glistening where the moonlight fell on the polished straws. It was a wide field, sloping away down to some trees and the harder dark outline of a barn. It seemed to be quite empty of tree or man, an autumnal homestead field which would be pale gold and peaceful in the sunshine, man's labour over for the season and the hens wandering and picking their gleanings from the carried harvest. But in the night, the dark surrounding hedges looked menacing, as if they were peopled with waiting presences, and the empty field were to be their meeting-place.

Kate, peering out from her clump of brambles, strained her eyes across the wires of the fence that glittered theatrically here and there in the moonlight, to see again, if she could, that man's shape that had crept so purposefully across the ground.

She could see nothing, but now she could hear something—a soft, slurred, continuous swishing sound, as if the night were saying hush! to itself. There was nothing in the field that she could see to account for this, there was not a shadow of movement there, and she had to take herself firmly in hand to suppress the onset of a sort of panic terror at the continuance of that unexplained sound.

She was about to emerge from her ambush to get a better view of the far reaches of the field when she drew back. The figure of a man passed within six feet of her. He had been close to her all the while. He was moving alongside the wire fence with the same slow, silent, crouching movement she had seen from the road. He was holding a staff taller than himself aslant in his hands. There was a second man some distance on the far side of him, also holding a staff slanting forward against his slanting, crouching body. As they passed beyond Kate's clump of brambles, keeping their silent way parallel to the wire fence, Kate saw that they carried between their staves a sort of darkness that hid the glistening stubble, yet caught the moonlight here and there itself— a net. It was the lower edge of the net that had made that brushing sound against the stubble. The men themselves walked silently, as if shod with felt.

As she watched, her heart pounding with the shock of discovering them so near when she had been scanning the distance for them, she heard a sudden sharp whirr and a flurry. There was a quick movement from the two men as they cast down their staves, the net lay flat upon the ground, and the two men ran together to where a great flutter and commotion was going on below the net.

Poachers! Kate had seen the nearer of the two men plainly as he passed her. It was Davis Pentrewer. There was no mistaking the angle of the cap, the benignant downward curve of the profile, the melancholy moustache. What birds those were fluttering and squawking under the net and sending a flurry of feathers up into the air above the men's heads, Kate was not countrywoman enough to guess, and it did not matter. Nor did it much matter who the second of the two men was—it sufficed that he was certainly not a boy, not Sidney.

Was this what Sidney had wanted his net for? It seemed probable, for he had visited the Davises and the gipsies at Pentrewer, and from what Ronnie Turner had said, had become enamoured of their lawless lives. Perhaps it was on a poaching expedition that he had set forth on the night of his disappearance. But then—where was he? The worst that could have befallen him, had he joined the gipsies in some such activity as was now going on, would have been a night in the lock-up and a talking-to from a magistrate! Poaching was a lawless, but not a dangerous, pursuit. Was it possible that Rosaleen and Ronnie, who had both made the same romantic suggestion, were right, and that Sidney was in hiding with the gipsies?

As Kate thought this, a third figure emerged from the darkness of the hedge and crossed the field towards the two men who were now, Kate judged, busily wringing the necks of their covey. This third figure was a woman, carrying a large covered bag or basket over her arm. The light broke on her spectacles, and Kate saw that it was Mrs. Davis.

Kate lingered a moment behind her brambles, considering what she could best do now. She had acted on Ronnie's inspiration, she had come out and followed Sidney into the night that had swallowed him, she had encountered a human activity that seemed at least connected with Sidney's own activities: but there was little purpose in waiting here and following the Davis's and their companion through what would no doubt be a long night's work. Kate rose and crept back to the shelter of the hedge. If poaching was connected with Sidney's disappearance, the kindly-seeming Davises might also be connected with that disappearance. The best thing Kate could do was to get back to the road, find her way to Pentrewer Farm and, if possible, search the house and buildings.

The track that ran up towards Pentrewer Farm was rutty with cartwheels, and narrowed, Kate judged, as it went on. Kate decided to leave her bicycle where it was, and go on foot.

The chattering little stream made the night more friendly than it had seemed in the field. Gwyn Lupton's cottage blinked at her with blind eyes as she went by. She wondered whether it was Gwyn who was out in the fields helping the Davis's with their nets, or whether he was sleeping the sleep of the innocent under that stone-tiled roof. There was not a sound except the drowsy cluck of a hen re-settling herself on her perch in the fowl-house. A little way beyond the cottage, the track crossed the stream, and a stepping-stone tilted under Kate's foot, and she continued her journey wet over the ankle and wishing she had come out in her gum-boots.

About a quarter-of-a-mile up from Gwyn Lupton's cottage, the track forked around a copse of young oaks and hazels that sloped up the spur. It was the left, and more open fork that Kate had to take. The wooded and widening spur was on her right. There were open, if steeply sloping, fields on the other side of the hedge to her left hand, and, a little way beyond the fork, standing up on the left bank, its gable-end towards the track, a small cottage with a huge yew tree, black as night itself, standing behind it.

This must be Pentrewer Farm. It looked as blind and quiet as Gwyn Lupton's cottage, and scarcely larger. Kate slipped over a gate in the hedge a few yards below the house, and approached up the field track towards the front. It seemed, with the moon full upon it, to be a simple box-like one-storey cottage with a stone roof beetling down over its tiny upper windows. A barn was built on to the cottage at the side farthest from the lane. It was certainly a farm of sorts, but Kate could well believe that poaching was a more profitable occupation than farming this rough land.

She moved cautiously to the shelter of the hedge, for although Mr. and Mrs. Davis were both out in the fields, she could not be sure that the house was empty, and that an eye might not watch from a crack in the blinds at one of these dark windows that faced her approach, The back of the cottage, which would be out of the moonlight and sheltered by the yew tree whose thick fringed boughs drooped over the chimney, would make a better approach for investigation than the front. Kate made her way between the cottage and the hedge, past a great woodstack and a water-butt, into a small enclosure that seemed, as far as she could judge in the darkness here, to be a sort of kitchen-garden and backyard combined. The cobbled space between the cabbage-bed and the back of the cottage was nearly taken up with a dog-kennel—empty, Kate thanked heaven, at the moment—a tin-bath full of potatoes, and a wheelbarrow. In the shade of the yew tree it was very dark indeed. A galvanised iron rain-tub stood close to the back door, and she avoided stumbling against it by a hair's-breadth so narrow that the mere thought of the noise which might have terrified the night caused a dampness to break out on her forehead.

Very cautiously she put her hand on the door-latch. It lifted, and the door gave. She stood a moment, reflecting, hesitating, with her hand on the latch. Should she go in? There was not a sound to be heard. The chances were that the house was empty, and that she would be able to walk through all the rooms and return unchallenged.

Standing there in that lonely and dark place, listening to me silence across which her own heartbeats struck like faint, far warnings, Kate realised for the first time how very light-heartedly, how unimaginatively, she had entered upon this search. She had seen herself trailing a lost boy across open country. She had not seen herself, as with a glimmer of common-sense she might have done, entering people's houses at dead of night, investigating their cellars, braving not only their righteous wrath and the law, but those unseen forces of the dark with whom, ever since an over-imaginative childhood, she had never quite managed to come to terms.

Before she went in, perhaps she had better track out the lie of the house and barn, so that if she had to beat a quick retreat she would know how best to do it. She softly let the latch fall, and, leaving the door ajar, crept up into the shadow of the yew tree. The yew tree stood on a little bank some fifteen feet or so behind the cottage, and the darkness under its boughs was intense. Leaning against the immense rough bole in the protecting darkness, Kate could see, out in the field beyond the gate, one or two stacks, paler than the hillside against which they stood. Farther out in the field, she could see against the sky an outline that was unmistakeable. In that crowded week in Dorset with Colin Kemp she had seen too many round-barrows not to know one when she saw one, even though it was by night, and only the top of the crouched shape was visible against the moonlit sky. There was the tumulus, Pentrewer Tump, large, flattened with the feet of the centuries, and with that regularity of outline which proclaims to the hastiest eye, even after the lapse of ages, the work of man's artist hands.

It was, so far as Kate could judge, a simple round-barrow. The field was fairly level here, and there seemed to be no ditch or vallum around the tumulus, which Kate guessed to be about twelve feet high. She wondered whether Colin Kemp had come across Pentrewer Tump in his recent wanderings through this district. She also wondered passingly what he thought he was doing, in this year of turmoil 1940, wandering solitary about the countryside, making drawings of abbey ruins. Colin had had a very affirmative, adventurous nature, the kind of nature that readily accepts a challenge: it was the thing Kate had liked about him— one of the things she had liked. She could not imagine him attempting to keep clear of any fight that his friends were involved in.

Perhaps he was finishing off some big piece of work before giving up his beloved archaeology for the duration. But he had been away from England, among the Incas, when she had last heard from him: it would have to be a magnum opus indeed that would take in Welsh mediaeval abbeys as a pendant to the remains of the Inca civilisation! And Colin had never been much interested in mediaeval ruins, regarding them as things of yesterday. It was a puzzle, but Kate was not likely to solve it now, and anyway she had something else to do.

Yet, not only because the dense outline of the tumulus standing up against the lighter indigo sky brought Colin back so clearly to her mind, but also perhaps because she had not yet nerved herself to break into the house, she remained standing there. She wondered how long Colin had been in England and had not let her know?

The night was so still that she could have heard a spider moving in the shaley bark of the yew tree at her back. The black tassels of foliage hung, quite unmoving, against the sky. So that when she did hear a sound, it disproportionately startled her. It was the full, thudding sound of a spade being struck into earth.

It seemed to come from the direction of the tumulus. Kate stepped cautiously away from the yew tree and advanced across the yard, remembering that it had been to see the tumulus that Sidney had first visited Pentrewer. She had a vague hope that he might, from whatever hiding-place he lay in, be re-visiting the tumulus at night, digging in it, perhaps, looking for another coin of Ceowulf. Unlikely in the extreme that he would find one, for Saxon coins were not indigenous to Stone Age barrows! Gwyn Lupton's find must have been the merest chance, the picking-up of a coin dropped accidentally hundreds of years after the barrow was raised. But neither Gwyn Lupton nor Sidney would be likely to know that.

Kate was almost at the yard gate which led into the field when, this time indubitably from the tumulus, there came a cough. She stiffened, and stood still. It had been a man's cough, she thought, deep and rattling, though suppressed. Unwelcome fantasies— stories about revenants and haunted places, quasi-philosophical theories about time and vibrations, a fearsome short story she had read once about a mindless elemental whose habit it had been to cough around people's house-doors in the dusk, rushed into her mind. She took herself in hand, reminding herself of all the sensible things she had said to Ronnie Turner. There was no need to start inventing Grand-Guignol one-acters in her head, just because a man was out at night taking up rabbit-snares or burying a dead sheep!

Her self-admonitions braced Kate so much that she was about to open the yard gate and go and investigate, when the dark curve of the tumulus against the sky was broken. I he figure of a man rose quietly and stealthily on to the top of it. A tall, lank figure, but with a crouching, earthward stoop of the broad shoulders and head. He stood back to the moon, and Kate could not see his features. In spite of her self-admonitions, she did not want to. A tumulus was, after all, a grave. And this man carried something in his hands—a spade.

The moonlight was full on Kate. Whoever this man was—for of course it *was* a man—she must not be discovered before she had carried out her plan of searching the house. She turned as quietly as possible, and made her way back to the yew tree, but she had no cover as she went over the miry yard, and the figure on the tumulus was facing her way, and she had small hopes of not being seen.

When she arrived back at the cover of the tree, she looked round, and saw that the figure had disappeared. Had she frightened him into retreat? Or—had there really been no man there at all, but only an appearance, a picture of some long passed episode upon the moon-struck air?

Kate had better not think about it, but do what she had come to do without delay. She was here to look for little Sidney Brentwood, who might be facing worse things than the remembered fragments of old, foolish stories, and the sight of a man digging in the moonlight. She went quietly to the back door, this time carefully avoiding the galvanised iron tub.

She had left the door ajar, and a gentle push would open it. She had her torch ready to put on as soon as she entered the dark house. She gave the door a gentle push, but to her surprise it did not open, though the latch was certainly up. There seemed to be some obstruction inside—perhaps the doormat was lying crooked. Kate gave another, slightly stronger push, and this time the door opened so quickly and so wide that she was startled.

The next moment she was paralysed to perceive that there was somebody standing there in the dark, on the threshold, holding the door open. Nothing was said. In the silence, Kate could hear breathing, her own and another's, and the hammering of her own heart.

Chapter Eleven

On the slim chance that she was not visible, in the shadow of the house, to the person who stood there, Kate backed cautiously against the house-wall, intending to make her way as silently as possible round to the barn door.

"Who is it?" asked a man's voice sharply.

Kate felt her way along the wall, and was just beginning to hope she was not going to be followed, when her foot made a scraping sound, and the figure emerged from the doorway.

"Is that you, Mrs. Davis?"

The tone and accent surprised Kate, even in her alarm. Her ears had become very much attuned to the border inflections in these two days: or why should a man's voice in the dark, simply because it lacked those inflections sound like Colin Kemp's? She did not reply. The man took a step towards her, and hastily turning she caught her shin against the bathtub full of potatoes.

She saved herself from falling by putting out a hand and grazing it badly on the house wall. It was painful, but not so painful as her shin. Like most people who bark their shins, she became instantly at enmity with all mankind, and when, standing on one leg and clasping her agonised shin tightly in her hands, she found a torch being played over her, it seemed like the last insult to misfortune. Even the fact that the man holding the torch and now uttering exclamations of surprise and concern, actually was Colin Kemp, seemed only a god-sent opportunity for letting herself go.

"Colin! Why the *devil* didn't you say who you were? Look what you've done! Nearly broken my leg! You've no *business* to frighten people out of their wits like that!"

Colin characteristically did not reply to her absurdity. He did not even laugh, though the next moment Kate had to do so, if grudgingly, for the echoes of her hot accusations struck comically on her ears.

"I thought you were an elemental," she grumbled, putting her foot to the ground. Her pain had abated.

"A *what*?"

"An elemental! There's one on the tumulus. Did you know? Digging."

"Somebody digging on the tumulus?" echoed Colin, his professional zeal aroused. "Nobody's got any business to be digging on the tumulus. It's scheduled under the Ancient Monuments Act. How's your shin, Kate? Better now?"

"Awful. I'm lamed for life," replied Kate briskly. "Colin, what are you doing here?"

"Staying with Mr. and Mrs. Davis and making some drawings at Llanhalo Farm. What are *you* doing, Kate, in this back yard at this hour of the night?"

"I didn't know you were in England."

"I haven't been—long," said Colin, rather evasively, for him. "Well, Kate, hadn't you better come in and rest your broken limb? Did you come to pay a midnight call on the Davises? They're out, at the moment."

"I know they are."

Kate entered the dark house door, and Colin opened an inner door on to a small kitchen where an oil lamp shed a circle of light over a crimson chenille table-cloth, and a few embers glowed in the little oven grate. It was not such a cosy, nor such a well-polished kitchen as the one at Sunnybank, but comfortable enough, with two armchairs covered in American cloth drawn up close to the fireplace, and a fine oak dresser occupying almost the whole of one wall. Colin groped under a side table for some logs and thrust them endwise into the dying fire, and applied a very large pair of bellows.

"Sit down, Katy. Don't stand and suffer."

"I don't think I want the Davises to find me here," said Kate uneasily.

"They won't be back just yet."

"Do you know what they're doing?"

"Do you?" parried Colin cautiously.

"Yes. I've just seen them at it."

"Well, it's their delight on a shiny night in the season of the year," said Colin. "Nothing to do with me. I'm only the lodger. I promised to have the fire going and the kettle boiling for a cup of tea at three o'clock, and there my responsibility ends. I'll just fill the kettle, and then I think, Kate, if you don't mind, I'll leave you to puff the fire while I slip out and see what this person you spoke of is doing on the tumulus. Was he really digging?"

"He had a spade," said Kate, sitting down and taking over the bellows. "But I think he saw me, so he may not be there now. I don't suppose he was really an elemental, Colin. Just somebody digging out a badger or something."

"Nobody digs out a badger on the tumulus while *I'm* about," said Colin firmly.

He departed. Kate, puffing energetically at the weak fire, admitted to herself that she was delighted to see Colin again, and to see him looking exactly the same as ever, too. She did not know what she had expected—possibly an impressive beard, or a skin burnt to mahogany by South American suns, or anyway the remote and unfamiliar manner of one who has had strange experiences in foreign lands. But Colin's chin was as smooth, his complexion as light brown and his manner as matter-of-fact as it had ever been. He had the same perky and intelligent looking sprout of hair sticking up out of the crown of his head, and Kate was almost sure he was wearing the same tweed jacket. Of course, there was no reason on earth why he should have informed Kate of his return to England. Probably in those two years he had come to agree with her about the incompatibility of earthworks and theatres. Still, he might have just looked her up. If she had found herself among the Incas, she would certainly have looked him up.

The weak flame caught on a splinter and began to lap and curl, and Kate put the bellows down and stood up. She determined to search the house thoroughly before Colin returned, in case he had scruples about letting her do it.

The little scullery, examined by torchlight, proved to contain no hiding-place and no way of egress except into the yard. In the passage, and the frozen little parlour into which it led, there was nothing to rouse any suspicion—-in fact, respectability was written so clearly in that little parlour, with its Victorian sideboard and marble clock, that its owners' nocturnal occupation seemed almost too fantastic to believe in. Kate also searched the three bedrooms upstairs, and even looked up the wide chimneys, but there was nothing to suggest that anybody could be hidden there. On the upper landing she stood and called once or twice urgently and clearly. "Sidney! Sidney!" but only the ticking of a grandfather clock, and the roaring sound of the fire, now well alight, answered her.

She returned to the kitchen and opened the deep cupboard alongside the fireplace. It contained a small quantity of tinned food and groceries on the shelves, a large wooden trough on legs which proved to be full of flour, a quantity of rabbit-wires, a ball of twine, and, on the floor, a pile of kindling wood. Pentrewer farmhouse seemed to contain nothing more criminal than a poacher's paraphernalia.

"I say, Kate," said Colin, when he returned a moment later, "there *has* been somebody digging on the tumulus. Not a sign of a soul there now, but some silly ass has dug quite a hole on the side of it. It's filled in with loose earth and roughly re-turfed—you wouldn't notice it unless you were looking for it. There's no question of digging out a badger, or anything like that, either. Somebody's been digging there quite methodically, looking for something—or burying something."

"Burying!" cried Kate involuntarily. She faltered: "How—how big is the hole?"

"About two-feet square. Why?"

"Only, there's been a boy missing from Hastry for nearly a month, and—"

Colin smiled faintly.

"You could hardly bury a cat in this hole. I should think it's more likely some silly ass has got the idea there are antiquities buried in the tumulus, and doesn't realise that they'll only be bones and bits of earthenware if he ever comes to them—which he never will the way he's digging. It's certainly not anybody who knows anything about excavating tumuli. The digging's been done thoroughly, but childishly, more or less down from the top."

"Gwyn Lupton, perhaps," murmured Kate. "He did say most firmly that he was *not* for ever delving in the ground after treasure. So perhaps he is."

"Who is Gwyn Lupton?"

"Oh, Colin, you can't have missed seeing Gwyn Lupton! Or rather, hearing him!"

"I've only been here two days and spent most of the time up at Llanhalo. Why should this Gwyn Lupton delve in the ground for treasure?"

"Well, you see, some weeks ago he found a coin on the tumulus."

"A coin!"

"Yes. A silver penny of Ceowulf, 874."

"*What!*"

"Well, of course, Colin, it was just chance. Somebody must have dropped it there some time, but he wouldn't know that. He probably thinks the tumulus is simply full of silver pennies. And as he sold this one for five pounds—"

"Cheap at the price, if it was a good one. Who did he sell it to?"

Kate explained, and added that the silver penny of Ceowulf was at present in London, but that Mr. Morrison had promised her a sight of it as soon as it returned. She remembered as she spoke that Colin had met the Morrisons, and asked him how he liked them. But Colin was still pre-occupied with the violation of Pentrewer Tump.

"If it's really this chap Lupton who's doing the digging, I shall have something to say to him."

Kate laughed.

"He'll have something to say to you! He's a descendant of the ancient Welsh bards, I believe. He's got everything except a harp. Oh, by the way he told me he had a putty impression of that silver penny he'd show me some time, if I liked. So if you want an excuse to make his acquaintance—"

"If I find him digging on the tumulus, I shan't want any excuse," said Colin severely. "I shall walk straight up and ask him what the blazes he's doing. And then, if he's really a bard, we shall have quite an Eistedfodd. And now," he went on, sitting down and holding a hand to the now blazing fire, "what *are* you doing here, Kate? You were the last person I expected to see tumbling over pails of pig-food in this backyard! It's grand to see you again. Are you staying near here? How's the theatre? Is it evacuated to this part of the world? Or have you got a new job?"

"I haven't got a job at all," said Kate, sitting down in the other armchair and sharing the blaze. "Unless trailing a forlorn hope is a job."

"It depends on how forlorn the hope is, I suppose. And on how important the issue is."

"A child's life," said Kate, and told him about Sidney Brentwood's disappearance and her own determination to find out what had become of him. Colin listened with that agreeable attentiveness which she remembered as one of the things that had always endeared him to her. Colin had a nice, orderly, well-trained mind, and never interrupted the recital of facts with exclamations and surmises. When she had finished he said thoughtfully:

"Well, Katy, I wouldn't say the child's life is at issue, exactly, would you? Either he's already dead, in which case you'll only find his body. Or he's still alive, in which case you'll only satisfy yourself and others of the fact. There's no reason, from what you've said, to think his life's threatened."

Kate was now not so sure that mental orderliness is an endearing trait.

"No *reason*," she admitted. "But—"

"But what?" asked Colin.

Kate replied with another question:

"Colin, are there any chambered long-barrows on these hills?"

Perhaps her dread showed in her face or sounded in her voice, for Colin replied in a reassuring tone:

"Not one, Katy. I can assure you of that. Lots of little burial-mounds, like the one out here, but nothing elaborate at all. I know these hills well."

"Do you? What *are* you doing here, Colin?"

"I told you—making measured drawings of the Llanhalo ruins."

"Yes, but—"

"For a survey of border antiquities," added Colin.

It had not occurred to Kate that the Office of Works would be publishing surveys of antiquities during wartime.

"The army's doing without me for a month or two while I finish my job here."

"I see..."

It sounded reasonable enough, but it was a little unlike Colin, and oddly disappointing, that he should allow the army to do without him while he finished such a job. The antiquities would still be there, when the war was over. Or, if they were not, the survey would be out-of-date!

"There's supposed to be the beginning of an underground passage at Llanhalo, did you know, Colin?"

"Are you thinking your boy may be hidden there?"

"Well—Gideon Atkins is a queer man," said Kate slowly. "Nobody seems to know much about him. And he swears there isn't a tunnel, and won't let anybody look for themselves."

"Probably he's right. Most underground passages only exist in the local imagination."

"If it doesn't exist, he might prove it once for all by letting some responsible person see the cellar it's supposed to lead out of. But he won't. He won't let even Mr. Morrison from the Veault satisfy his curiosity, and Mr. Morrison's an antiquarian."

"Atkins may be afraid that if he gives an enthusiast like Morrison permission to explore whatever old vault opens out of his cellar, he might be pestered ever after to let people dig in it for subterranean passages."

"Well, if he's such an old dog in the manger, he can't be surprised if people explore that cellar of his without permission!"

Colin stood up and swung aside the bracket chain from which the now jovially steaming kettle depended.

"If by 'people' you mean yourself, Kate, I do hope you don't intend another dead-of-night adventure. If I were you, I'd give up these secret nocturnal investigations. They're not safe."

"Safe! Really, Colin, is this the sixteenth century?"

"The twentieth century's got dangers of its own."

"What, *here*? And anyway, how can I find Sidney without meeting whatever dangers he met? I want what happened to Sidney to happen to me."

Colin stirred the logs in the fire and a new flame sprang to roaring life.

"What happened to Sidney was, that he disappeared," he said quietly. "I don't want that to happen to you, Katy. Why don't you take the Davises into your confidence? They're perfectly sound people, I believe, apart from this little matter of the shiny night. Ask them whether your Sidney was ever mixed up in one of their poaching expeditions, for instance. They may know something about him they haven't seen fit to tell the police."

Kate agreed.

"They *will* be surprised to find me here!"

However, Mr. and Mrs. Davis, when towards the hour of four they returned, seemed disposed towards jocularity rather than surprise. It was certainly an unconventional hour for calling, and Kate did not attempt to explain her presence except by saying that she had been looking for Sidney.

"He ben't here, Missie," said Mr. Davis, hanging up his cap and disclosing a surprisingly venerable-looking high bald crown with a fringe of grey hair. Apart from the two slinking dogs who followed them into the room, there was nothing about Mr. and Mrs. Davis to suggest their nocturnal occupation. Probably, thought Kate, they had left their tackle and booty in some outhouse, so as not to pain the susceptibilities of their law-abiding guest. Mrs. Davis busied herself with cups and saucers and plates, and soon the four of them were drinking tea, and Mr. and Mrs. Davis were eating cold bacon and potatoes. When Kate inquired whether Sidney had ever visited them again after the first occasion on which he had cycled over to see the tump, a look passed between husband and wife sitting at the table.

"Well, no," said Mrs. Davis briskly, "he never come again. But Mrs. Howells and us is not well acquainted, and I think she would not like him to be coming over here too often. Hastry people likes to keep theirselves to theirselves." There was an indescribably ironic note in her clear high-pitched voice as she said this.

"Only," said Kate rather nervously, looking at Colin for encouragement. "I've found out that Sidney was interested in making nets. And I wondered—"

"Nets! What would that be for, I wonder?" commented Mrs. Davis blandly, again with a glance at her husband that had, Kate thought, a warning in it.

"Well—" Kate hesitated. Her eye caught Mr. Davis's, and, disregarding his wife's warning look, he allowed a sort of foxy grin to creep under his ragged moustache and curve the long lines of his leathery cheeks. He spoke to his wife conciliatingly in Welsh, and she replied very spiritedly in the same language. An argument seemed to develop, of which, after a minute or two, Mr. Davis had the better. He turned to Kate, still smiling, and began:

"Well, you see, Missie, since I expect as your friend has told you about us it were like this. The day as Sidney were here, were mending one of the nets I uses of a night-time, and Sidney—"

But if there was talking to be done, Mrs. Davis, now that her desire for caution had been over-ruled, was evidently going to be the one to do it. She broke in:

"Sidney was a very noticing, lively kind of boy! And he had been talking to my relation, Mr. Dai Lewis," she gave her head a little jerk in the direction of the road, and Kate understood that her relation, Mr. Dai Lewis, was the proprietor of the caravans and tents at present pitched in the field opposite Gwyn Lupton's. "And like a boy he wass wanting to know all about what the nets wass for, and if he could go with George and Mr. Dai Lewis one night. And to pacify him, George said he would have to show first he could make and mend his own nets. Because, of course, we wass not wanting children with us in such night work, dear me, no! And Sidney said at once he would learn to make a net. And nothing would please him but he must get a ball of silk for net-making off Mr. Lewis— exchanged a knife, he did, for a ball of silk. And off he went with it, telling us as he'll be back to help us with his own net one night before long."

"I did not think as he would come, though," said Mr. Davis, meditatively sucking his moustache, putting his cup and saucer neatly on his plate and feeling in his pocket for his pipe. "No, I did not think as he would come. Boys likes to think they will go out of a night-time, but when the time comes their beds claim them. Oh ah!"

"Do you think, then, that Sidney may have been coming to you the night he disappeared?"

"Oh ah, I shouldn't be surprised," said Mr. Davis, stuffing his little pipe with his large forefinger. "He wass asking me when we wass next going out, and I was telling him, most nights that is fine either me or Dai Lewis is out."

"Was it a fine night, the night he went?"

"Oh ah, it was fine, but there wass no moon, if I remembers, and I was bad with my back, and we didn't none of us go out that night, because Dai Lewis wass gone on into Breconshire. So Sidney would have been disappointed if he had come. Perhaps when he could not find us, he went off somewhere else, looking for something to do. It wass not a very good night to be out. Very dark it was, if I remembers."

"We did not say anything about it," said Mrs. Davis, rather defensively, getting up and putting the cups together on the tray, "because it would have made a lot of trouble for us and not have done any good to Sidney. Besides, we does not know he wass coming to us! Poor boy! I would give a lot if George and my relation Mr. Lewis had never put such ideas into his head!"

Her glasses flashed reproachfully at her husband, who replied philosophically, puffing at his pipe:

"A boy like Sidney wass, will have his head full of ideas, anyways, I reckon, and if they doesn't get put in one way, they will another."

A little silence fell. Mrs. Davis with a sigh picked up her tray and carried it out to the scullery.

Colin asked, after a pause:

"Did you know somebody was digging on the tump, Mr. Davis?"

"Oh ah? Well, they are not likely to find anything, whatever."

"Whoever it is mustn't be allowed to go on. Pentrewer Tump's protected under the Ancient Monuments Act."

"Ah, I knows. We had a paper about it," said Mr Davis, who was evidently less perturbed than Colin about the violation of Pentrewer Tump.

"If it's excavated without permission from the Office of Works, I'm afraid you'll be held responsible, Mr. Davis," said Colin.

"Oh ah, I daresay," said Mr. Davis with the utmost tranquillity, applying another match to his pipe. "It were all in the Government paper we had sent us, if I remembers."

But the Government was a long way away and occupied at the moment with other things than tumps. And Mr. Davis himself had more serious things to think about than the preservation of a rough grass-covered mound that was very little use even for grazing. So his easy-going tone conveyed.

He got up, and stretched, and belched softly, and lifted the corner of the black-out curtain.

"Her's nearly light," he observed. "Nearly light her is. And a fine day her'll be, I shouldn't wonder."

Chapter Twelve

Kate and Colin left Pentrewer and its inhabitants to a late sleep, and walked back down the track to where Kate had left her bicycle. Colin wheeled his bicycle with him, for he was going to Llanhalo, he said, to put in a little work before breakfast.

"Do you mind if I come with you, Colin? I want to see Aminta."

This was slightly disingenuous, for Kate did not, except in the most general way, want to see Aminta. She wanted to see Gideon Atkins again. And she very much wanted to see the dairy at Llanhalo again, and if possible, in spite of Gideon Atkin's hostility, the cellar that led out of it.

She left Colin to his measurements in the Abbey ruins, and turned into the farmyard. It was now quickly growing daylight, and the farmhouse looked still and dark, but there was a thin pencil of light showing at the side of the black-out curtain at a ground-floor window.

She went quietly to the dairy door and found it, as she had expected, open. There was no light inside, and as she entered Kate put on her torch for fear she might trip over a bucket or a churn in the cavernous darkness. There was the warm, sweet smell of new milk in the dairy from two tall frothing pails, and from somewhere in the farmhouse a faint scent of woodsmoke from a new-lit fire crept to this dark, cold place. Kate went quickly towards the door at the end of the short passage which Aminta had told her was the entrance to the cellar. The walls of the passage were of stone, rough-hewn in large blocks, and probably of great antiquity, and the barrel-vaulted ceiling reminded Kate of a church crypt. What a lot of *things* a farmer possesses! she reflected, running her torch over the barrels, the mole-traps, the coils of rope, the buckets, the brooms, the trestles, the oil-drums, all at present out of use and apparently surplus to other barrels, traps, buckets, brooms and trestles in use elsewhere! What a lot of props, what a complicated life! reflected Kate, thinking of her own life and greatly preferring it, forgetting for the moment that it had come to a full stop and a blank wall.

The cellar door handle was a large iron ring, like ice to the touch. Kate's heart beat fast as she put her hand on it, and she felt a little like Bluebeard's wife at the door of the secret room. Only, Bluebeard's wife had had a key, and Kate had not, but expected the door to resist when she turned the ring. To her great surprise, it did no such thing. The ring turned, and to a gentle pressure the door swung heavily away over two or three stone steps. What luck! But there was a light in the cellar. And where there was a light there was probably a human being. Quickly Kate made to draw the door silently shut again. But in her surprise at its opening, she had allowed the iron ring to slip out of her hand, and the weight of the door hanging over the steps carried it on slowly, swinging wide before her.

Kate made a grab, but she could not reach the handle. Had she been able to do so, it would have been too late, for there was a woman standing below in the cellar staring up at her with an expression of the utmost astonishment. She was holding, Kate instantly observed, a large knife in one hand and in the other something horribly red, and raw, and bloody.

Kate's first impression was of the contrast between the dank, dark stone cellar, empty, unwhitewashed, with an earthen floor, and the starched shirt-blouse and spotless apron of the neat, fragile, elderly little figure that stood there. Her startled eyes focussed upon the knife and the other horrible bleeding thing in the little grey-haired woman's hands.

The next moment she saw that it was only a piece of raw lights or something of the kind. There was a bunch of the stuff hanging up on a nail over a stone shelf. And three tabby cats were rubbing themselves against the woman's stiff apron.

"I—I'm sorry if I startled you," said Kate. "I'm looking for Aminta. I thought, perhaps—"

She had enough presence of mind to descend into the cellar as she spoke. She might not easily get such an opportunity again.

"She's still out milking, I think," said the little elderly woman in a rather toneless, grating voice. She had coarse grey hair tightly drawn back from her florid-skinned, pink-nosed, plain little face, and her neck was so bent and stiff that she appeared almost hump-backed. She added: "I'm just getting some breakfast for my cats to keep them quiet. They try me so with their mewing."

Kate tried not to look too eagerly round her, nor to reply too absently as she looked. The cellar was a square stone place, vaulted like the dairy and two or three feet lower in level. The floor seemed to be of earth, and there was no window. Quickly scanning the walls, Kate could see no sign of a door, nor even of the outline where a door might have been bricked up a long while ago. But close to the floor, in the corner of the wall opposite the steps, was an iron grating about two-and-a-half feet square, with pitchy blackness the other side of it. Kate tried not to keep her eyes focussed too eagerly on this. If there were an ancient entrance to any secret passage in this cellar, that must surely be the place!

"This must be tremendously old a cellar," she observed, lingering and gazing.

Miss Atkins, if it were she, gave a toneless little laugh.

"Eh, it's old enough, and cold enough, too. I've got a fire in th'kitchen, Miss—"

"Mayhew. Are you Miss Atkins? I hope it isn't very tiresome of me to come so early, but I thought I might catch Aminta before she started work."

"Eh, we start work here a lot earlier than this," said Miss Atkins. "Miss Hughes'll be in presently. Please to come to th'kitchen."

Kate had no excuse for lingering here, and followed Miss Atkins perforce up the steps. Miss Atkins took a large key from the pocket of her apron and locked the cellar door. Then she proceeded to cut the piece of lights she carried into three rough portions, and calling "Puss! Puss! Puss!" opened the door into the yard, and threw the gobbets up and out. The cats streaked out and up the steps after them, and the door was shut. Kate thought of Miss Brentwood's three cats and their saucers of sardine-bits perched on table and piano. It took all sorts of cats to make a world! Kate followed Miss Atkins along a stone passage to a large kitchen where a glittering kitchen-range was roaring, and a candle in an enamel stick provided all the light there was. Miss Atkins blew out the candle she was carrying as soon as she entered the room. Economy was the order of the day at Llanhalo. Kate could have guessed that from the speckless, but somehow rather worn and bleak, aspect of the kitchen. Kate, whose idea of a kitchen until recently had been an apartment five-feet square, or a gas-cooker on the landing, or even a gas ring in a sitting-room, was becoming quite a connoisseur of kitchens. There was a nice old settle and a wicker basket-chair or two, and a very large table and an enormous deal dresser loaded with ugly plates. There was also, standing on a low wooden stool in front of the fire, a large red earthenware crock with a piece of white table-cloth draped over it. It roused Kate's curiosity. It had such a ceremonial and secret air, enthroned there and jealously covered over like one of the properties of a magician which has been carried on to the stage and left to excite the audience's speculation.

Like the magician, Miss Atkins made no comment on this object, but offered Kate a seat on the settle, and began to take some cups and saucers off the huge scrubbed dresser. Miss Atkins was Chloe or Amaryllis of the dairy, grown old without her swain. Her long white apron and her neat shirt-blouse seemed positively to crackle with cleanliness as she moved about, and her crumpled face was as pink as if it had been scrubbed with a scrubbing-brush, like the silvery shelf of the dresser behind her. She was the first shy person Kate had met in this countryside. The remarks they made to one another expired one by one on the well-whitened flags until, glancing at the clock and approaching the range with the teapot, carefully skirting the sacred object under the cloth, Miss Atkins shot a glance sideways at Kate under her bristly grey eyebrows, and said in her low grating voice:

"You're the lady who's come to look for the little boy that's missing, aren't you? Miss Hughes told me."

Before Kate could speak she went on, tipping the black-leaded kettle towards the teapot:

"Eh, there's those that have children and doan't value them, and there's those that knoaws how to value them and hasn't got them."

"Did you know Sidney Brentwood, Miss Atkins?"

"Nay, it isn't often a leaves th'house, and th'master doan't often have people here," said Miss Atkins, stirring the tea in the pot three times round and putting on the lid. She spoke gravely and hesitatingly in her low toneless voice, as though words were too precious to be poured out like boiling water. "But I heard about the boy, He was a good boy, they tell me. A nice-looking boy, too, big for his age."

Her voice was as inexpressive as ever, but her meek pose as she stood with her hands crossed in front of her, with her stooped stiff neck, looking at the fire, expressed all that there was of a sort of wistful resignation.

"I wonder you don't have one or two evacuees here, Miss Atkins, if you're fond of children. They'd be company for you."

"I did put down to have one," said Miss Atkins, "but I didn't get one. I reckon they thowt as we're a bit far away here. I'd like it well enough."

"If you had a boy with a bicycle, it would be all right. It's not so far as all that," said Kate. She was thinking of Ronnie Turner. An idea began to germinate in her mind. "Would Mr. Atkins mind having a boy here, if it turned out there were one wanting a billet?"

"Eh, he'd be willing enough, if it was a quiet boy," said the little woman, putting her teapot under a cosy on the tray. "I could keep a boy easy on the billeting-money. The master'd have nowt to say against it."

Any further discussion at the moment was stopped by the appearance of the master, followed by Aminta. When he saw Kate sitting by the fire he inquired with dry amiability: "That bike o' yourn punctured yet?" He seated himself in the basket chair opposite.

"No. I carried it all the way down your awful lane, you see."

"That's a lie," said Mr. Atkins genially, rubbing his large mauve hands together and holding them to the blaze. "I saw ye through th' byre door, biking up alongside his lordship the stone-picker out yonder. Happen he'd like a cup o' tea, too?"

"Happen he would," replied Kate, "if the rations'll run to it.

"Maisie can water the pot down, can't you Maisie. Miss Hughes, lass, go and tell th'young man out yonder there's a cup o'tea for him in her alongside his young laedy."

"I'll go," offered Miss Atkins eagerly yet hesitatingly, as Aminta rose from her seat on the settle beside Kate. "You don't want to go out there again, Miss Hughes, you want a rest, I know! You sit you down, love, by th'fire I lit for you."

"No, really, I'll go," said Aminta, and went. She had spoken pleasantly but indifferently. Something in the look on Miss Atkins's face as she glanced after Aminta's sauntering figure, something baffled and sad, touched Kate, and also reminded her of Aminta's mild complaint that Miss Atkins mothered her more than she cared for. If Miss Atkins, poor lonely creature, nourished maternal yearnings, it was hard luck on her that Aminta, of all the girls in the W.L.A., should have been deposited at her welcoming hearth!

"Lit the fire for *her*, did ye?" commented the brotherly Gideon. "I thowt as ye'd lit it to do the cooking, but I were wrong, maybe.

Pour out the tea, woman, pour out the tea! There's work to do about the plaece! Happen you've coom over to lend a hand wi' it?" he added to Kate.

"No, I didn't," replied Kate, taking her cup of tea. "I came to see Aminta."

"Eh, well, ye're a bit laete, lass. We're working people here, and milking's at five," said Mr. Atkins, helping himself to a large quantity of sugar. When Aminta and Colin entered, he inquired at once with a kind of attacking geniality whether Colin had counted his old stones and found them all in place? Colin replied gravely that he believed there was a small piece of mortar missing from above the west doorway.

"The whole damned thing'd be missing, if I had my way," said Mr. Atkins, taking a long draught of tea and lingering over his moustache.

"I know," replied Colin pleasantly. "That's why I'm making a scale drawing of it. By the way—" he fished in his trouser pocket— "here's to-day's gate-money before I forget it."

He handed a sixpenny bit to Mr. Atkins, who took it with a nod and laid it on the mantelpiece.

"I think I ought to have a season-ticket, really," observed Colin. "Or anyway a workman's ticket, if I come before breakfast."

"Eh, ye can go hoame to your breakfast, lad, wi'out stumping up again," said Mr. Atkins, who perhaps disliked Colin's occupation more than he disliked Colin. "Ye can spend all day among them stones, and sleep on 'em, too, for owt I care. There's no accounting for the taeste of you educated chaps."

The redoubtable Gideon seemed in a mood this morning to be tolerant even of archaeologists. Kate decided to put his tolerance to the test.

"Mr. Atkins, if it's really true that you've got a romantic underground passage here, why don't you throw that open to the public, too?"

An indescribably wooden look came over Mr. Atkins's round bristly face.

"Why doan't I? Well, I doan't because nobody in theer senses'd pay good money to see what's oanly an old drain, young laedy."

"Are you sure it's only a drain, though? Have you looked?"

"I've looked as far as any man in his senses'd want to look. I haven't knocked th'wall down, nor yet taeken the floor up."

"Have you moved the grating?"

Mr. Atkins, pausing with his saucer halfway to his lips, gave her a quick, hostile look.

"What do *you* knoaw about th'grating?"

"Eh, Gideon, I was down cellar getting food for th'cats when the young laedy came in by th'dairy," said Miss Atkins placably.

"Oh, were ye?" grunted her brother, as if he would have found fault, if he could, with this innocent occupation. "Well then, young laedy, I *haven't* moved th'grating, and I doan't intend to! And I'll tell ye why I don't intend to. There's three reasons. One, there's only an old draen, or maybe a ventilation shaft, t'other side o' th'grating. Two, th'grating's rusted and fixed in so firm it'd taeke dynamite to shift it. And three, I'm not going to give the run o' my house to all and sundry to come gaeping about in it. And that's flat. It's bad enough to put up wi' them gaeping about th'yards and buildings. But a man's house is still his own, I reckon, even in these days!"

He spoke with a heat of resentment and a determination to keep his cellar inviolate that roused in Kate an answering heat of curiosity and an equal determination to make her way, by force, cunning or blandishment, into that close-kept cellar. She tried blandishment straight away.

"Would you let *me* look at it, Mr. Atkins, just once?"

He stared at her with a partly puzzled, partly hostile look in his sharp little eyes.

"What in thunder's naeme do ye want to look at it for?" he inquired. "There's nobbut to see but an old rusted-in grating, with an old draen the other side, I tell ye."

"But you say you haven't looked, so how do you know? Oh, Mr. Atkins, I'm awfully interested in—"

But Kate had made a false step, she saw at once, in casting an aspersion on her host's omniscience. Rising and putting down his cup with an indignant rattle, he said roughly:

"Eh, well, your interest mun be your master, my dear! I've no objection to you, and I've no objection to Miss Hughes having her friends here, wi'n reason! But I'll not have her friends, nor anybody else, poking their noses round i'my house! Next thing'd be, yon smart Percy from the Veault'd be here again, talking the hind leg off a cow about his interest in old houses, and such flim-flam! He's got an old house o' his own, let him pull that to pieces and leave mine aloane! I'm fed up wi' talk abut old houses and old ruins!" he went on, becoming more and more righteously wrathful at the sound of his own voice, and fixing Colin now, with an unloving eye. "I tell ye straight, mister, when I bought this plaece two years ago, it was my intention to pull down yon abbey, as they calls it, and build a fine new barn wi' the stoanes. There's a tidy lot o' stoane out there, and it was that decided me to buy th'plaece. But I hadn't been here six weeks when I was served wi' a damned paper from th' Government to say as I'd be liable to go to quod if I built a good barn out o' yon damned useless ruin, even though it's my own, bought and paid for! And I had to *buy* th' stoane to build the barn I wanted, and leave all that clobbering mess standing in my yard, just to please the damned Government!"

"I know," said Colin, apologising on behalf of the Government. "It's hard lines on you, but—"

"But nowt! I can't stop ye from waesting your time out in th'yard but I'll stop ye from bringing your damn-headed nonsense inside my house! And if I ever find any of yer, or any of your smart-Percy friends nosing i'my cellar, I'll—I'll lock ye in, and ye'll be welcome to crawl out by any underground passage ye can squirm into!" said the wrathful Gideon, and departed heavily from his fireside. Even in his wrath, he carefully skirted the covered crock which still nursed its secret before the fire.

Aminta rose, stretched herself and remarked:

"Well, I must measure up the milk and take it over to the Veault."

"Do you do an early delivery there every day?"

"Yes, generally. They'll be good customers later on, for all sorts of things."

"And *such* an early delivery, too!"

"Oh, I don't know! It's getting on for half-past-six," said the early-rising Aminta. "Rather late, for me. I'll see you again soon, I expect, Kate." She added: "You would have it my respected employer was meek and mild, you know, Katy. I told you he wasn't, didn't I?"

And with some satisfaction at her own unusual perspicacity, she strolled off towards the dairy.

Kate was beginning to think that Mr. Atkins was anything but meek and mild. She was determined to find her way again into that cellar, and with leisure, this time, to draw her own conclusions about the rusted-in grating and what lay the other side of it. She needed a collaborator. But Aminta, who had not in a year had sufficient curiosity even to go and look at the grating which was reputed to conceal an age-old subterranean passage, was scarcely the right partner for the enterprise.

"Miss Atkins," said Kate, reverting to the idea which had occurred to her ten minutes ago, "if you would really like an evacuee here, there's a boy in Hastry the school-master wants to find a new billet for. A nice boy, twelve years old—"

Miss Atkins was by nature inexpressive both in face and voice, but it seemed to Kate that her response to this suggestion was sincere. They decided that Kate should tackle the head-master, and that Miss Atkins should apply to the billeting officer, and that a little wire-pulling should soon remove Ronnie Turner from the barren land of the Cefn to the good pastures of Llanhalo.

"I'd like well enough to have a boy here. I could manage on the billet-money, and I like to see a boy eat," said Miss Atkins simply. "I mun go and start on my bed-making now, but doan't you hurry away. You bide here a bit by th'fire, you and your friend."

When the kindly little woman had gone rattling away with her dustpan and brushes, Kate said to Colin:

"I wonder why Mr. Atkins is so keen not to let anybody see the cellar."

"Just what he said, I should imagine. He's an obstinate kind of chap whose home is his castle. And he's got a grievance about the ruins—a fairly legitimate grievance, from his point of view."

But Kate, whose mind was obsessed with hiding-places and the lost child who might be hidden in them, saw Gideon Atkins in a more sinister, if flickering and uncertain, light.

"I wonder if there *is* a secret passage here?"

"I dare say there was, even if there isn't now. After all, this house is built on very ancient foundations."

"And if there is a secret passage or the remains of one, what's in it?"

"Just the usual things, I expect. Earth, and worms, and bits of broken stone, and insects. Don't let your imagination trot away with you, Katy. I've excavated all sorts of sites, and I can assure you the usual things nearly always are in the usual places."

"A boy's a usual thing, one would think, but this boy Sidney isn't in the usual place."

Colin said gently:

"I'm afraid he probably *is* in the usual place for little boys who've been missing a month, Kate."

"Meaning heaven?"

Kate was not going to waste her energies quarrelling with Colin about this.

"I've been thinking, Colin, about what Mr. Davis said. It was a dark night when Sidney disappeared. A bad night to be out on, Mr. Davis said. Well, to-night was a lovely night to be out on—you could see for miles. I ought to have thought of that. If I want to do what he did, and have a chance of finding what he found, I ought to come out on the same sort of night. The dark's different from the day, and dark nights are quite different from moonlight ones. You lose your way, perhaps. You mistake things for other things. You get frightened."

"Look here, Kate, if you want to experiment again, let me know beforehand."

"Why? So that you can jump out on me from behind a hedge?"

"Just because I'd rather you did. I know you wouldn't let me come with you, or I'd suggest that. But I'd rather spend only one night wondering what you're up to, instead of half-a-dozen."

"All right, if I can, I will," agreed Kate, standing up. "But as you're not on the telephone, I may not be able to."

"I'd better be getting back to my ruins, I suppose," said Colin without much enthusiasm. "Miss Atkins's dough is rising nicely, isn't it? It's making quite a hump in the cloth."

"Oh, is that *dough*? I've been wondering what it was all the time!"

Colin smiled.

"What did you think it was, Kate?"

"I don't know! It looked so mysterious sitting there all veiled, with everybody skirting round it."

Colin lifted the cloth and revealed the whitish spongey mass.

"*Not* the Doom of Llanhalo, after all, you see! Just the usual thing in the usual place."

Kate laughed, and went with him through the dairy to the yard. It was nearly light. The sky had that greenish tint of morning, and all the stars were gone.

"I think," said Colin, "after all I'll go back to Pentrewer and get a bite for breakfast, as Atkins has kindly given me a season ticket."

"Colin, surely if you're doing this job for the Office of Works you don't have to keep doling sixpences out to old Gideon?"

Stooping over his bicycle and pinching a rather flabby tyre, Colin answered:

"I didn't say I was doing this job for the Office of Works, did I? Dash. I must pump this tyre, or I'll have a puncture."

Watching him, Kate felt a little puzzled and a little chilled. No, he had not definitely mentioned the Office of Works, but surely he had conveyed the idea that his work was sanctioned by interests greater than his own?

However, his manner somehow discouraged her from pursuing the subject further. And when he had blown his tyre hard, he changed the subject, or had forgotten it. They talked about London, and the theatre and Maiden Castle and the old days, most of the way back.

Chapter Thirteen

When she returned to Sunnybank, Kate found a letter from Sidney's great-aunt awaiting her. Drinking her third lot of tea since midnight and eating the hearty breakfast of bacon and fried potatoes that was more welcome than usual after the exertions, Kate read the underlined, effusive little missive:

"I have not heard from Sidney's father yet, but he always was a bad correspondent, and I expect I shall see him before I hear from him. Poor Dick, I am really *dreading* his arrival, though of course, nobody could blame me for what has happened... I am sure you will excuse only a short note when I tell you I am in *great* trouble! Bobbie is lost! In fact, he has not been home since the morning you called, when you so kindly tried to catch him for me! I don't know whether the *raids* upset his *nerves*, or what, I am always *most careful* not to allow my pets to go out anywhere but in their own back garden, but Bobbie has been trying for some time to get into the street, though I never thought that he would get *lost* like this. I am really *heartbroken*, as I am afraid he has met with an accident, or caught cat-flu! There is such a lot of it about! I have advertised for him and offered a reward, but I am beginning to feel that my poor pet must have *gone to heaven*, as he was so devoted to me and such a *loving, timid*, creature, I know he would come home if it were in his power. I am sure if you have any news of poor little Sidney, you will let me know at once, *by telegram* if possible, so that I shall have *something* to tell his poor father when he arrives."

Kate did not know whether to laugh or cry over this effusion. As she folded it up and put it in her pocket, however, a memory of the raffish leer with which the devoted Bobbie, sitting on the pavement of Tranchester Terrace, had received her admonition to go home, made her decide to laugh. If the loving, timid creature could have spoken, its farewell message to its mistress would, Kate felt sure, have shaken that lady's dream world to its foundations.

This was not the first time Kate had been up all night, and she had not expected to feel any reaction during the day. But either the open air or the fried potatoes proved too much for her, and she spent the first part of the morning sleeping on the settle in front of Mrs. Howell's kitchen fire, with the noises of pudding-mixing, the oven door being opened and shut, and the melodious tinkle of the shop-bell as a dim, pleasant accompaniment to her dreams.

At eleven, she roused herself and washed in ice-cold water at the sink, and went out into the sunny, blue and tawny November day to call upon Mr. Pilgrim at the school. Mr. Pilgrim, a man who did not readily allow the eccentric or the unexpected to disturb the findings of his practical common-sense, had firmly placed Kate, in spite of her disclaimers, as a relation, or at least an old acquaintance, of Sidney Brentwood; and therefore it seemed natural to him that she should be exercised over the comfort of Sidney Brentwood's ally Ronnie Turner. He readily accepted her assurance that there was a good billet waiting for Ronnie at Llanhalo, and promised straight away to make representations to the billeting-officer.

Kate decided, in case the billeting-officer required more positive evidence than Mr. Pilgrim was able to provide, that she would visit the Cefn and form her own conclusions, and that the dinner-hour would be the most profitable time for a visit.

The Cefn, approached by a track running almost vertically up Rhosbach, except where it swung aside here and there to avoid outcroppings of grey stone, was a cottage of the smallest, plainest, one-storey type, built of the stone from the hill it stood on and looking itself almost like an outcropping of limestone and slate.

Kate knocked on the door, and Miss Gilliam herself, looking oddly untidy without her pixie-hood, her thin, grey-streaked bobbed hair hanging raggedly to her shoulders, opened the door, not very wide, and said good-morning, not very cordially.

However, when Kate had expressed a desire to see Ronnie Turner before he went back to school, Miss Gilliam seemed unable to think of any plausible reason why she should refuse her and, rather unwillingly, let her in to the living-room upon which the front door opened, Ronnie was sitting at the table eating a lot of sodden boiled potatoes with a very little pale gravy.

Miss Gilliam, it seemed, had her own dinner after Ronnie had gone back to school. She liked, she said, to eat in peace. Judging from a savoury smell that came from the oven, Kate thought that she also liked, perhaps, to eat in secret, and not be reproached, however silently by Ronnie's boiled potatoes.

"They say as potatoes is very good for children!" remarked Miss Gilliam gratuitously and with an ingratiating air. "There iss vitamins in them!"

"Not when they're boiled to a mash."

"Oh, very often we hass them baked in the skins. Doesn't we, Ronnie bach?"

"Yep," replied Ronnie indifferently. He had put his knife and fork down, less, Kate thought, as a protest against the watery mess on his plate than in excitement at seeing her. He had flushed, and his eyes shone expectantly. He was transformed, in the extraordinary lightning-like way of children, from a pale and torpid little boy ploughing his way through his dinner into a creature of fire and light.

"Children iss mostly very fond of potatoes," said Miss Gilliam, cutting the slice of white bread that was evidently to be Ronnie's afters.

Kate had not come here to talk about potatoes, but Miss Gilliam's uneasy defensiveness irritated her.

"I don't think they're enough in themselves for a kid's dinner."

"Oh no, indeed, I should think not!" cried Miss Gilliam in high-pitched and insincere agreement. Keeping a minatory eye on her evacuee, she added: "Ronnie hass plenty other things to his dinner, doesn't you Ronnie? Good gravy from the joint, greens when I has time to clean them, rabbit-stew, tinned salmon, apple-pies! Doesn't you, Ronnie?"

Ronnie, evidently a polite as well as a truthful child, looked a little surprised and said nothing. Miss Gilliam's hand, grasping a table-knife, hovered above a bowl of pallid dripping which was standing on the table.

"You'd like a nice piece of bread-and-dripping now, wouldn't you?" she asked winningly. "Or—" she hesitated, glancing first at Kate and then at a corner-cupboard, and screwed herself to the sacrificial point, "Or would you like jam to-day? Nice apricot jam?"

"Jam, please," said Ronnie, looking very surprised indeed. Jam was evidently a rarity.

Miss Gilliam unlocked the corner-cupboard door with a key out of her pocket, and whisked out a pound pot of shop jam with a very gaudy label, and shut the cupboard as quickly as if there were rabbits in it who might jump out But Kate had had a glimpse, not of rabbits, but of shelves laden with pound pots of grocer's jam. She looked thoughtfully at Miss Gilliam, remembering the trouble there had been in Mrs. Howells's shop over the sultanas, and Mrs. Howells's remarks about Miss Gilliam's nose for scarce confectionery. There were plenty of other cupboards in this kitchen—one on each side of the fireplace and others under the dresser. Kate wondered if they were all equally handsomely stocked.

"Ah," said Miss Gilliam, spreading apricot jam very thinly and lingeringly on the slice of bread in her palm, "it iss not easy to satisfy a boy's appetite with nine shillings a week, but we must not complain when there iss a war!"

Kate took the opening and observed that she believed Ronnie was soon to change his billet. Ronnie looked as if he could hardly believe his ears. So did Miss Gilliam, but the delight in the child's face was quite absent from hers. She paused, with the slice of bread and jam in her hand, and a look of thunderous wrath gathered on her brows.

"Oh, indeed, and who hass been complaining?"

"I don't know that anybody has."

"I will go and see the billeting-officer this afternoon I will go, and see him? Does they think that with nine shillings a week we

can feed people on chickens and ducks and plum cake?"
demanded Miss Gilliam shrilly, energetically scraping off most of
the jam she had spread on Ronnie's slice of bread before thrusting
it into his hands. "Well, if there iss people that can afford to keep
other people's children for nothing, let them do it! I am sure I am
glad if Ronnie goes! I have had nothing but work and worry with
Ronnie, and all for nine shillings a week, too! I hope he will be
moved this very day, and not come back here expecting jam and
eggs and cake, and his washing done for him, and all for nine
shillings a week! Indeed, I have been out of pocket, I can tell you! I
can tell you I would not have taken the boy at all, except that I was
sorry for him, and I am sure I did never expect such ingratitude!"
cried Miss Gilliam, more in anger than in sorrow, turning her
batteries on Ronnie now.

That philosophical child, however, rose with the remains of his
slice in his hand, and remarking:

"It's ten to two, Miss," picked up a satchel from the table,
retied a shoelace, slung his gasmask over his shoulder and looked
expectantly at Kate.

They departed, leaving Miss Gilliam still vociferously arguing
with her own conscience. As they walked down the hill, Kate told
the excited Ronnie of the possibility that he might be removed to
Llanhalo Abbey, and that there he might be able to help her in her
search for Sidney. Ronnie walked beside her as if on air, skipping
every now and then and kicking a small stone joyfully down the
slope in front of him.

A couple of days later, when Miss Atkins's and Mr. Pilgrim's
appeals had had their effect and the transfer had been sanctioned,
Kate enlarged further on the subject as she and Ronnie once again
strolled down from the Cefn. Ronnie was carrying a little suitcase
tied together with string, a gasmask, a pair of football boots, an
overcoat and a satchel, and Kate was bumping Ronnie's bicycle
down the steep and rocky path.

"When you have an opportunity, find out, if you can, what that grating's like. Whether it's really rusted in and can't be moved, or whether it's loose in a frame. The cellar's usually locked, but Miss Atkins keeps cat's-meat there, and I don't suppose she'll mind you going in. Only remember Mr. Atkins doesn't like talk about underground passages, and keep quiet about it in front of him."

"O.K., Miss!" said Ronnie, with so much zest and gladness that Kate was constrained to say firmly:

"But, Ronnie, don't on any account try to loosen the grating or take it out, will you? It wouldn't be safe. And it might spoil all our plans. Leave all that till I come."

"O.K."

"I think you'll like it at Llanhalo. Miss Atkins is nice. And my friend Aminta's there. If you're in a hole and want to talk to anybody talk to her. You've been having rather a thin time of it at the Cefn, haven't you?"

Ronnie made his indifferent, humorous underlip grimace:

"A bit lonely, it was, Miss."

"Did Miss Gilliam always give you a dinner of potatoes and bread?"

"Pretty near always, Miss," said Ronnie cheerfully. He added, in fairness: "I had rabbit, sometimes."

Chapter Fourteen

The following night Kate set out on a second expedition in Sidney's wake. This time she went earlier, before the waning moon was up, leaving Sunnybank before darkness through which a little chilly wind blew from the north. Mrs. Howells had done her best to dissuade her from going to-night, for two or three bombers had throbbed through the dark early in the evening, with that low, purposeful, threatening throb of aeroplanes in open country, far from balloon barrages and ack-ack guns, and Mrs. Howells was not as inured as Kate to the presence of enemy aircraft.

"The waterworks is only four miles away, the other side of Rhosbach," said Mrs. Howells uneasily. "There has been plenty bombs dropped not so far off, too. I wishes you would not go. There was bombers over the night Sidney went."

"But they didn't drop any bombs."

"Not near here they didn't, but they dropped some the other side of the hills. And you never knows with them Nazis. They're sly."

"They'll have to be awfully sly to hit me. Awfully extravagant, too. I'm not worth a bomb to them."

But Mrs. Howells's rustic superstitions were not in favour of joking about disaster. She sighed.

"I can see as it's no use me talking, so I'll hold my tongue. You're more used to being bombed than we are, I expect." She added, with a faint unwilling smile: "People does get used to things, whatever! First time we had the planes over here, Corney and me went in the cupboard under the stairs, but we never thinks of it now."

Kate could just see the outline of the hill above her on her right against the higher-toned sky, but it was some time before she was sufficiently accustomed to the darkness to distinguish between the different tones of road and hedge, and she had to cycle slowly in the little sphere of light cast by her darkened bicycle-lamp, for fear of running over the grass verge or into a telegraph-pole. Nobody passed her, and in the chill of the night even the animals in the fields were quiet. Down in the valley to Kate's left an occasional small spot of light beamed out, from a pedestrian's torch or a bad black-out.

Kate pedalled slowly on. Her thoughts, like the night, were uneventful, and a sort of feeling of frustration began to creep over her. Perhaps it had been, after all, rather foolish of her to suppose that by following in Sidney Brentwood's tracks through the darkness she might meet with whatever inspiration or danger he had met with. There was a time-lag of four weeks; and Kate Mayhew was a different person, differently susceptible, from Sidney Brentwood. If Sidney Brentwood's mind on his going out had been as dull, as empty, as Kate Mayhew's, he would have met with neither danger nor inspiration: he would have gone home to bed. A dark night like this was neither dangerous nor inspiring; it was empty, it was dull, it was silent, it gave rise to no fancies, as the moonlight did.

Thinking thus and mechanically pedalling on, Kate came around the spur where the road swung a little away from the hills down to Pentrewer Bridge. The cold wind had made her nose drip, and at the bend she got off her bicycle to fish in her pocket for a handkerchief. As she stood there, blowing her nose, her bicycle propped against her, a light, a point of yellow light, flashed out and quickly off again, then on again, then off again, ahead in the complete blackness of the hill.

Had Kate been moving, she might have thought the trees were obscuring and revealing to her as she went some careless cottage black-out. But she was standing still.

Queer, thought Kate, standing and straining her eyes into the distant dark. She mounted her bicycle, and rode a little way down the road. The light disappeared. She returned to where she had been standing, and watched again. Once more flick, flick went the little yellow point of light in the black distance, with a deliberate, precise effect, as if some infant troll among the hills were playing with a light-switch. Signalling came at once to Kate s mind, as it must have come to any mind, however untutored in radiography, at such a time in history as this. Kate knew nothing about the morse code, but it seemed to her that sometimes the light stayed on for longer, sometimes for shorter, flicks. Signalling—but to whom?

When the eyes are being strained to the utmost, the ears perhaps perform their function indifferently. As the question entered Kate's head, she heard very plainly and all of a sudden what she might well have heard before, the distant, menacing thrum... thrum... thrum ... of an unfriendly aeroplane somewhere in the sky. Good God! thought Kate, with an intensity of feeling that had been quite off her spiritual horizon five minutes ago, I believe somebody's signalling to that damned Jerry! She looked around the dark sky in which, had there been a hundred planes, she could not have seen one. She felt an impulse to rush on her bicycle towards the place where that light was, and put it out. But where was the place? There was no building nearer than Pentrewer, so far as Kate knew. Could it be from Pentrewer that that intermittent light was coming? Flick—flick. Flick—flick. And thrum... thrum... went the engine overhead, closer and closer, with a rhythmic greed that seemed to eat the air.

There was nothing for it but to cycle on down the road towards Pentrewer. Kate jumped on her bicycle and was off. When she moved on, trees, or the lie of the land, blocked her view, and the light was no longer visible.

In a very different mood from that of a few minutes ago, Kate cycled on as fast as she could go, keeping her eyes now on the perilous dark road, now on the distance quite unpointed by any speck of light, and feeling as if her bicycle were racing the huge engine that seemed to fill the empty night with its menacing throb, so that it was difficult to believe that it was not flying almost within crashing distance of the hill. Long before she had arrived at Pentrewer it had passed, grown remote and faint, and faded out of hearing.

At Pentrewer Bridge, Kate dismounted. The darkness and the silence were now unbroken, except for the sound of the little stream and the faint noise of the wind in the trees. She put her bicycle in the ditch as before, and advancing cautiously to the hedge, shone her torch into the gipsies' field. The gipsies' encampment was still there, dark and silent, everyone asleep. Gipsies could not light campfires and sit round them, nowadays, in the night-time.

It had been growing colder during the past two days, and there was a thin crackle of ice on the water that filled the ruts of the rough track. As Kate approached up the track to Pentrewer Farm, of which she could just distinguish the outline of roof and chimneys up on the bank, she thought of Colin. She had not, as she had half-promised, given him warning of this expedition. She had not decided on it until to-day, but that had not been the only reason. A sort of reticence surrounded her friend Colin, and bred an equal reticence on her. She had freely and fully explained to him what she was doing in Radnorshire, but he had not responded with an equal confidence about his doings, but played her off with amiable prevarications. As for the nonsense he had talked about the dangers of solitary nocturnal expeditions she might have been listening to some great-aunt, not to Colin, and it had never been Kate's habit to defer, except politely, to the opinions of her great-aunts on such matters.

Pentrewer Farm, like the cottage below, was dark and silent as the grave. And the grave, the tumulus, whose shoulder Kate thought she could just see rounded against the open darkness of the sky, was silent, too. No light in any of the windows here.

There remained Hymns Bank, the empty house whose ghostly reputation had on a previous night caused Ronnie to abandon adventure and flee. And standing there hesitating before Pentrewer Farm, Kate recalled that Ronnie had claimed to have seen a man, a strange man, not Gwyn Lupton nor Mr. Davis, walking up towards Hymns Bank that night.

A piece of ice cracked under her foot, and instantly a dog set up a volley of barks on the bank in Pentrewer yard. It was a startling sound in the stillness, loud enough to call Mr. and Mrs. Davis and Colin from their beds, and even, perhaps, the elemental from his age-old grave.

"Sh! Good dog! Good dog!" said Kate, very foolishly, from the lane below, at which the dog redoubled his efforts to rouse the countryside. And another dog, farther off, perhaps at Gwyn Lupton's cottage, awoke and joined in. Between them, they made din enough to warn any night malefactor to be on his guard. She hurried back away from that noise, and made her way up the fork which led to the empty cottage. The track here, unused was narrow and overhung with trees, and very wet as she went farther up it in the shelter of the hill-sput. The barking of the dogs, thank heaven, soon died down.

Before the peaceful normality of Pentrewer Farm, under the silent empty sky, Kate had been inclined for a moment to discredit her fifth-column fancy, and to think that, after all that light must have a more or less innocent explanation. But now, as she ploughed her way up the narrowing trackway, treading on she knew not what uneven ground which sometimes sucked wetly against her soles and sometimes struck hard against the toe of her rubber boot, conscious of the smell of vegetable decay which hangs around such enclosed, neglected places, surrounded by a bosky darkness that she could almost feel upon her staring eyes, she heard again that ominous throb, throb, throb, of a distant bomber, and the notion of a deliberate signal did not seem fanciful. In fact, she half-regretted that she had not aroused Colin, she had a half-impulse to go back.

Recognising and sternly subduing the fright that underlay this impulse, she went on. The bomber came on, too, as if it were looking for her. She dared not put her torch on now, and floundered in and out of miry, crackling puddles which seemed all the more disgusting because she could not see them. Once she went right off the track into a bramble bush, which whipped her face and caught at her skirt as strongly as if a detaining spirit were in its hooks. She had to use her hands to free herself, and as she stood there struggling with the thorns, she became aware, by some graduation in the darkness that lay ahead of her, some freshness in the fir-scented air, that she was not far from a clearing in the trees.

She judged that she had come nearly half-a-mile from the fork at Pentrewer Farm, on a gradually rising track. The queerly named Hymns Bank must be quite close. But there was no light to be seen in or beyond the clearing, and no sound except the close throb, throb, throb of the bomber overhead. Kate got herself free from the brambles, and went on, and quite suddenly found herself dose up against a rough stone wall.

The bomber had passed and was nothing now but a faint warning in the distance over the hills, and Kate ventured to switch on her torch for a second, long enough to see that the wall was the yard wall of small stone house that stared at her with dark menacing windows like eyes that said: "I see you!" to her torch. She switched it off, and a darkness seemed to throw itself upon her like a wave. But she had upon her retina the picture of a gate in the wall, close to her left hand, a straight path up to the door of the house, a low-roofed, one-storeyed, darkly staring house of stone, with a tangle of wild leafless creeper hanging over a lopsided porch.

Kate dared not put on her torch again, for those windows must not cry "I see you!" to her as she crept up to the front door. She was glad of her silent-treading rubber boots. But when she felt for and put her hand on the gate to push it open, she felt something move, cold and clammy—a large slug, perhaps—under her palm, and it took all her presence of mind to repress a little cry of disgust. She did repress it, and at once, as if she had driven her disgust into her heart, her nervousness was enhanced, and she felt as if an omen of danger had been given her. She disregarded it, and went up, feeling her way by an overgrown box hedge that ran alongside the path, to the front door. A creeper-end, hanging from the porch, touched her face. She brushed it aside with a shudder, and stood there, not breathing, listening for she knew not what, considering what to do.

If there was no one in the house, she might safely feel for the door-handle, turn it, press on it, use her shoulder, break her way in. But it took a good deal of nerve to make a noise in this stillness, with the possibility of a silent someone in the house listening to her. Kate hesitated, her hand raised to feel for the door-latch or a handle. What else could she do but go boldly in? She could not, at least she would not, go away and leave the place unsearched. She might tiptoe round the house shining her torch in at the windows. But that would be simply to give warning to whoever was in the house—if there was someone in the house. But there was probably no one in the house. Why should she think, because from a mile away she had seen a light shining from she knew not where, that there was someone in the house?

Of course there is someone in the house! the dangling creeper, touching her shoulder, whispered. *Of course there is someone in the house!* swished the wind in the tree-tops. *Of course there is someone in the house!* the darkness bellowed in a sound as loud as silence round Kate's ears. There is always someone in the house. Do you think there can be a house, and no one in it? If there is no human in the house, there is someone there who is not human. Do you think that generations of people can live in a house, and go, and leave nothing, no one, huddling in the chimney corner or dragging a slow foot up or down the stairs? If there was no one in the house before you came, shouted the darkness, there is someone now! *You* know who is in the house! Your fear is in the house, all the fear of darkness and the unknown that has ever driven men mad, has taken shape in the house and is waiting for you.

Gosh! if I stand here listening to nothing any longer, I shall start running away! said Kate to herself. She heard a funny little noise very close to her ear. It was her own front teeth gritting together. The next moment she had the door-handle in her hand and her shoulder ready for the shove.

No shove was necessary, for the door opened to the turn of the handle, with a loud click that seemed to burst the dark in two. Kate stood on the threshold. Her eyes were no use to her however, she stared about in the blackness. Her ears heard nothing but the soft noise of the wind. Her nose smelt the odours, dank, close and cold, of dry-rot and damp earth and mildewed plaster.

The effort of entering had quieted the voices of the night, and though Kate was aware of the running of her pulse, she was not much frightened. There was nothing to hurt her in a dark, empty house but her own fears, and she had the remedy for those in her own hands. Action was the remedy. She had applied it, and had better apply it again. Leaving the door open behind her, she switched on her torch and looked about her.

The empty, low-ceilinged room, with its rusty oven grate and damp paper hanging from the walls, looked as she had expected from the smell of it—forlorn, damp, rotting. The brick floor was sweating, and the bricks buckled here and there by rats, and littered with dry, gnawed nut-shells. A jam pot, stained a pond-like brown with dirty water long since evaporated, was the only domestic property on the scene. The loose door of the stairway next to the chimney-breast hung ajar.

Kate supposed she had better go upstairs while she was about it. But first she went out to the scullery at the back, which was in much the same long-neglected, long-deserted condition as the living-room. Some small thing was hanging stiffly from a hook in the ceiling, and Kate, examining it, found that it was the body of a fox, no more than a skeleton clad in a mummified skin as hard as wood.

This was a very old cottage, Kate surmised, observing the heavy timbering, set close together, of the main wall, and remembering what Rosaleen Morrison had told her at the Veault. She thought of Mr. Morrison, that ardent antiquarian, as she went cautiously upstairs, and wondered whether any hidey-holes existed here. She went cautiously, because the floorboards had rotted through at the top of the staircase. A door led off the little room, or landing, in which she found herself when she reached the stairhead, and to get to the door she had to tread carefully, close to the big chimney-stack where the broken boards still stood firm over the joists.

The door stuck a little on the damp, swollen floor, and Kate gave it a hearty push, for she had quite recovered from the fear of making a sound that had at first afflicted her, and felt scarcely more nervous than if it were daylight and she, a prospective tenant with an order-to-view in her pocket.

This room, too, was dark and silent. But not empty. As Kate pushed open the door with her right hand, in which she held her torch, another hand, a gloved hand, soft and cold, came quietly from behind the door, and took her torch from her, and turned it out.

Chapter Fifteen

Half, perhaps a quarter or less, of a minute crept by like an age, before a man's voice said so close to her that she gasped:

"Excuse me taking your light. My ferret's got loose, and I doesn't want him to be frighted up the chimney."

Kate's first feeling was of relief at the amiable and commonplace tone, her next; an odd persuasion that she recognised, or ought to recognise, the voice. A light masculine voice it was, the local accent curiously overlaid on a sort of

Cockney intonation. But it certainly belonged to none of her local acquaintances, all of whom spoke with a much broader accent than this.

"Us'd better go outside and shut the door," suggested the voice. "Them ferrets is nasty customers when they gets frighted."

Once again, the tone was reassuring, but Kate was not entirely reassured. If there's a ferret loose in this room, she thought, straining her eyes into the darkness, it's a very silent ferret. Had its owner been looking for it in the dark? Certainly he must have been looking for it very silently, for the cottage, when Kate entered, had seemed as silent as the tomb. She backed out on to the landing, saying nothing. She heard a footstep and the click of the door-handle, and felt a living, breathing presence beside her near the chimney-breast in the dark.

"Mind they boards, them's rotten," said the presence, and switched on Kate's torch. He kept it directed downwards to the floor, but Kate, standing on the sound joists with her back to the chimney, looked, not at the floorboards, but quickly, keenly, at him. She could not tell what manner of man it was who stood beside her. She made a guess at a shaven, longish face under a battered hat, but whether old or middle-aged, or young she could not tell. She gained an impression of a dark tweed jacket and a medium-sized, upright figure. She had a good view of mud-caked shoes and stained grey flannel trousers. The hand that held her torch was wearing a leather glove—not a countryman's working glove, but one of brown calfskin.

"I asks pardon if I frighted you," said the man, who seemed less curious to get a view of Kate than she was to get a view of him, for he kept the torch pointing down towards the stairhead. "I didn't know who you was, and I isn't supposed to be keeping my ferrets here, see. I didn't make no noise when I heard you come in because I thought maybe you'd go, without coming up here."

Kate said, with uneasy sceptical bravado:

"Your ferret's very quiet in there."

The man laughed.

"I'm feared he's gone up the chimney! 'Tisn't easy looking for they creatures in the dark! And I didn't like to put my lights on whiles they planes was about."

"But you *did* have your light on a little while ago, didn't you?" said Kate. "That's what brought me here."

"Ah, I put my light on when I first come here, to get they creatures out of the sack and back into their cages," replied the man, still keeping his torch away from his face. "But when I heard that plane come over I put the light out pretty sharp, and it were then Ginger escaped out of the sack." He added hesitatingly: "Did you see the light, then?"

"I should think I did! If you're going on keeping ferrets here, I should put up a black-out curtain, if I were you."

"Reckon I'd better move my ferrets, now you knows as they're here. Or happen you won't tell?" said the voice on an ingratiating, humorous note that would have pleased Kate better had it not been for that uneasy persuasion hovering all the time in the background of her mind, that she ought to recognise the person who was speaking to her. Perhaps it was only the aftermath of her fear. She had been frightened, very frightened, when that hand had come silently from behind the door and taken her torch away from her. Perhaps the fear she had suppressed then still lingered like a warning in her mind, causing this uneasy feeling of recognition and of strangeness. If Kate could once get hold of her torch, she would soon settle this point!

"Could I have my torch back, please?"

"I'll see you down. I've left mine in the room. The stairs is dangerous."

"I can see myself out, if you'll give me my torch."

Once again that oddly familiar laugh.

"Nay, you isn't as used to the stairs as I is," said the other. He made a motion with the torch towards the stairhead, but Kate did not budge from her chimney, for she was not, if she could help it, going downstairs first! Queer that a note of recognition could seem more chilling, give more warning of danger, than something completely strange! Kate pressed her hands against the cold plaster. Her heart performed a heavy little gallop as she realised that the man had no intention of allowing her to see him clearly. She swallowed something in her throat, and asked boldly:

"Do I know you?"

"Happen you've seen me. I've seen you, Miss."

"Where?"

"About the place on your bike."

"Do you live in Hastry?"

"Nay!"

"Where, then?"

There was a little pause, then the man answered evasively:

"Oh, no place pertickerler. I moves about."

A light broke on Kate. She had an extraordinary sense of relief. Of course! Was not Mr. Dai Lewis's encampment still pitched in the field opposite Gwyn Lupton's? Were not gipsies notoriously evasive in speech, amiable in manner, secretive in action, as careless, no doubt, of black-outs as of property-laws?

"Are you—" Kate was about to say "one of the gipsies" but she did not know whether a gipsy might not resent this term. She substituted: "Are you Dai Lewis?"

"There, now, and you was asking did you know me!" responded the man in his soft and evasive way which yet, Kate did not doubt, could harden at need to the most definite and terrifying ruthlessness. There had been no hesitation, no ambiguity, about the way in which he had taken her torch out of her hand: nor about the way in which he had refused to give it back, affably as he had couched his refusal!

The worst of Kate's fears, the fear of what is unknown, went to rest. Dai Lewis the gipsy was, after all, a relation of Kate's friend, Mrs. Davis. A gipsy was the last person to be suspected of signalling to enemy planes, although no doubt the loss of a ferret might seem more dire to him than the loss of a country. If this were Dai Lewis, Kate could abandon the idea that there had been signalling from this house. She had something else to talk to Dai Lewis about.

"Mr. Lewis, I've been wanting to see you."

"That's very kind of you, I'm sure!" replied the man with a sort of jocose crude gallantry.

"You remember the boy who disappeared—Sidney Brentwood?"

There was a moment's pause before the other answered—Kate thought, rather guardedly:

"Ah, I remember him."

"He came to see you, didn't he, about making a net?"

"Aye."

Did you ever see him again? Did he ever come to this house? Or did you ever see traces of somebody having been here? You see," said Kate eagerly, as Dai Lewis remained silent, "if when Sidney came out that night he saw the same light that I saw—Mr. Davis says it was a dark night—he may have thought, as I did, that it was a signal, and he may have come here, as I did, to find out what it was."

"Well?"

"Well, you might have seen him."

"Wouldn't I have told the police if I'd seen him?" inquired the man. "Or does you think as I did the boy some harm that night—murdered him, maybe?"

Kate laughed, but nervously, at this grim note.

"No, no! But—"

"Nobody's bin here but me, as I knows on, and I isn't often here. I wasn't here the night as the boy went, so if he come here I shouldn't know."

"Oh, no! I remember now, Mr. Davis said you'd gone into Breconshire."

"That's right."

Something in the intonation with which Dai Lewis uttered these two simple words caught Kate s ear, perplexed as it already was by that sense of vague recognition.

"Are you a Welshman, Mr. Lewis?" she ventured.

"Why does you ask?"

"You don't talk like a Welshman, it seems to me."

"There's different kinds of Welsh talk, I reckon," replied Mr. Lewis cautiously.

"Of course, there must be," agreed Kate, noting at the same time that her question remained unanswered.

"I guess you hasn't been here long enough to know how Welsh people talks," said Dai Lewis tolerantly.

"No, perhaps not. But in my job one gets interested in how people talk, one gets to listen to people's intonations."

"Aye? What is your job?"

"The theatre," said Kate, and suppressed a sigh: the theatre seemed so far away.

She could not be sure, but it seemed to her that she had startled Mr. Lewis. There was something rigid about the silence which followed. Then he echoed indifferently:

"The theatre, is it? You're an actress, are you, miss?"

"I do a bit of acting sometimes. But stage-management's my job. Well, if you'll give me my torch, Mr. Lewis, I'll make my exit."

"Til shine you out," replied he courteously but firmly, and stood aside to let her pass, shining the torch upon broken boards so that she could pick her way.

There seemed nothing for it but for Kate to skirt the damaged floor and descend. Mr. Lewis followed, keeping his circle of torchlight shining ahead of Kate down the stairs. Its shifty, stagey light fell on stairs deeply ingrained with the grey dust of ages, on the matchboarded walls puffed and splitting with damp, on the door at the bottom hanging on long iron hinges.

As the circle of light fell over the door, Kate almost stopped dead on the fourth step from the bottom, almost gave a cry. Stuck to the blistering, thickly painted boards of the rough door, about a foot from the top, was a small square of bright green tinfoil, such as is used for wrapping toffees.

Then Sidney *had* been here!

"What's the matter?" asked her escort from behind her, as after that involuntary jerk she went on down into the room, following the shifty circle of light closely with her eyes for other signs. Sidney *had* been here! Kate was not in the mood to weigh any other possibilities. Sidney had left that green square of tinfoil as a warning and a sign. Green for safety: but not this time!

"I thought I saw a mouse," said Kate calmly, holding out her hand for her torch.

Dai Lewis switched it off, and for a moment Kate's primitive fears threatened to return upon her. But, of course, to open a door in the black-out, one must switch off one's torch! Kate heard the wind in the trees, and, she thought, once again, far off, that stubborn steady thrum of planes forging through the dark.

"Good-bye, Missie. Don't put on your torch. There's planes about, I hears them."

Kate thought this was rather cool advice from one who had been guilty of blazing lights out of windows with enemy planes abroad.

"And don't *you* forget that black-out!" as she took her torch from him in the darkness.

He laughed. It still seemed to Kate that his laugh, even more than his voice, was vaguely familiar to her. No doubt she had seen and heard Dai Lewis in Hastry village shop or elsewhere. A stage training develops an ear for voices, but not always a methodical memory for placing them.

"Aye. I'll hang up my jacket!" he replied, as Kate felt her way down the garden path and out of the rickety gate.

The plane was coming closer, and Kate, who dared not use her torch, made slow and floundering progress. When it had passed overhead, she heard the unmistakeable, sickening, earth-heavy crash of an exploding bomb. A pause, then another, farther off. Impossible for an ear attuned to town bombing to determine how far away those bombs had fallen. Not so far as they sounded, Kate guessed, for the plane that dropped them had been more or less overhead only a few seconds ago.

No more bombs fell, and for the present no more planes were to be heard. As she returned down the difficult path, Kate's thoughts returned to Sidney Brentwood. If Sidney had stuck that piece of tinfoil on the door on purpose, as a despairing sign to friends who might follow on his trail, it must be that he had been constrained, unable to escape, unable to send any other message. Coming downstairs at Hymns Bank—perhaps being dragged downstairs—he had managed to stick that piece of green toffee tinfoil upon the door, knowing that Mrs. Howells, anyway, should news of it ever reach her ears, would connect it with him. But who had constrained him? Not Dai Lewis, for Dai Lewis and his tribe had been in Breconshire at the time that Sidney disappeared. Besides, even if Sidney had found Dai Lewis at Hymns Bank, why should Dai Lewis have done more than send him off with a flea in his ear? There was nothing dangerously criminal about using an empty house as headquarters for poaching in the woods, and Sidney knew all about the gipsies' poaching exploits.

But that Sidney Brentwood had been at Hymns Bank that night, Kate felt sure. Her night's search had led her one step in the right direction. It was from Hymns Bank, not from Hastry, that she must track Sidney now.

Who owned Hymns Bank, she wondered? It should not be difficult to find out. It lay at least two miles from Llanhalo Abbey and Gideon Atkins was scarcely the man to be encumbered with such derelict and unprofitable property: otherwise Kate might have played with the notion that it was his. Her thoughts continually reverted to that fabled subterranean passage, and to Gideon Atkins' wrathful denial of its existence. She had to check a tendency to exaggerate Gideon Atkins' unamiable denials into sinister and monstrous signposts to secret guilt.

Chapter Sixteen

When, about two o'clock, Kate arrived back in Hastry, she found both Mr. and Mrs. Howells up—she feared, on her account, although they assured her they had got up entirely for their own satisfaction. However, they were both so relieved to find that neither of the bombs they had heard had landed anywhere near her, that she remained unconvinced that their vigil had not been on her account.

"Berminster waterworks, that's what they be after," said Mr. Howells, looking less than ever like a postman, with his thatch of grey hair standing on end and his collarless shirt open around his sleep-dishevelled beard. "Every time I hears a bomb, I thinks of my sister's brother-in-law, Jeff Dew, listening up at the control-station to hear if this'un or that'un's going to send him to glory, and I has to laugh. Because he's right as rain, they fellows never hits what them's aiming at, my God, no."

It appeared from Rumour, who arrived in the village before the dawn and hung around on the doorsteps waiting for the taking down of the black-out, that Mr. Howells' laughter was justified. Five, ten, twenty sheep—the number varied—were a dead loss, and there were two craters on Mr. Jenkins's, Mr. Jones's, Mr. Richard Hillier's, Mr. Meredith's land—Rumour was impartial in distributing the glory—big enough to put a house in, pretty near. But the Berminster waterworks and Jeff Dew remained unscathed.

Colin, when Kate told him of her night's expedition, did not express concern so loudly as Mrs. Howells had done. In fact, he said nothing for a moment. But he looked serious, and Kate could feel the air, already cold enough for sitting out in, grow cooler still with his silent disapproval. They were sitting on Pentrewer Tump, where Colin had been showing Kate the patch of recent digging cunningly covered over with fresh turves and replanted foxglove stems. The day was bright, with a snap in the air, and Mr. Davis, like any respectable farmer, was making a bracken-stack in his yard.

"Mrs. Howells was afraid a bomb had dropped on me."

"Well, it might have done," said Colin, and Kate could not deny it. He added amiably, having evidently decided either that warnings were wasted on Kate or that she had the right to disregard them if she chose: "where did you go? Did you find anything?"

"I went to Hymns Bank. And I found a light, and a piece of green tinfoil. The light hadn't anything to do with Sidney, but the tinfoil had."

Kate had expected Colin's curiosity to be aroused by that piece of tinfoil, and looked expectantly at him. But it was the light that seemed to interest him.

"You saw a *light*, Kate?" he asked quite sharply. "What sort of light? Where? A light in the black-out, do you mean?"

Kate told him the story of her night's adventures. She expected Great-Aunt Colin to draw the moral, as he would have been justified in doing, of the dangers that lie in wait, even in the twentieth century, for unaccompanied females who make nocturnal journeyings about the countryside. But he did not do so. In fact, Kate was a little disappointed to find how little her terrors seemed to interest him. He examined her, with a closeness that made her feel she was in the witness-box, on the subject of the light she had seen.

"I'm afraid my education in the morse code's been neglected, Colin. All I know is, there are such things as light-signals, and so when I heard that old bomber, I feared the worst. But if the light came from Hymns Bank, as it probably did, I was wrong. It was Dai Lewis signalling to his ferrets, as I've told you."

"I don't believe looking for ferrets with a torch would give the effect of signalling through a window," said Colin slowly. "Though of course we can't be sure without experimenting."

Kate laughed.

"Well, we can't experiment without getting locked up! So I vote we take Mr. Dai Lewis's word for it. He seemed perfectly candid. Except—"

Colin looked at her sharply.

"Except what?"

"Well—Except that he wouldn't let me see him properly. He wouldn't give me my torch till I was out in the black-out with a bomber overhead and couldn't put it on. And all the time he had it, he held it directed at the floor. That was one thing. And the other was—"

"Well?"

"Something about the way he spoke," said Kate slowly. "Such a queer intonation. Not at all like the local accent."

"He may not be a local man."

"He's a cousin of Mrs. Davis."

"But he may have been brought up in another part of the country, and got a different accent, all the same."

"Oh, I know. But that wasn't it. It was—That I seemed to recognise something queer about his accent. I've heard the same kind of accent before, not here, somewhere quite different, I don't know where. Also, I thought I recognised his voice, but that isn't so puzzling, because very likely I have heard it, in the post office or somewhere."

Colin agreed:

"And as for his accent, no doubt you heard that at the same time! To me, the fact that he avoided being clearly seen is much more odd."

"Yes, but not so very odd, when you think what queer fish gipsies are. It worried me at first, but when he said who he was, it didn't worry me any more. And, of course, Colin, a gipsy would be the last kind of person in the world to be signalling to the enemy, though he might be the first person to be careless about the black-out. I don't see, either, how Dai Lewis could have had any connection with Sidney's disappearance, because he was in Breconshire the night Sidney disappeared, Mr. Davis said so."

"Then, if you think Sidney stuck that piece of tinfoil on the door to show that he was a prisoner at Hymns Bank, it follows that somebody else, not Dai Lewis, was keeping him a prisoner there?"

"Yes—I suppose so."

"Then somebody else—not Dai Lewis—was using Hymns Bank for some secret purpose?"

"Yes, probably."

"It would be very queer if two people, quite unconnected with one another, were using the same empty house for two different kinds of villainy, wouldn't it?"

"Yes, I suppose it would."

"And queerer still if they didn't know of one another's existence."

"Yes," admitted Kate, feeling a little like a witness whom a clever barrister has driven into an uncomfortable corner. "But the only other thing one can think is, that Dai Lewis *was* signalling to the enemy, and that he *is* responsible for Sidney's disappearance. And I don't see how one can think that, if he'd wandered off into Breconshire before Sidney disappeared."

Colin murmured:

"'Here awa', there awa', wandering Wullie.'"

Kate sat up suddenly.

"Say that again!"

Colin looked at her in some surprise.

"'Here awa', there awa', wandering Wullie,'" he repeated, rather sheepishly. "Why?"

"Say some more."

"The rest of it isn't at all appropriate."

"Never mind that! Say some more!"

"But why—oh, all right! 'Loud blew the cauld winter winds at oor parting, It was nae the blast brought the tear in my e'e! Now welcome—'"

Colin, who, though not a Scotsman, was a Burns addict, was beginning to enjoy himself, but Kate had heard enough. She sprang to her feet.

"I know now what it was that worried me about Dai Lewis's accent!"

Scotch?"

Kate gave a little excited laugh. She had not time at the moment to tell Colin what she thought of his attempt at a Scots accent.

"Scotch! No! Phoney! Colin, you know—or perhaps you don't—how sometimes on the stage an actor who's doing a dialect part drops out of the dialect he's supposed to be using for a moment? Unless you really know a dialect well, it's a most difficult thing to keep it true! He'll seem to be getting along all right in his Irish, or American, or whatever it is, a bit hollow, perhaps, but you feel it'll pass muster with anybody but a *real* Irishman or a *real* American. And then suddenly for a few words he gets the intonation quite wrong, and you hear his ordinary accent quite plainly. He hears it, too, and snaps out of it at once, but the illusion goes for a second. Well, that was Dai Lewis last night. His local accent wobbled about. When he said 'That's right,' he might really almost have been a north country comedian. And every now and then he might have been a coster."

"Gipsies get about the world," murmured Colin, looking at her thoughtfully.

"I know, but not into repertory companies!"

Colin also got slowly to his feet.

"Did this man *say* he was Dai Lewis, Kate?"

"He didn't contradict me when I asked him if he was."

"What made you ask him?"

Oh—because when I asked him where he lived, he said he lived 'nowhere partickerler.' And of course, the ferrets."

"Did you see the ferrets?"

"No, as a matter of fact I didn't. Nor hear them, nor smell them."

"And did Dai Lewis say he was in Breconshire the night Sidney went?"

Kate reflected: "No, I don't think he did. He just said he wasn't at Hymns Bank."

"In fact, he didn't really say anything to suggest that he was Dai Lewis, at all?"

"No, I don't think he did, Colin! I just concluded he was, and he didn't deny it."

The bracken wagon, empty, came lumbering out of the yard, with Mr. Davis at the horse's head. He had a companion with him now, Gwyn Lupton, his greenish hat at the back of his head, a pitchfork in his hand, his voice raised in a dignified monologue above the creaking of the axles.

Kate hailed the two, and ran down the side of the tumulus as Mr. Davis whoaed his horse to a standstill.

"Mr. Davis!" she cried impulsively. "Can you tell me—what is your cousin Mr. Dai Lewis like to look at?"

Mr. Davis looked a trifle surprised at this bald question and the eagerness with which it was uttered. He slowly took off his cap as if about to scratch his head, slowly decided not to scratch his head and put his cap slowly back again. Then he said slowly:

"Oh, ah, Missie! He be a tidy sort of a man to look at, I reckon. He do weigh well."

"What height?"

"Ah, a lot taller than I be, Missie. A lot taller'n you be, too, though you be a tall un for a female. Six foot pretty near, Dai Lewis be, I reckon. Oh ah. Pretty near six foot."

The man Kate had seen in Hymns Bank had certainly not been anywhere near six feet, but about her own height, which was five feet eight. However, before she could ask for further details Gwyn Lupton observed:

"Young lady, Dai Lewis and me is of a height, though we is not of the same girth, no, indeed, for he is more like an oak tree, and I am more like a spindle now that I am advanced in years, though when we was young it was the other way about. The years adds flesh to some men and wears the flesh off others, it is according to the constitution. Dai Lewis is a fine man to look at, a fine handsome man, and if you do not know him by anything else, you will know him by the limp he has, which he has had ever since he broke his leg getting off a tram in Llanfyn sixteen years agone.

Sixteen years agone it was, I remembers, for I broke my leg the autumn following, falling off a stack where I was pitching bracken, as I might be doing this morning. But I had not the weight on me Dai Lewis had, and did not fall so fast, and so I mended proper and does not limp at all. For them that weighs well does not mend well, Missie, and a heavy belly is a deceiving thing."

Kate was now certain that the man she had seen in Hymns Bank was not Dai Lewis. But they were all doomed, she feared, to hear a good deal more about the handsome Mr. Dai Lewis and about his inferiority, in spite of appearances, to Mr. Gwyn Lupton, unless she could find some means of stemming the flow of Mr. Lupton's sonorous discourse. He stood there, holding his pitchfork like Britannia's trident, his other hand on his hip, a look of rapt inspiration on his dark, distinguished face, with an eye upon Kate whose stern spell she positively feared to break.

Colin, however, held Mr. Lupton, whom he had reason to suspect of secret digging on Pentrewer Tump, in less awe, and, somewhat to Kate's relief, stemmed the flood for her.

"I'm told, Mr. Lupton, you took a mould of that coin you found on the tumulus, and I've been wondering whether you'd be so kind as to show it to me?"

"Yes, indeed, I will show it you with pleasure, if you will step along to my house," said Mr. Lupton graciously, transferring his hawklike glance from Kate to Colin. "A very old ancient piece of money it is, older than the days before the Romans was here, I did believe, but Mr. Morrison at the Veault said that it was from after those days, but none the worse for that. Five pounds he gave me for it. It may have been worth more?" said Gwyn Lupton interrogatively. "Well, Mr. Morrison is a very pleasant gentleman, an antiquary gentleman he is," he resumed, as Colin non-committally shook his head, "and I wass glad to let him have the piece of money for five pounds, since he wished it. It cost me nothing. I was taking up a snare upon the tump—and I had set my snares on the tump not only to get rabbits for myself, but also because the tump is a valuable ancient thing that the Government is interested in," said Mr. Lupton virtuously, "and it iss a pity if the rabbits should make their burrows in it and disturb the bones of the kings that is decaying there—I was taking up my snare, look, and I put my hand to the ground, and in my hand I found the piece of money."

He laid down his pitchfork and demonstrated in a very lively and graceful manner the casual stooping of the rabbiter, the delighted wonder of the treasure-finder.

"I wass not looking for treasure, I wass not thinking of treasure. It is when we is not looking that we finds treasure. When we is looking for treasure, it hides away from us," said he improvingly.

Colin also felt that he might improve the occasion.

"There's no more treasure to be found in the tump, anyway," he said firmly. "Just old bones."

"I am sure I do not know about that," said Gwyn Lupton with the greatest indifference. "I has never thought about it. But I knows, of course, that whatever treasure is there, belongs first to the king that is buried there, and after him to the king that is not buried, which is His Majesty King George."

"His Majesty King George wouldn't thank you for an old clay pot, which is probably all you'd find, apart from the bones inside it." Colin added quickly, as it was obvious that Gwyn Lupton was about to launch another and stronger repudiation of any further designs on the tumulus: "May I come and see the putty mould this evening?"

"You will be welcome, young gentleman, at any time you chooses to come. And I will show you at the same time some other curiosities which will interest you—an old book of the Bible, with pictures in it, that my wife had left her in a will, and a thorn tree root that is almost, but not quite, in the shape of a weazel," said Mr. Lupton graciously, and, somewhat to Kate's surprise, allowed Mr. Davis to gee-up his horse, and strode off beside him across the field towards the brackeny upper slope.

"You seem to have a slightly damping effect on Gwyn Lupton, Colin."

"He's wondering how much I know about his excavations on Pentrewer Tump."

"Has he been digging there again, do you think?"

"No. He's waiting till I've departed, I expect. It's a great pity that Saxon coin couldn't have been found somewhere else! Nothing I can say will ever convince these people now that Pentrewer Dump isn't just full of silver pennies waiting to be dug up and exchanged for five-pound-notes! Well, I've reminded Mr. Davis he's laying himself open to heavy penalties if he allows digging to go on, so perhaps he'll do something to curb Mr. Gwyn Lupton's enthusiasm."

"Perhaps he daren't. Perhaps he's got a skeleton in his own cupboard. Mrs. Howells says Gwyn Lupton is intimately acquainted with all the skeletons in the local cupboards, being a house-carpenter, you see, and having had a good deal to do with those same cupboards at one time and another in a professional way."

Colin smiled.

"Yes, really, Colin. It never occurred to me before what a grand opportunity a carpenter has for knowing all about skeletons. But one day Miss Gilliam from the Cefn was making herself disagreeable in the shop. And Gwyn was there, and he fixed her with his beady black eye and made some vague remarks about an occasion when he had earned somebody's gratitude by not saying something he *might* have said. And Miss Gilliam crumpled up in the most dramatic manner and trickled out of the shop as if he'd put a spell on her. And when I was up at the Cefn a few days later, I guessed why. She's the uncrowned queen of food-hoarders, and Gwyn Lupton, you see, having worked at the Cefn recently, knows it."

Colin laughed.

"Well, not being the owner of a skeleton in these parts, I stand in no awe of Gwyn Lupton. And I shall take the opportunity, when I go to see his mould to-night, of impressing him with the risks he's running in trying to acquire a skeleton of his own. If only I could make him believe that a skeleton is, literally, all he'll find!"

Some gruesome application of these last words to her own case took place in Kate's mind against her will. Stifling a sigh, she said buoyantly:

"Well, let him! Compared with other things, it doesn't matter much!"

Colin, unaware of the shiver Kate was stifling with these unusually philistine sentiments, remonstrated:

"It does matter, Kate, a good deal, if valuable antiquities are allowed to be destroyed by avaricious ignoramuses!"

"Compared with life and death, it doesn't matter!"

"Perhaps not. But nobody's life's in danger, is it?"

"Yes! Sidney Brentwood's is! And here we stand talking about bones that have been buried about three thousand years as if they mattered! Colin, that man I saw at Hymns Bank *wasn't* Dai Lewis!"

"So I gather."

"Why did he pretend he was?"

"He didn't want you to know who he really was, I suppose. And he wanted you to go away without suspecting anything seriously wrong."

"He didn't want me to see him. Was that because I should have recognised him if I had?"

"Either that, or he was afraid you might see him later and recognise him."

"And he didn't want me to see into that upstairs room. What had he got there? Not ferrets!"

"Probably something more incriminating than ferrets."

"Such as?"

"Well, say, an apparatus for signalling to the enemy. You saw a light flickering from the house, didn't you? Perhaps a secret radio transmitter too."

"Ronnie said he heard a clicking noise coming from the house," said Kate thoughtfully.

"Well, there you are. I doubt if whatever's going on there has anything to do with your Sidney, Kate."

"But the green tinfoil! He had been there!"

"Perhaps. But keeping a small boy prisoner—if Sidney is being kept a prisoner—certainly isn't the *raison d'être* of what's going on at Hymns Bank."

"Well, I'm here to look for Sidney, and I must follow up every possibility."

"Kate," said Colin earnestly, "if you want to find Sidney, the first essential is, not to lose yourself. Don't take absurd risks. Every soldier, everybody's who's got a serious job on hand, knows better than that. Don't go to Hymns Bank again alone. Let me go with you. Or let me go instead of you. But don't go alone. Promise."

Kate hesitated, for form's sake, and promised. She had, as a matter of fact, no desire to go alone again to Hymns Bank, which, terrifying enough at the churchyard hour last night, loomed now, since her talk with Mr. Davis, full of more tangible terrors than ghosts and voices on the wind.

"I wonder who the place belongs to."

"As it happens, I can tell you. Mrs. Davis told me, when we were having a chat about the de-population of the countryside yesterday. An old aunt of Mr. Davis lived there till about seven years ago, when she died, and left the place to a cousin of Davis in Australia. The cousin's never shown any interest in his property, and as this country was getting more and more de-populated and tumbledown cottages on the wilds were practically a drug in the market, nobody's ever wanted to buy it off him. Legally, it still belongs to the absentee."

"I see," said Kate, dismissing rather regretfully her notion that it might be the property of Gideon Atkins.

"But I don't think it matters who it belongs to," said Colin. "Anybody can get into a tumbledown cottage and use it for whatever purpose they please. The doors and windows won't be burglar-proof, if it's been tumbling down for seven years."

"Only seven years! It looks as if it had been tumbling down for centuries. It's a very, very old cottage," said Kate, who was no more averse than most people from trotting out a newly- acquired piece of knowledge. "Mediaeval, in fact."

Colin glanced at her with a smile.

"Kate taking up architecture? How do you know?"

"By the wall-timbering," said Kate with dignity. "Very heavy timbers, and set close together. Rosaleen told me. I'm going up to Llanhalo this afternoon to ask Aminta how Ronnie's settling down."

She did not add, that she was expecting a report from Ronnie on the condition of the iron grating in Llanhalo cellar, for she did not want to be damped further by Colin's talk of danger.

"Don't tell anybody about Hymns Bank and what happened there last night, will you, Kate?"

There he went again! Colin nowadays seem obsessed with the necessity for caution.

"Not if you think I'd better not. I probably shouldn't anyway."

"Not even Aminta. Not anybody."

"All right," said Kate, puzzled, but willing to oblige.

"And don't tell the police either—just yet."

"Why not just yet?"

"Well, because country police are a bit heavy-handed sometimes, and might put their foot in it."

Kate reflected that, after four weeks, the police had not succeeded in tracing Sidney, and agreed.

"Don't tell them, or anyone, without consulting me. Trust me, Kate."

"I do, of course. How could one help trusting anybody so cautious as you are these days?" inquired Kate, not quite without friendly malice. "You remind me of the old family lawyer who comes on in a white wig in the middle of the first act to advise the heroine not to go on with the plot of the play."

Chapter Seventeen

Aminta was over at the Veault, carting litter. Miss Atkins, who appeared at the scullery door with drifts of steam about her and a wash-day spongy pinkness of face and forearms, remarked in her odd, grating little voice which always sounded as if she grudged words, that Miss Hughes would be back at milking-time, and Miss Mayhew might come in and wait, if she wished.

But Miss Mayhew judged that even the most hospitable of housewives does not really want visitors on washing-day, and preferred to walk on to the Veault across the field-track she had taken with Aminta. Before she went she inquired, however, after Ronnie Turner. Miss Atkins' small inexpressive eyes, which the daylight showed to be of a child-like sapphire blue colour, blinked shyly. She smiled her rather difficult but sincere smile.

"Eh, he's a good boy. He's na trouble."

"What does Mr. Atkins think about it?"

"The maester's reckoned out on paeper as I can feed the lad and keep him nicely on tha'billeting-money. So he doan't object."

"Ronnie eats a good deal, I expect."

"He doan't sleep so well as he eats, I reckon. He got up this morning wi' rings under his eyes. The raid kept him awaeke, maybe. I didn't hear nothing of it, and the master's a sound sleeper, too. But Miss Hughes and Ronnie was full o' it this morning." With a faint smile she added: "I like to hear them chattering at breakfast-time," before going to attend to her noisily-bubbling copper, from which great clouds of steam were now rising and hanging under the ceiling, obscuring the rafters.

Kate, walking across the field, reflected that it was fortunate that Mr. Atkins and his sister were sound sleepers. If the bombers, to say nothing of the bombs, last night had not awakened them, it was unlikely that any nocturnal experiments of her own with the cellar-grating would do so.

Kate was struck anew by the drowsy charm of the Veault as she approached it down the sloping field. Lucky little Londoners, about to be evacuated to such a spot, where nature and art had provided such beauty, and money was providing such comforts!

In the sun-trap of the sheltered courtyard outside the back door, Rosaleen was sitting on the old mounting-block, swinging her trousered legs, with her satellite Major Humphries, whose small green car stood out in the farmyard, dose at hand. Nurse Maud was spreading newly-washed teacloths over the stone wall in the sunshine.

"There, they'll soon be dry!" said she, approaching and adding her amiable if off-hand nod to Rosaleen's attentive and charming greetings.

Rosaleen cocked an eyebrow at the display.

"They'll soon be dry, honey, but will they be so very, very clean?"

"I've rubbed and I've scrubbed, and they won't come cleaner than that."

"Gee, let us hope then that a domestic or two'll turn up here before those forty infants!"

Kate, realising that she had not on her previous visit seen any sign of a servant in the house, remarked:

"You'll need them, won't you?"

"I should just say we will! At present our domestic staff is limited to a gardener living out in a cottage, and his wife, who comes in daily and obliges us. I don't know if the gardener will survive the impact of forty infants, but I am sure his wife won't unless we can provide her with some underlings. Uncle tells us he has fixed up with a butler to come from London to-morrow, and his presence may help to save the situation—if he truly comes, but Auntie and I are not pinning our rosiest hopes on his arrival. Also, we do not feel so confident as Uncle does that butlers make good mothers. That reminds me, Maud. Did you remind Auntie about ordering those mackintosh sheets?"

"You bet I did!"

"It would be just too harassing if the first consignment of infants arrived before the first consignment of mackintosh sheets. Did Aminta tell you, Miss Mayhew, we've heard the first batch of five kiddies is coming at the end of next week? Auntie is very, very excited. She's indoors writing orders for food and soap, and ultimatums to all the servants' registry offices in England. You'd think there'd be plenty of domestics just too anxious to get away from London and the bombs, wouldn't you? But no, it seems finding domestics for country places is the same old forlorn hope as ever."

Major Humphries cleared his throat and muttered something about "taking it." Rosaleen nodded sympathetically, but Kate thought a faint flicker of amusement went across her fair charming face as she scored up the cliché.

"And after all," went on Major Humphries, rather pompously, "there's no such thing as safety anywhere. Two bombs last night fell within five miles of here."

"Lord, what we country-dwellers go through!" said Nurse Maud, who seemed unable to handle Major Humphries gently.

"Now, Maudie, a bomb's a bomb whether it drops on you in the country or in the town!" said Rosaleen placably. But neither the Major nor Maud seemed anxious to be placated.

"In London there's more risk from raids, certainly!" said Major Humphries stiffly. "But there are other dangers in the country, you know! Invasion—"

A look of exaggerated incredulity came over Nurse Maud's large handsome features.

"Invasion! What, *here*?"

"It's on the cards, I assure you, Nurse."

"Where'd the Jerries come from? Up the river Wye in canoes?"

"Troop-carrying planes and parachutes! We don't know what that feller has up his sleeve. Got to be prepared."

"And what'd they come *here* for? To study botany?"

"Plenty of good landing-places on these hills. You don't think a troop-carrying plane'd try to land the troops in Piccadilly Circus, do ye, Nurse?"

"Och. Major, all these Home Guard exercises have gone to your head!" said Maud, rudely.

Major Humphries' already rather boiled-looking eyes became still more suffused, and Rosaleen interposed, rather hurriedly:

"You mustn't mind Maud, Major Humphries! She's a cynic about just everything! I'm sure *I* sleep all the sounder in my bed for knowing the Home Guard's at its post, if *she* doesn't! Kate, that nice Mr. Kemp was here yesterday afternoon, and wasn't Uncle just pleased to see him! The way they enthused together about a place called Avebury, you'd have thought it was their old school they were talking about, until you found out it was just a place they'd both been to, where there are some stones."

Major Humphries, evidently still somewhat sore from Nurse Maud's handling, remarked gruffly that this feller Kemp seemed to be quite a young feller, and therefore he supposed, damned queer as it seemed, that archaeology was a reserved occupation.

Rosaleen laughed.

"Well, if you'd heard Uncle Doug and Mr. Kemp yesterday, and seen them mingling their sighs and smiles, Major, you'd *never* have thought that archaeology was a *reserved* occupation! This Mr. Kemp is making a survey of the ruins at your great friend Mr. Atkins' place, isn't he, Miss Mayhew?"

"He is," said Kate, amused at the half-unwilling thaw that took place in Major Humphries's umbraged expression when he met Rosaleen Morrison's long-lashed, serious glance. He blinked once or twice, as if the light were too much for him, and the lines around his eyes softened. He muttered, however, that it struck him as dashed queer that such a footling occupation as archaeology should still be allowed to carry on.

"Oh, but Mr. Kemp's doing this survey for the Government, I'm told!" said Rosaleen, smiling softly at Kate, as if asking her to excuse, on Colin's behalf, Major Everyman's ill-manners.

"The Government!" echoed the major, snorting. "Don't tell me that!"

"Yes, really, Major. The Office of Works, it is, I believe."

"If he told you that, he's pulling your leg," said Major Humphries. "There aren't any of these Government surveys being made in wartime."

Rosaleen looked inquiringly at Kate, but Kate could only reply:

"I really don't know who Colin's making the survey for."

"Dark horse, evidently," said Major Humphries.

"Well, Major, you certainly never set eyes on anybody more candid and confiding and less resembling a dark horse than this friend of Miss Mayhew's!" said Rosaleen spiritedly. She was evidently a little put out at having her suave social atmosphere ruffled by these arguments.

The appearance of Aminta, leading a farm-cart piled high with bracken through the gate and into the farmyard, created a welcome diversion. Rosaleen stood up and hailed her joyfully over the low wall of the court.

"Major Humphries, I guess your car's in the way."

"No it isn't," called Aminta. "I haven't time to unload this lot now. I've got to get back for milking. I'll take old Lion out and leave the load in the cart till to-morrow."

She began to undo the traces. Nurse Maud went out to help her, and then strolled off by herself towards the field gate. Maud still had a suppressed but dangerous sparkle in her eye from her exchanges with Major Humphries. She seemed queerly intolerant of that conventional but harmless gentleman, Kate thought, considering for how short a while she had been acquainted with him, though what were the sources of their antagonism Kate could not see.

"I've got a letter for you, Kate," said Aminta, when she had, with Kate's admiring assistance, come-upped and whoaed her horse out of the shafts. She put her hand in her breeches-pocket and fished out a rather crumpled envelope, which she handed to Kate, and led her horse away.

Kate went with her, leaving Rosaleen to pour balm on whatever soreness Nurse Maud's caustic tongue had left on Major Humphries' simple soul. Nurse Maud, evidently in a misanthropic mood, leant against the gate and surveyed the rest of them from a haughty distance.

"*Dear Miss*" ran Ronnie Turner's letter, "*the key of the cellar is on a nail by the kitchen fireplace. Last night when the bombs woke me I went to the cellar like you said. I had my torch. The grating comes out. There is a little tunnel the other side, all dark. There is not very much room there. I did not see anything of Sid.*

Yours truly,

Ronnie.

P.S. I would like to try and go down this tunnel."

So would I, said Kate to herself. She was all in a hurry now to get away and be back in Hastry before school was over, or, if that was impossible, to meet Ronnie cycling home, and arrange a midnight meeting in that cellar. She must remember to take some candles with her, and plenty of matches, to get a new battery for her torch—

"Look out, Kate!" said Aminta, just in time to prevent her abstracted friend from tripping over a shaft of the bracken-cart.

"What are you going to do with all this bracken?"

"Leave it out in the cart till to-morrow. It won't hurt. To-morrow I'm putting it in one of the barns here, that old Gid rents off Mr. Morrison."

"I suppose all these farm-buildings are let, are they?"

"No, they're all empty, except that one. Mr. Morrison doesn't like letting his buildings for some reason. He didn't really like letting the barn to Gid, but as Gid had an unexpired agreement with the former owner of the Veault, he has to put up with it till next Lady Day," said Aminta cheerfully from the stable which stood alongside the wall of the cobbled courtyard.

When, having fed her Lion, she emerged, and Rosaleen suggested that she might have a lift back to Llanhalo in Major Humphries's car, Kate eagerly claimed one, too. Nurse Maud opened the field-gate for them with the detached air of a professional gate-keeper. She scarcely responded to Major Humphries's stiff salute, but winked sadly at Kate as they went by.

Since Aminta was taking a couple of large milk-cans and a small dog back with her, Kate sat in front and conversed on the local scenery with Major Humphries. She spoke with the false brightness of the mentally abstracted, for her thoughts were all the time running on plans for the investigation of Llanhalo cellar.

"I beg your pardon, Major Humphries! I didn't catch what you said."

"I said: awful there's been no news about that boy. Mrs. Morrison tells me you're connected with him. Dreadful thing for everybody concerned. Feel it myself, though God knows *I* couldn't have done anything to stop him running off like that. Good billet, too, nice people the Howells, best billet in the village. Got homesick, I suppose, the silly young owl. Didn't know what was good for him."

"What do you really think's happened to him, Major Humphries?"

How often Kate had asked this question since she arrived in Hastry, and how often received the answer she now received, she had lost count. What parrots people were! she thought with gusty impatience. Or did they all give the same reply, not because they were parrots but because it was the only conclusion to which thought led? Was it in hopefulness, or in folly, that Kate stood alone? The major drew down the corners of his mouth under his trim and bristly greying moustache.

"I'm afraid the river'll give the answer one day, Miss Mayhew. The river, or the hills. Don't like saying it, but there it is. No use blinking facts."

He drew the car up at the bend of the road where Kate had first seen Gideon Atkins trimming his hedge. Aminta's little dog sprang out, and there was a clanking of cans as Aminta descended.

"Can you manage the door? Let me," said Major Humphries, stretching across Kate.

But it was not a difficulty with the car door that had frozen Kate for a moment, half turned to get out, her foot on the step. She had the door, in fact, open in her hand. And at the bottom of the door, stuck on the dark green leather, was a small square of bright green tinfoil.

Kate managed to say:

"No, I suppose it isn't any use blinking facts."

She got out. She did not want to get out. She wanted to stay in Major Humphries's car, in the company of Major Humphries, to whom she had paid so little attention, to have another look at him, to study him, to listen to him.

"Everything O.K.?" asked Major Humphries breezily, putting in his clutch. "You quite O.K., Miss Mayhew? You look a bit off-colour, doesn't she, Miss Hughes?"

"I'm quite all right," said Kate, smiling the dim, mechanical smile which had no doubt caught the Major's eye. "Thank you."

"Not at all! Glad to be of service. Good-bye."

He drove off.

"Aminta," said Kate, looking after him, "how tall would you say that Major Humphries was?"

"How *tall*? I'm sure I don't know! Taller than me. About your height, I should think. Are you going to be sick, Kate?" asked Aminta curiously. "You do look a bit peculiar, now I come to look at you."

Chapter Eighteen

Over tea with Mrs. Howells, Kate led the conversation via the Home Guard, to Major Humphries. Major Humphries, it seemed, though now a character well-known in the district, a member of the local council, a churchwarden, vice-president of the local horse show and secretary of the local hunt, had not been living long in the neighbourhood. He was a retired Army man, a bachelor, who had come to settle down two years ago in a house with a small estate between Hastry village and the railway station. He was a bit of a busybody, Mr. Howells opined, with a finger in everyone's pie. But Mrs. Howells's opinion seemed to be that he had a kind heart, and that Hastry folk did not on the whole object to having their pies stirred by him.

Two years, thought Kate: the same length of time that Gideon Atkins has been at Llanhalo. She remembered that Humphries, even while expressing the liveliest contempt for Atkins, had admitted frequent visits to Llanhalo. Perhaps those visits had not, as he claimed, been made purely in the interests of the hunt?

They seemed unlikely partners, on the face of it, Kate reflected, the rough-and-ready money-grabbing farmer and the gentlemanly army man. But at once it occurred to her that Major Humphries would not be a difficult part to play. The man who could put up so creditable an impromptu performance as a gipsy ferreter would have no trouble in studying and maintaining such a stock part as that of Major Everyman!

She had made her appointment with Ronnie at Llanhalo for three o'clock next morning. The waning moon would be high then. Moonlight or none would seem to be a matter of indifference to the adventurer in cellars and secret tunnels beneath the earth. But Kate's experiences at Hymns Bank last night had given her a strong distaste for darkness.

The wind was in the south, and the distant bells of Hastry church tower struck three as she stood at Llanhalo dairy door. A voice breathed hoarsely, sibilantly in the doorway:

"Is that you, Miss?"

She slipped into the dairy, and softly shut the door.

"Well, here we are, Ronnie."

They looked at one another by the light of a candle on the dairy shelf, Ronnie with eager, bright-eyed trust in Kate and the hour, Kate with more tranquil assurance than she felt. Ronnie looked smaller than usual by this light, slighter, younger, and more vulnerable. She noticed that he was dressed for adventure, in a corduroy wind-sheeter zip-fastened up to the neck and his trousers tucked into the tops of his gum-boots.

"Everybody asleep?"

Ronnie nodded.

"You got a torch?"

He nodded again.

"Come on, then."

Kate took the candle in her hand and followed Ronnie to the cellar, shutting the door softly after her and locking it. The earthy, vault-like chill of a little-used cellar to which the daylight scarcely penetrates, struck coldly on her bones, with a foretaste of what might be expected in a subterranean tunnel. There was a faint unpleasant smell in the damp air, too, which probably came from the bunch of uncooked lights hanging on a nail, the cats' dinner, the only commodity kept in this place. The doorway through which they had just come was, Kate observed, arched, and the stone spandrels were finely moulded. This place had never been built as the cellar of a farmhouse. Like the ruins outside, it was a relic of the mediaeval abbey which had once existed there.

"I've took the grating out, Miss. I thought it'd save time."

"Good. Did it come out easily?"

"Quite easy. Miss. It just lifts out."

Ronnie crouched and grasped the heavy grating in his thin hands to demonstrate the extreme ease of lifting it, but it seemed to Kate that the effort was as much as he could manage, and, afraid that he would drop it on his toe and hurt himself, or against the stone wall and rouse the house, she restrained him.

A hollow, two foot square, yawned in the dark stone wall. Kate, lying on the ground and shining her torch into the aperture, could see a low arched tunnel about two feet high and three feet wide, walled and roofed with rough masonry, extending away from her for a distance that was difficult to assess—perhaps twelve feet or so. It appeared to end disappointingly in a rough stone wall.

"Ronnie, I'm afraid this tunnel's a wash-out," said Kate, withdrawing her arm and looking up at Ronnie, who crouched eagerly at her shoulder. "It only runs for a few yards."

Ronnie shook his head vehemently. His narrow, clear-skinned face, pale, not flushed, with excitement, wore quite an exalted look. His grey eyes were very dark.

"Miss, that's not the end you can see! It's a sort of cave, or something!"

"How do you know?"

"Well, I've got a stronger torch than you, I believe, Miss. And I—I wriggled a little farther in, Miss, when I was looking. I didn't go down the tunnel. I kept my feet this side of the hole," explained Ronnie. "I just—wriggled in a bit. And I could see there was a kind of hollow place at the end that seems to go up and down."

Kate borrowed his stronger torch. It certainly looked now as if there were a gap in the floor at the end of the tunnel before that rough stone wall blocked the view. It looked as if a well existed there. A little shudder ran over Kate, not only at the bare thought of a well in such a place as this, but at the possibilities which fringed this bare thought with horror. Wells did exist within doors in ancient houses, she knew. She pictured the deep shaft, the ancient masonry of its rounded sides extending downwards, downwards, far beyond the light of any torch that might be shone down it, so far that the black water at the bottom would send up only one small reflective gleam. What old secrets, and new ones as well as old ones, might not such a well conceal?

Ronnie's face fell when Kate told him that he must wait in the cellar until she had investigated as far as that well, but he did not protest. There was scarcely room for two in the tunnel together, since the roof was so low that it would be necessary to crawl along almost at full length.

Kate had rarely seen a less inviting ingress. She pushed the lighted candle in its enamel stick ahead of her into the narrow earthy place in which, as she went head and shoulders, she imagined she could indeed smell the waters of some ancient spring, and crawled after it, pushing it ahead of her along the ground at the point of a walking-stick she had brought with her. The candle-flame burnt clearly enough, though it flickered a good deal in a draught that seemed to come from ahead of her. The air was all right, anyway. But Kate would not care to proceed far along a subterranean passage in this snakelike fashion. And reflecting as she went upon the arrangement of the ground floor at Llanhalo farmhouse, she realised that the tunnel she was in could not be much below the ground, and was unlikely to proceed far at this level. The kitchen was only two or three steps up from the level of the dairy floor, and the dairy was three steps up from the cellar. The floor of this passage ran level with the cellar floor, and therefore its roof was not much below the ground-floor level.

Kate's torch, combined with the candle-light, showed clearly now that the tunnel she was in ended in a kind of well that extended upwards as well as downwards, a narrow rounded shaft of rough masonry. She crept cautiously along to the end, and, peering over with a faint dread of what it might be her fate to see, found that she was looking down the dark well of a very narrow staircase that dropped, steep as a ladder, to a ground-level about ten feet below. Looking up, she saw that the circular well extended about four feet above the roof of the tunnel in which she lay.

She could stand upright now, her feet on the top step, in a circular well of masonry which she could touch all round at the stretch of her arms. Ancient timbers covered the well just above her head. She lifted her hands, and pressed upwards. The timber did not yield and, rapping softly on it, Kate had the impression that the well was ceilinged, not with boards, but with baulks of great weight and thickness.

Kate did not know Llanhalo well enough to say where she was now. She guessed, under the kitchen. But if ever there had been an egress here into the house from the ancient stone stairs which led who-knew-where beneath her, it had been blocked up long ago. It was downwards that she must go. With her bicycle-lamp hooked on to her belt and the candle in her hand she went cautiously down, backwards, as down a ladder, for though a couple of iron rods stood up out of the narrow flight the chain or rope that had once connected them and formed a handrail was no longer there, and the flight was very steep. At the bottom, Kate found herself in the entrance of what was apparently quite a spacious tunnel, in which even she could stand upright. The walls and arched roof, like those of the little tunnel she had just come through, were of rough masonry. The uneven floor, in which, in the slanting light of Kate's lamp, bumps and hollows appeared, and rough-edged stones cast sharp, exaggerated shadows, was, she judged, a floor of the natural rock of the hillside. She could not tell how long the tunnel was, which slanted at a narrow angle off from the direct line of the stairs. Its dark walls, and roof, and floor, seemed to swallow the light she cast into it and reveal nothing that was not very close. She stooped and spoke along the tunnel: "Sidney!" and her voice seemed to echo softly away from her for an immense distance. If it had been cold in the cellar, it was colder still down here. But there were no signs of flooding, the floor was dry and the air, odorous of cold rock, was breathable.

Kate was about to re-climb the stone steps to summon Ronnie to a view of Llanhalo tunnel, when she heard a scrambling noise, and the child's head appeared in the aperture at the top of the stairs. In the macabre shifty light of his own and Kate's lamp, in these grim grey stone surroundings, his face looked luminous, fragile, and intensely alive.

"Ronnie, I thought—"

"Miss, I had to come! I heard a noise in the dairy. Somebody in the house. Somebody after us, there is, I believe, Miss! I didn't dare wait!"

Drawing his knees up, crouching and then standing erect, the child slithered helter-skelter down the stone steps.

"I pulled the grating to behind me, Miss, so if they gets into the cellar they won't know we're down here. I couldn't get it quite into the frame. I think I got it the wrong way up, but I reckon it'll be all right."

As he spoke, a loud hollow clang! from the cellar seemed to indicate that his reckoning was at fault.

"There goes your grating, I'm afraid, Ronnie! Gosh, I hope it doesn't sound as loud in Mr. Atkins' bedroom as it does down here, it might do what the bombs couldn't do and wake him up! Who was it in the dairy, I wonder, Ronnie? Did they speak?"

Ronnie shook his head.

"Come in from outside, I think, Miss."

"Outside!"

"I heard the dairy door go first, the outside door, and then somebody walking softly in the dairy."

"Outside!" repeated Kate again. She did not like the suggestion this word gave rise to, of others beside herself with secret business at Llanhalo to-night, secret business in the dairy, the cellar, perhaps in this subterranean place which, in spite of Gideon Atkins' ill-humoured denials, existed secretly under the commonplace comings and goings of farmhouse life.

"Well, thank God I locked the cellar door, that'll hold them up for a moment or two, anyway."

They listened, they were all ears, both were quite unconscious that they were tightly clasping hands. From a long distance away, from somewhere down the tunnel behind them, Kate could hear drip... drip... nothing else, not a sound. Then, just as she was relaxing and deciding that Ronnie must have been mistaken, she heard a noise—the grinding, low noise of a door-handle being quietly turned. There was somebody in the dairy, trying the ring of the cellar door, trying it cautiously, as though he, too, whoever it might be, feared to arouse sleepers in the house.

With one accord Kate and Ronnie broke hands and turned and hurried down the tunnel, walking quietly and not speaking at all. Kate's heart was beating loud enough, it seemed to her fancy, to be heard all over the house. She did not think that Ronnie's pulse was accelerated at all, so quietly and circumspectly did that admirable child walk along beside her in the strange, mine-like darkness over which their lamplight irregularly swung from its focus upon the possible pitfalls of the rough floor, now upon the distant ceiling, now upon the walls, casting black exaggerated shadows which made the rough masonry look even rougher than it was, dwindling the dark ahead of them to a black ever-receding hollow: until glancing sideways at her, he said suddenly with a little scared, excited laugh:

"Miss, I thought at first somebody was running after us, but I believe it's my heart beating."

"So's mine. There's nobody coming, yet."

"Miss, I wonder if this tunnel comes out anywhere or just leaves off?"

Kate was wondering that herself, with a sharper anxiety every moment, as they continued their way along the tunnel, which showed no sign so far of coming to an end. In spite of Gideon Atkins's firm, and, Kate suspected, disingenuous denials, Llanhalo tunnel existed, a well-constructed passage made in the dark ages for who knew what sinister traffic between Llanhalo Abbey and Heaven-knows-where? But it was only too probable that somewhere along its considerable length a blockage of fallen earth had long ago closed it in, and that soon these twentieth century traffickers would come to a blank end. Then, they would have to return by the way they had come. Then, they would have to be prepared to meet whoever it was they had heard turning the handle of the cellar door.

"Ronnie," asked Kate suddenly, "how do you like Mr Atkins? How do you get on with him?"

She did not know whether to be relieved or not when Ronnie replied in a rather surprised tone:

"All right. Miss. I reckon he's a decent sort. He gave me a ride on his horse."

"He said there wasn't any tunnel here."

Ronnie grinned.

"Then I reckon he never looked, Miss." He added: "Miss, I think this tunnel comes out somewhere all right. Do you know why? Because I reckon if it was stopped up the air wouldn't be like it is. I reckon we wouldn't be able to breathe, Miss, if it didn't come out somewhere."

Kate wondered whether this piece of ratiocination were based on a science lesson or merely on a yarn about treasure seekers in a penny comic. It sounded reasonable, anyway. The air, though it struck chill as the tomb, was not stagnant.

There had been one or two curves in the tunnel, probably made to avoid cores of hard rock, and Kate was no longer conscious of direction. They had come quite a long way, the drip... drip... they had heard while they listened to the movements in the dairy, was louder now. Taking another curve round a great boulder of natural rock which had been left by the tunnel-makers as part of the tunnel wall, they came to a place where a trickle of water had worn shallow fissure in the rocky floor of the tunnel before it found its perennially trickling way through the masonry overhead. Kate lifted her lamp to look at the great drops, black as ink, that trembled on the edge of the crack, before falling drip, drip, into the shallow pool upon the floor that overflowed into the fissure and was carried off by the perennially trickling stream.

"This is where the tunnel will collapse one of these days," murmured Kate, scanning the walls and ceiling. "Seems all right for the present, though."

But Ronnie, who had his torch turned upon the floor, clutched at her arm.

"Miss! Miss!"

"I wish you wouldn't hiss at me like that, Ronnie, can't you call me Kate?" said Kate, a little irritably. But when she saw what he was pointing to, she forgot this hyper-criticism. A little way the other side of the shallow pool of water, on the dry earthy floor, faintly but unmistakably impressed, was a footmark. Further on, much fainter, was another one. Somebody had trodden in the pool of water, and his wet shoe, picking up the dry earth from the floor at the next step, had left its faint, shallow imprint there.

"Somebody's been here," said Kate, stating the obvious.

"A man. Going the same way as us."

"Not necessarily. He might have come the other way, without treading in the water, and trod in the water when he went back. I wonder how long a footprint like that would last," mused Kate. "Quite a long time, probably. There's nothing to disturb it. No rain. No wind. Nobody to tread it over. Perhaps it's been here for years."

Ronnie looked very sceptical. And Kate herself did not know why she felt this disposition to minimise the importance of that footprint. The anxiety with which she had heard that soft turning of the cellar door-handle, and which had sent her scurrying with

Ronnie down the passage, was fast becoming an acute sense of danger. She had not thought sufficiently before setting out so gaily, and with this child in tow, on this night's adventure. She had imagined herself making leisurely investigations in Llanhalo cellar and then going home to work out a plan of action based on her discoveries. She had envisaged dearly enough the possibility that there was no tunnel at all, not even the beginning of one. She had never, she realised now, clearly enough envisaged the possibility that there was an easily negotiable tunnel. She had not considered at all the possibility that she would find herself followed down it by she knew not whom! *That's you all over, Kate*, she said to herself bitterly: *act first and then discover it's too late to think, that's you, you fool. What a piece of management!*

She did not speak aloud, but she made a little uneasy, impatient noise, and Ronnie looked up at her, and she recalled herself, to the necessity of keeping a brave front. She was all the while listening for the approach of pursuing footsteps, but could hear nothing yet, only the drip, drip, of the water behind them now. She needed all her bravery when she perceived what looked like the blocked, blank end of the tunnel ahead of them: a blocked blank end of masonry, a rough stone wall of large irregular blocks roughly mortared together.

She bit her lip to suppress a cry of dismay; and the next moment hope sprang up the more strongly for that moment of blank distress. There was an aperture at the foot of the wall, which, always supposing that there was no blockage the other side, would, if they crawled upon their stomachs, amply let them through. Blocks of loose stone lay in the tunnel, as though they had fallen out from that aperture; or rather, been deliberately removed, for they were piled roughly aside against the wall of the passage. Kate thought in passing that some of the surfaces had a clean, new-quarried look as though they had not long been hammered and chiselled out of place, but she had not time now to reflect on the implications of this. Getting down on her stomach, she dragged herself through, torch in hand, into what appeared to be a small, rounded chamber, earthen-floored, vault-roofed—a simple circular chamber like the burial chamber to which the passage of a Stone-Age long-barrow may lead, except that it was larger and the stonework of comparatively modern date.

But such a comparison only flickered across Kate's mind as she drew herself through. For there was somebody lying on the ground, covered in brown blankets, at the farther side of the little chamber, looking at her with a white, blank face on which not even surprise was pictured. All excursions into ancient history, and all reflections on the art of masonry, all sense of danger and urgency, even, vanished from Kate's mind at the sight. She drew herself slowly to her feet, and looked down at a fair, thin, ghostlike boy, who stared back at her with eyes that looked blind and black, with lips expressionlessly parted and darkly caked. His chin and even the modelling of his forehead had a strange sharp look, and the whiteness of his cheeks made Ronnie's normal pallor look like that of a different race, said never a word, and Kate said never a word. She realised, with a sort of amazement at herself and circumstance, firstly, that she had truly found Sidney Brentwood, and secondly, that, driven by the sense of danger to herself and Ronnie unpremeditatedly down this passage, she had for the last half-hour or so quite forgotten Sidney Brentwood.

But Ronnie had not forgotten, or he recovered more easily than Kate from his amazement. He stared a second, and then, with a face of exultation, fell on his knees on the other boy's blankets.

"Hey, Sid!" He paused a second, disconcerted perhaps by the lack of response in his friend's face and perhaps also by the sharp pallor and the cracked lips and the flat hair. Then, in the touching, half-earnest, half-playful tone in which children comfort one another, he went on:

"You know *me*, Sid! You know old Ron!"

It was not plain that Sidney Brentwood knew old Ron, nor that he knew anybody or anything. But he was alive, and that was all that mattered to Kate and Ronnie in that first amazed and exalted moment.

But very soon Kate realised that to have found him was one thing, to rescue him another. They were in danger themselves, she and Ronnie, and Sidney was in danger, too, and their respective dangers reacted upon one another to create an appalling danger. It was plain the boy was ill, feeble, semi-deaf and semi-blind with darkness and loneliness and privation. His life was in Kate's hands now, as well as Ronnie's and her own.

Gideon Atkins and his accomplice Major Everyman had spared Sidney Brentwood's life: even professional criminals, let alone amateur traitors, would jib at committing murder, if it could be avoided. But if it were their only hope of escape from discovery and the law, they would not jib.

Kate stooped and put her ear to the aperture in the chamber wall through which they had just come. She could hear nothing as yet but the drip, drip of the water from the roof. The locked cellar door had served them well, but it was only a matter of time before pursuing footsteps came down the tunnel. Then what would Kate do, alone with these two frail kids?

Kate felt in all its force the deep dismay of the too-sanguine adventurer who sees for the first time that his adventure will not end at all in accordance with his glowing plans. It did not surprise her that the pale boy kept his lips expressionlessly parted and did not respond to her smile, for her smile felt as if fastened on her face. Oh God! said she to herself under that stiff, mechanical, pinned smile, oh God, what a fool I was not to bring Colin with me!

Chapter Nineteen

But work in the theatre induces above all things a habit of buoyancy and strong, quick reaction to ill-hap. While Ronnie knelt and uttered consolations to the unresponsive Sidney, Kate examined rapidly with her torch the place in which they were. There must, she thought, be some further exit from this place— unless, in the course of centuries it had been blocked in. So well-constructed and lengthy a tunnel could not have been contrived to lead only to this little chamber, but must surely have been a communication between two places of importance in their day.

The vaulted ceiling seemed to terminate in a kind of central chimney-like shaft, probably a ventilation shaft, and the cause of the comparatively good air they had breathed in the tunnel. But it was very narrow, not more than eighteen inches across, and even had they been able to reach to the centre of the ceiling) it would have been futile to think of escape that way. Kate next examined the walls, and found, to her relief and joy that there was another aperture in the wall, opposite to the one by which she and Ronnie had struggled in, dose to where Sidney was lying. Examining the wall more closely, she found that this aperture was at the base of what had once been a doorway, filled-in now with mortared stone. There was a timber lintel about five feet from the ground, and the narrow rectangular outline of the filled-in doorway could be traced in the masonry. And looking more carefully at the entrance through which she and Ronnie had come, she saw that it also was at the base of a blocked-in doorway. Two sizeable doors had once, in the heyday of the secret passage, led into this chamber, which had probably been a storeroom. Both doors at some time in the passing centuries, perhaps by agreement between the owners of the connected properties, had been built in. And recently, quite recently, Kate judged from the clean broken edges of the stone, both had been opened again sufficiently to allow an uncomfortable passage through. There was a chance, and it was worth taking, that the other half of the secret tunnel was negotiable and might lead to escape, if not to safety. She knelt by Sidney Brentwood and said softly and clearly:

"Sidney, we've come to take you back to Hastry now. We must be quick. Do you think you can come with us?"

The boy only stared at her. She thought of the smiling chubby face in the photograph she had seen in the Edgware Road She would not say the child was quite unrecognisable: the width across the eyes, the proportions of nose and upper lip, were unmistakeably the same. But there was no other resemblance to that photograph in the white-faced wraith with the earth-coloured circles below the eyes, so stupefied and shrinking. Kate had sometimes pictured herself meeting Sidney Brentwood for the first time, coming to his rescue: and always, so uncalculating in the sanguine spirit, she had pictured a lively, joyous, candid boy whose friendship and trust would spring to meet her overtures.

"You don't know me yet, but you know Ronnie, don't you?"

"Ronnie," repeated the boy hoarsely and faintly, licking his cracked lips. Yes, evidently he knew and trusted Ronnie.

"Well, Ronnie and I have come to take you home."

Sidney had his clothes on under the blankets that lay across him. A half-burnt-down candle in a brass stick stood near his bed, and a box of matches, and also a plate on which were several apples and a half-eaten, stale-looking loaf. There was a jug of dusty water, too. Sidney was not starved, then, and he could probably walk. But when Kate told him to get up and took him encouragingly by the arm to help him, he seemed unable to rise, he whimpered that his feet hurt, and Kate, pulling the blankets away, found that his ankles were hobbled together with strong wire.

She gave one energetic curse which she hoped would find its way on to the heads of Sidney's mishandlers, and set herself to untwist one of the wire fetters, while Ronnie did his best with the other. It was a laborious job, and the impatient Kate had three broken finger-nails by the time she had loosened hers and was ready to finish Ronnie's. Kate wondered for a moment that Sidney had not managed to undo that wire himself before he became too feeble to attempt it. Then she noticed faint dark marks like old bruises on his wrists. No doubt the necessary precautions had been taken.

"Come on, son!" said Kate anxiously, for if he could not walk at all, she and Ronnie should they be intercepted, would indeed by almost hopelessly handicapped. She had had a momentary thought of leaving Sidney here while she and Ronnie went to fetch help: but she had decided that the risk for Sidney was too great. She would not let him out of her sight now till there was a fair prospect of safety for him.

He made one or two feeble steps, and would have collapsed had it not been for Kate's arm. And when Ronnie with his torch had crawled first into the aperture in the wall and had reported space for three, and Kate, subduing her galloping impatience and sense of danger, was urging Sidney to follow his friend, a sort of desperate, lost look came over the child's white face, on which even this small exertion had brought out little points of sweat, and he turned back towards his bed.

"Come, Sidney, come!"

"My net— my net—" he stammered hoarsely, and groping in his bed found and dragged out a large square-meshed net of brown silk.

"Oh, must you bring that?"

Evidently, he must. Kate rolled it up and put it under her arm; and giving Sidney gentle and unhurried directions as if he were a child of three rather than thirteen, she persuaded him to crawl after Ronnie through the hole in the wall. She followed.

The passage they found themselves in much resembled in proportions and construction the one from which they had entered the central chamber. They walked along, slowly, Ronnie ahead, and Kate supporting Sidney with an arm around his waist. But before they had gone far it became evident they were not going to have so easy a passage at this end of the tunnel. The earthen floor became rough and covered with rubble and loose broken stones, against which Sidney perpetually stumbled. And it seemed to Kate, playing her torch anxiously ahead, that the ceiling sloped lower and lower towards that uneven floor. Before long, Kate found that she could not stand upright, but must walk crouching over the thick layer of loose stones, with the sensation of the whole earth suspended over her bent head. She longed after a while, more acutely than she remembered ever longing for anything, to stand upright. She could see nothing ahead of her but Ronnie slowly and cautiously making his way along, and for all she knew this narrow tunnel might bore on for miles—to Wigmore Castle, Aberystwyth or the Garden of Eden, as Aminta had said, and she more or less on all-fours all the time!

"Can't you see anything yet, Ronnie?"

Ronnie did not answer for a moment. Kate, who had noticed that the tunnel ceiling seemed to be getting even lower, for Sidney at her side, as well as she, had to stoop now, was about to repeat the question more sharply and anxiously, when he replied in a low voice:

"Miss, I believe the tunnel's blocked."

There was a sob of despair in his voice, and Kate acutely realised that she was not the only one of the party who felt the strain of the danger they were in. But the next moment the boy said hopefully:

"No, I reckon we can squeeze through all right!"

Kate, brought to a halt while Ronnie investigated what lay ahead of them, sat crouched against the wall beside Sidney Brentwood, She took his hand in hers, but he made no sign except a little sigh. Shining her torch down the way they had come. Kate realised that the reason this tunnel was narrowing was that it was filled with debris of stone and brick. It was not the ceiling that sloped down, but the rubble-covered floor that sloped up. The blockage ahead of them seemed to consist of a heap of stone and brick rubble and earth. Ronnie was already crawling across it, head-first, head-first, at full length; she could see the soles of his gum-boots disappearing between the blockage and the ceiling. A moment later his stooping, flushed face appeared at the opening.

"It's all right here!" he breathed joyfully. "Miss, you can stand up here! There's steps, too! I believe we can get out here!"

Kate's heart leapt. But when she tried to persuade Sidney to follow where Ronnie had gone, he became limply obstinate and despairing, shaking his head to all her coaxing.

"No. No."

The clammy skin of his puckered forehead was wrinkled like an elderly person's. He looked as if he might faint, and Kate was in despair. She could not go through herself until Sidney was through, but to unburden herself she passed over the rubble to Ronnie the net she had been carrying under her arm.

"My net!" said Sidney faintly and despairingly.

He looked as if he were about to cry.

"Oh, Sidney, it's all right. You put your hands up there to Ronnie and he'll give you the net," said Kate.

Sidney obeyed, and Ronnie, who had been anxiously adding his persuasions to Kate's, took his friend's hands firmly.

Kate half-lifted, half-pushed, and Ronnie, clutching his friend now under the armpits, tugged until Sidney was through, lying on a floor of broken stones and bricks, coughing and weakly shedding tears, but through.

"Gosh, Miss!" said Ronnie, stooping and looking under the ceiling-arch to where Kate crouched on the rubbly ground and prepared to follow. "Sid doesn't weigh much!"

"That's a good thing," gasped Kate, struggling head first and at full length through the gap, to find herself lying beside Sidney on the hard, unwelcoming stones.

"That's a good thing," said she picking herself up, her heart expanding with joy because at last she was able to stand upright, "because we may have to carry him before we've finished. I'll take your net, Sid. I'll take care of it. You hang on to me. We're nearly home now."

Ronnie gave her an odd, intelligent look, half-hopeful, half-sceptical. Clearly he would have liked to think that her remark was addressed to him as well as to Sidney, and was true.

They were standing in a narrow circular shaft, rather like the one at Llanhalo which had led down to the passage-entrance, but half-filled in with a floor of broken stone and brick that reached up to within two feet of the arch of the entrance-way to the tunnel. A flight of narrow stone stairs, this time of spiral form, ran round the narrow well and finished some three feet above Kate's head. Above that, the shaft narrowed to little more than a chimney's size. Undoubtedly, this must be the other end of Llanhalo secret passage.

This end had been filled in with stone and debris, probably long after its time of usefulness was past, but some property-owner who did not care for mysterious secrets and relics of the dangerous past and tunnels down which people could, after all, come as well as go. Thank Heaven the debris had sunk and slipped down the sloping tunnel in the course of years and made room for passengers again, or Kate and the boys might have found themselves, after all their pains, faced with impenetrable mass of broken stone and been forced to return to the perils that awaited them at the Llanhalo end. Kate wondered if Gideon Atkins ever struggled along so far as this, whether he knew what awaited them at the top of that flight of stone steps; or whether, content with using the central chamber as a prison, he had abandoned further researches when he found the tunnel half-filled with debris, deciding that he was safe from discovery from the forgotten and deserted further end?

At the top of that flight of steps, what awaited them? The lone hillside? Or some ancient ruin whose connection with Llanhalo Abbey had been long forgotten? Probably, thought Kate, the latter; for ground level must be about three feet above her head, where the stairs ended, yet the narrow shaft of masonry continued for six feet or so above that. Utterly ignorant of where they would find themselves, they must go up and look for a way out. Well might young Ronnie have looked sceptical to hear her say "We're nearly home now!"

Once again it seemed expedient that Ronnie should go first, Sidney next, and then Kate. There was no handrail, but Ronnie did not seem to mind, gripping the rough stonework of the shaft with his left hand, and with his right assisting Sidney along behind him. At the top of the stairs, he drew Sidney up to him, and to allow Kate room to emerge upon the top stair, moved into a very narrow passage which seemed to be the only egress from the stairs. Kate, on the top stair, found herself in a narrow circular shaft of rough masonry, with little more than room for one person to stand upright, so much did the stair-shaft narrow above the stair-head. The circular shaft was broken at the stair-head by the narrow space, about eighteen inches wide, through which Ronnie and Sidney had passed. Kate followed them. They were now all three in a narrow passage, or space between two walls, not more than about eight feet long, of which one end gave on to the stair-head and the other end was blocked.

Ronnie and Kate had agreed before coming up the stairs, not to speak to one another until they had made sure of their whereabouts. But Ronnie's interrogative and amazed look, as he shone his torch up to the cobwebbed grey boards which formed the ceiling of this narrow space, down on the earthen, dusty floor and along to the end where a brick wall, roughly mortared, blocked them in, made Kate break her silence. Sidney stood between them, leaning against the wall, his eyes shut, indifferent to his surroundings, quite exhausted. Kate leaned across him and uttered intensely in Ronnie's ear:

"There *must* be a way out of this!"

"I reckon we'll have to knock the wall down," said Ronnie, half-ironically, half-trepidantly.

They stood one at each end of the narrow place, and examined it with their torches. One wall was of rough stone, and showed no sign of having, or ever having had, an opening in it. The opposite wall was of timber and brick. The wall-plate was a great timber baulk, white with dust from ancient stone and mortar. Four heavy upright oak timbers, rough-adzed, unstained and pale in colour, supported the beam upon which the ceiling lay. The spaces between these upright timbers were filled with unplastered brick panels, dried mortar bulging between the bricks. Kate remembered what Rosaleen Morrison had told her at the Veault about the timbering of old houses. Heavy upright timbers, close together, with no cross-pieces, meant a very old building.

If there was any way out of this place, it must surely be through the timber and brick wall. But brick is an unyielding substance, and these wall-timbers showed neither crack nor hinge. Kate rapped them with her knuckles. It was like rapping the trunks of great trees.

Kate was beginning to get desperate. The thought of attempting to take Sidney back through the hazards of the underground passage appalled her. There must be a way out here! The air in this little space between two walls was none too good, and their presence seemed to have disturbed age-old dust, which was dry now in her throat and nostrils. When Sidney suddenly opened his eyes and looked at her in a lack-lustre fashion, she was alarmed at the dumb distress of his look. He sighed, and slipped down against the wall, Kate's arm supporting him, and sat on the wall-plate.

As he did so, and leant his head on his hands, Kate fancied or was it an illusion of her moving torchlight?—that the great upright timber at the back of him shifted slightly outwards at the base. Coaxing and pushing, she induced him to move a little way along the wall-plate and lean against the brick panel. As he did so, it seemed to her certain that the upright timber slipped back into position, level with the bricks.

Playing her torch over it, Kate saw now that the base of this timber was darkened and soiled and a little battered, compared with the others, as if it had frequently in its long life been kicked and pushed at. Ronnie at her side, she knelt down and pressed her weight steadily against it where it adjoined the wall-plate. It gave silently to her push, and as she relaxed pressure, slipped silently back to the vertical. Hinged, or more probably pivoted, at the top, the whole heavy timber hung from the ceiling-plate. The other two uprights were truly morticed into the wall-plate and truly supported the ceiling. This one was a false support, and formed, in fact, the hidden door of the secret place in which the three of them now stood.

Kate switched off her torch and signed to Ronnie to switch off his, and pushed again. Once again, the timber yielded. Kate holding it open, supported on her arm, listened intently. No sound. Absolute darkness.

"I'll go first, Ronnie," she said in a low voice. "Then Sidney. Then you."

Kate had the impression, as she slipped out under the lifted timber, that she was stepping into a large, high, indoor place. It was quite dark, and she hesitated to use her torch. There was smooth stone on the floor: she had touched its cold surface with her finger-tips as she had slipped the wall-plate.

She helped the boys out, and carefully let the timber drop back. It made only a soft thud as it fell into place.

"Where are we?" whispered Ronnie.

"I don't know," said Kate irresolutely, fingering her torch, straining her eyes into the darkness, which was as quiet as if it were posted with waiting people. There was a smell of chrysanthemums in the air.

"Shall I put on my torch?" asked Ronnie, and before the irresolute Kate could answer, had clicked it on. Its beam fell startlingly and closely across the Jacobean pattern of a linen-covered settee. Kate switched on her torch too, for, if they were going to have a light, they had better have plenty. The smell of chrysanthemums came from a great bunch of them in a terra-cotta jar on an oak table. The lone hillside, the ancient ruins, the barns, faded and departed out of Kate's fancy. She turned sharply and looked at the broad dark-stained timbers and light-coloured plaster panels of the wall through which they had just come: the wide, open fireplace in which a few burnt-out embers lay: the wide stairs with the turned newel-post and twisted balusters. Then she relaxed and laughed softly, if a little wildly. She could almost have dropped on to the comfortable settee and had her laugh out, with hysterical relief. They were in the hall of the Veault.

"And Mr. Morrison said he was afraid there weren't any hidey-holes in his house!" she murmured. Ronnie looked at her with dazed, inquiring eyes. "It's all right, Ronnie. You can relax. Let Sidney lie down on that settee and forget his troubles. We're with friends."

Chapter Twenty

On the table, as well as a jar of chrysanthemums was a silver two-branched candlestick. Kate lit the candles, smiling to herself, feeling quite lightheaded with relief from the long strain. The bracket-clock on the high mantel marked twenty minutes past four.

"Where are we, Miss?" asked Ronnie at her elbow. He had helped Sidney to a seat on the settee, murmuring to him and patting him like a horse. Kate met the eager look of his clear grey eyes, and the thought of the dangers he had just been through in her company made her heart contract. She pushed the quiff of dark hair off his eyebrows.

"The Veault. People I know live here. They'll look after us," she whispered. "They're nice. I'm going to wake somebody now. You stay with Sidney. We'll soon have him in bed.'"

When the relief of their escape from immediate danger had worn off, Kate would be able to reflect on the fact that she had actually succeeded, as she had believed she would succeed, and as very few others had believed she would succeed, in finding Sidney Brentwood.

In a relaxed and almost light-hearted mood she tapped on the door of the small bedroom over the porch in which, she remembered, Rosaleen had said she slept. When there was a responsive rustle and a sigh, she opened the door a little and whispered to the darkness:

"Rosaleen!"

Rosaleen woke with the wary, instant liveliness of an animal.

"Yes? Who is it?"

There was a creak of springs and an upheaval of white sheet in a darkness faintly modified by the square of the uncurtained window.

"Kate Mayhew. I say, Rosaleen—"

Black-out or none, Rosaleen lit a candle and looked round at Kate with great, dark, startled eyes.

"Say, what the—Is anything the matter?"

She looked alarmed, as well she might, and, without waiting for an answer, flinging the bedclothes back, she reached out for her dressing gown.

"I hope I haven't given you a shock, I tried not to," prattled Kate in a whisper. "Only I had to wake somebody, and—"

"Yes? Yes?" interrupted Rosaleen, tying the sash of her dressing gown tightly round her waist.

Having made her concession to apology, Kate could not keep the lilt of triumph out of her voice:

"I've found Sidney Brentwood, Rosaleen! He's here!"

Rosaleen's little fingers froze on her sash.

"*What?*"

"Yes, only he's awfully exhausted, poor kid! There's all sorts of things to tell you, Rosaleen! A secret passage—you know, I told you there was supposed to be one at Llanhalo!"

"Sure you did."

"Could you possibly give Sidney a bed? He ought to have a doctor in the morning, too. He's down in the hall. I'll tell you all about it."

Rosaleen slowly finished tying the sash of her dressing gown with mechanically-moving fingers.

"Sure, we'll give him a bed," she said slowly. Her reactions to surprise were not, after all, as quick as her lively waking would lead one to expect. She seemed a little bemused, as though events were going too fast for her. "Sure we'll give him a bed," she repeated. "Is there anyone else with you?"

"Only Ronnie, the kid from Llanhalo. But he's all right, bless him. It's only poor little Sidney that wants coddling."

"And you say you found him in a secret passage! Well for land's sakes! You go on down, Kate, and see if the bellows'll get the fire up again! I'll just wake Auntie and be right down."

She smiled, her voice rose, fresh and charming, she had become hospitality itself as she hurried Kate out of the room and lit a candle on the landing. Kate had been a little disappointed at Rosaleen's first reception of the great news. But she reflected as she turned to go downstairs that great news is difficult to assimilate when flung at one without warning as one wakes.

Kate was still carrying under one arm in a bundle the net that Sidney Brentwood had insisted on bringing with him. It was not properly tied, and had become unrolled and somewhat of an impediment during their attempts to find an exit from the hiding-place in the wall: and as she started down the stairs one end dropped loose, and she caught her heel in it. Putting her torch down on the stair, she paused to extricate herself and to roll the end of the net up again. Since it was Sidney's dearest treasure, she must be careful of it. Sidney, when he was restored once more to his happy and active life, should not ask in vain for his handiwork. Rolling the net up in the semi-darkness, seeing over the slant of the balustrade, the soft glow light of the candles she had lit, and hearing the chirpy and soft little voice of Ronnie encouraging Sidney on the settee, Kate smiled to herself. Half-an-hour ago nothing seemed to matter for herself and Sidney and Ronnie but to get to safety. But now she could afford to dwell again on little happinesses, and to think it important that a boy should not lose his little treasure of handiwork.

The smile was still on her lips when she heard a low voice in one of the rooms off the landing—and her mind had to register carefully the fact that it was Rosaleen's voice, for, although it was Rosaleen's voice, it was speaking quite out of Rosaleen's part in this drama. It said:

"That blasted kid's escaped!"

The smile became fixed on Kate's face. She could feel it, after a second tightening her facial muscles. *That blasted kid's escaped!* No stretch of license could read the feelings of a friend into that choice of words. But it was not so much the words, as the tone, bitter, angry and agitated, in which they were spoken, which paralysed Kate.

"It's that bloody girl," went on the voice. "I knew there'd be trouble! We ought to have got rid of the damn kid as soon as she turned up. Now what? Now what?"

As if the overheard question, which was uttered in a voice of anguished fury, had been addressed to her, Kate came suddenly to herself; and without waiting even to call herself the fool she suddenly knew she was, she had seized off her shoes— for shoes were noisy on these wooden stairs and stone floors —and was down in the hall.

"Quick, Ronnie! We must go! Quick, quick!"

The child's look, startled, wide-eyed, dismayed, touched Kate's heart and irritated her both at once. He had been sitting, curled like a little dog, in the corner of the large settee, with Sidney leaning against him. She shook him impatiently.

"Quick! There's danger here! The back door! I'll show you!"

Sidney, thank Heaven, was docile, not obstinate, in his weakness, and only sighed when Kate roused him and walked him to the door. It was an old door, probably one of the original doors of the sixteenth century house, with a great old wooden bolt as well as a more modern chain and socket. Ronnie's small fingers could not manage the bolt, and he looked at Kate in anguish, and she quickly handed him the torch and tackled the door herself. All was still quiet in the hall. No one had come down yet. No doubt Rosaleen thought that Kate was innocently blowing up the embers and awaiting her hospitable hosts.

But as the bolt grated softly back, and the chain, flung dangling, struck against the door-frame, a voice behind Kate said softly:

"Why, Kate, where *are* you going?"

It was Rosaleen, who had approached down the back stairs and through the kitchen. She had put on slacks and a blouse. Perhaps it was the moccasins on her feet that had made her approach so silent. In the light of Ronnie's torch, without her make-up, she looked much older than by daylight, and at the same time even more fragile and appealing. The expression on her face was one of simple astonishment.

Kate was at a loss.

"Sidney wanted air," she improvised. "He nearly fainted. I thought we'd go out for a bit."

"Why, of course! But—without your shoes, Kate?"

"I've blistered my heel."

"That's too bad! I must find you some slippers."

The wide door swung open to Kate's hand on the latch.

"I'll take the kiddie out for you," said Rosaleen. "You can't go out without your shoes."

I think *I'd* better, he knows me," said Kate hastily, retaining hold of Sidney's arm. Rosaleen had put her little hand on the boy's shoulder. Kate felt quite a horror of that little hand with its long painted fingernails: it lay there so lightly, yet looked as if at any moment it might sink, like a claw, in the boy's shoulder. Kate knew that Rosaleen had no intention of letting them go. Kate's only advantage was, that Rosaleen did not know that she knew this.

"Then we'll both go," said Rosaleen with a little laugh. But it seemed to Kate that she was holding Sidney where he was, and that her laugh lifted her upper lip stiffly. While Kate was wondering what to do, a little tug came at her sleeve. It was

Ronnie. His lips were pursed in a soundless whistling, and he was carelessly allowing his torch-light to play about here and there; but a flick of his eyelids and his torch together directed Kate's glance towards Rosaleen Morrison's other hand, her right one. And Kate saw that what she had taken to be a torch in that hand was not a torch at all, but a small pistol.

She looked up, and met the wary stiffness of Rosaleen's smile. And at the same moment she knew that she had a second advantage over Rosaleen, the most ancient, the most primitive, advantage of all. She dropped her hand from Sidney's arm as if she were relinquishing him to Rosaleen, and, stepping back a pace or two, clenched her right fist and with all her weight behind it drove on to Rosaleen's chin.

Pugilism had formed no part of Kate's stage-training, she knew nothing of the science but what she had seen in films, and the success of her blow positively took her own breath away. Rosaleen went over like a ninepin, leaving Kate open-mouthed with an odd reprehensible exhilaration, modified by the fear that she had cracked Rosaleen's skull for her. There had been a horrible thud as she went down, and she showed no lightning-like disposition to get up again.

Well, after all, Kate did not want her up again! Kate picked up Sidney and heaved him over her shoulder. He was lighter than she might have expected, but not so light as she had hoped, or else her strength was not quite what she thought. Saying to Ronnie:

"Put your torch out, and come on!" she staggered out into the courtyard. It was moonlight now, not bright, the stars were small and there were thin clouds about the sky. But the outlines of the barns and out-buildings, and the wall that ran around the courtyard, stood out so clearly that Kate could but pray that no one was looking from a window. Thank Heaven she had thought of taking off her shoes, cold and uneven as the cobbles were! Silence was the thing. Silence, so that no one knew where to follow, since they could not have speed.

Kate was prudent enough not to yield to the temptation to cut across the courtyard, but went round it, keeping in the shadow of the outbuildings. She was scarcely through the gate, however, when she heard angry voices in the house, and dots of swinging light from somebody's torch ran like will-o'-the-wisps about the barn walls. Rosaleen had been found, and pursuit was not far off.

If Kate had felt vaguely that there was danger in Llanhalo tunnel, she knew now quite definitely that there was danger, terrible danger, at the Veault. All the hazards of this night seemed to come to a climax here, as she stood panting, Sidney still in her arms, in the lee of the stables, out of sight of the back door, shadow over her, but moonlight all around, with Ronnie at her shoulder looking up at her with the wary and rather grim expression of a lieutenant who is beginning to believe that circumstances are after all going to be too much for his sanguine leader. His little chin quivered once. Oh God thought Kate, what now?

A sort of paralysis came upon her. If we go into the stables we'll be just caught in a trap. If we make a dash for it, we'll have the damned moonlight all over us. She balanced in a horrible, nerveless equilibrium.

It was Ronnie who broke the spell for her. As a man's voice sounded from the back door:

"They've gone this way, you bet! " he startled Kate by breaking away from their little group and climbing back up by the wheel on to the wagon which Aminta had left there yesterday.

"Quick, quick, in here!" he muttered, shoving aside armfuls of bracken, burrowing a hole in it.

It was a faint hope. Kate half-lifted, half-helped Sidney into the wagon, but she shook her head when Ronnie held out a tense hand to pull her up too.

"No!" she whispered. "I shall try and get help!"

"Oh no!"

"Yes, it's safer so. Lie down, I'll cover you up. Keep Sidney quiet. And, Ronnie, whatever happens—whatever happens—don't make a sound or move. I trust you not to."

With the two children buried deep in the bracken, the cart stood, half in moonlight, half in shadow, with supine shafts that rested on the ground. Oh, if Kate could but hitch those shafts to a hundred-horse-power engine, a Pegasus, a flight of magic geese, and drive it miraculously away! She had said that she would try to get help. But, of course, she could not leave the Veault while the children were hidden there! It was to draw the enemy's fire that she had decided to remain in the open: so, she would not be staking everything upon one chance.

Yet it was hard, when footsteps and torch-light came across the courtyard towards that cart, to tear herself from it, to leave it undefended and slip around the corner of the stable. She felt that the once-friendly-seeming bracken had turned traitor now and cried aloud to be searched; she felt that no one, looking for fugitives, could fail to look in that obvious, self-advertising place.

Yet the two who came through the courtyard gate ignored it. Kate, listening with stopped breath around the angle of the building, recognised the voices as those of Mr. and Mrs. Morrison. It was by pitch and tone she recognised them, for the accent was strangely harsh and coarsened version of their gentle American drawl.

"Well, they can't have gone far without shoes, that one thing! And with a sick kid, and only five minutes start—"

"Jesus, Ellida, quit handing out the sunny stuff! They can git far enough to finish you and me and all of us if we don't stop them! I'll go up the field-path, in case they've scooted back to Llanhalo. You search the barns."

"What'll I do with them if I find them, Doug?"

"Hold 'em up and holler to me to come."

"And then what?" asked the woman, with a strange nervous dread in her voice.

"Leave that to me and Joe. I ain't taking risks *this* time to please you, Ellida! I guess *this* time your soft heart'll just have to gush in vain!"

"And suppose," said the woman tremulously, "the girl left a message to say where she was going?"

"Then we'll be for the high-jump anyway, I guess, and all the blitzed kids in London won't be able to make us look like respectable philanthropists."

"Doug, couldn't we just keep them here, like we did the boy, till the day after to-morrow?"

"Nice little helper this girl'd be, wouldn't she? Not on your life, Ellida! She's got to have her mouth stopped for good, and stopped now, and the kids must go with her!"

"Doug, it's dangerous! I—"

"Sure, it's dangerous. It's *been* dangerous, it *is* dangerous, and it's going to be a whole lot *more* dangerous," said the twanging level male voice, moving closer to where Kate stood. Kate could see the circle of his torchlight now playing upon the yard gate and the field gate.

If by chance Morrison turned his torch her way as he went towards the field gate, he could not fail to see her. No doubt he, as well as Rosaleen, had a weapon in his hand. It was Kate's first intention to keep quite still, pressed against the wall of the stable, until he had gone up the field. But then it seemed to her almost certain that the man would play his torch in every direction as he went by, and that by remaining still she was simply waiting for him to see her. Too late, she decided to move.

Too late, because her movement in the semi-darkness attracted an attention that might have missed her had she remained where she was. She heard Morrison's footsteps come suddenly to a halt. The beam of his torch reached her; by its light she saw a burdock with its thistly flowers and one or two plants of white bitter-sweet in the rough grass near his feet, very clearly, like a botanical plate in an old book. Her cautious movement along the wall became a careless flight. As she reached the corner of the stable building and rounded it out of the light of that torch, she heard Morrison cry:

"Back to the yard, Ellida. Here's the girl!"

Skirting the stable wall, Kate found herself back again, by a lower gate, in the cobbled courtyard. Morrison was not far behind her, and she was dimly aware of Mrs. Morrison coming down from the barns towards the yard. She was cornered. She dared not rush out through the courtyard again into the open. Mr. and Mrs. Morrison no doubt had firearms, and it was too much to hope that they would be compunctious or inexpert in using them. The back door of the house stood open, and Kate's immediate craving was for cover. She fled in.

The kitchen facing Kate was dark, but the hall a little way up the passage still glowed with the candles Kate had lit. Kate made for the hall, for the light drew her: the light in which, if she could be seen, she could also see. The hall door was open, and there was nobody there. But as Kate hovered, making sure of this, on the threshold, she heard a crack! and the little spitting noise of a bullet burying itself in wood somewhere.

Kate had wanted light, but not to make herself a target, and as much as she had welcomed light she now desired the dark a ding-place. She flew on her stockinged feet for the stairs, pinching out the candles as she went. She did not know where she was going—just, away from that pistol. She had flown for the stairs instinctively. But half-way up she paused, since no one was following her, and listened. She could hear Morrison at the back door saying:

"What happened?"

Kate stole softly down the stairs again into the hall. She must not yield to the impulse to run upstairs and let herself be cornered in some unfamiliar room. Alongside the door, in the corner of the room, was a panelled oak chest. Picking up the two-branched candlestick from the table, Kate softly got up on this. Like most pieces of Sheffield plate, the candlestick was heavily weighted with lead at the base, and it was Kate's intention, when Morrison entered the room in pursuit of her, to use it as a club. A simple stratagem, but the only one Kate could think of.

"What happened?"

"Where's the kids?" riposted Rosaleen in a tone as sharp and hard as his.

"I heard a shot!"

"I missed her. She made a dash for the hall."

"You're too hot on your gun, Rosa. Next time, wait for orders!"

"All right, all right, I didn't shoot to kill! If I had, I wouldn't a missed."

"Where is she?"

"Went upstairs. We've got her cornered. Where are the kids?"

"They won't get far."

"If they do, we're sunk."

"Ellie and I can corner the girl, I guess. You take the car, Rosa, and go and fetch Joe. Go up the field way to the road. You may get a sight of the kids on the way. If you do, make sure of them. But don't stop looking for them, we'll do that directly. Go straight for Joe, and drive straight back here. Soon's we've fixed the girl, we'll make a search for the blasted kids. They wont've gone far. One of them's sick."

Rosaleen objected:

"Make sure of the girl and the kids first, and fetch Joe after, *I* say!"

"And if it happens we can't make sure of the kids? We got to get away somehow, haven't we? We're in a jam and we may have to break out of it. Do as I say! Get Joe! Jesus, it'll be daylight soon! Be serious, Rosa, can't you?"

"If you'd listened to me being serious a month ago, this wouldn't have happened! You risked the whole show, after all our work, for the sake of Ellida's mother-complex! God! Couldn't I just wring your fat motherly neck, Ellida?"

"Cut it out, Rosa!" said Mr. Morrison in a violently vibrating voice. "Go and fetch Joe!"

"You're boss here, but you can take it from me you're acting like a fool," said Rosaleen, and went out. One pursuer the less, and not the least formidable of the three. Where, wondered Kate, was Nurse Maud? She had an odd persuasion that Nurse Maud, were she here, would be the most formidable and relentless enemy of them all.

"I'll go up the back stairs," said Mr. Morrison. "You up the front ones, Ellida. You got your gun? Don't shoot unless you have to—we got to find out where the kids are. Don't let her get away, though."

Ellida moaned suddenly, and Kate had the impression she was shivering.

"I knew when the day was put off something awful'd happen! It's been put off and put off, and now I believe it's too late! The whole plan's gone wrong from top to bottom, if you ask me, and—"

"Oh, quit moaning, get on after the girl! Use your torch. She's got no gun. She can't hurt you."

Morrison's voice receded through the kitchen. Can't she, thought Kate. She hoped, she thought, she could. She gripped her candlestick, and waited. Now was her chance, probably her one chance. If she could eliminate Mrs. Morrison, there would, for a while at least, be only one enemy to cope with, a formidable enemy, and armed, but not, surely, entirely beyond Kate's skill to elude. Kate held her breath, as torchlight and footsteps came up the passage. All the strength in her body seemed to be in her right arm, gripping the awkward but satisfyingly heavy two-branched candlestick by the central stem.

But it is practice that makes perfect, even in violence. The unpractised arm swinging a candelabra, though it may feel as strong as Samson's will find itself subject to any sentiment or whim that may jump to the surface of the unpractised mind. When Mrs. Morrison, that elderly, commonplace, ill-conditioned woman, all of a sag without her corsets, her grey hair in a net that made an odd hard line above her coarsely-wrinkled forehead, her lips crimped together in a cruel enough line, but with a look of tragic care as well as the wariness of a hunted animal in her narrowed eyes, appeared in the doorway, a pistol gripped in her fat right hand and a torch in her left shining a beam into the ingle-nook and under the table and up the stairs, first Kate's heart faltered, and then her hand. Violence must be whole-hearted; half-hearted violence is of no avail. Kate could not feel afraid of this woman; and the amateur in clubbing, to use a club wholeheartedly, needs to feel urgently afraid.

Sidney's net lay on the chest beside her. She had felt it with her hand as she scrambled up. As Mrs. Morrison advanced a step further into the room, something in the opposite wall seemed to attract her attention, for she stooped and peered forward, and her huge shadow bobbed up over the ceiling like that of a nurse visiting a night-nursery, candle in hand. Kate swooped softly like a bird to the soft net, and picking it up by the corners, spread it out. The little careful noise she made in purring down the candlestick startled the woman, who turned sharply. As she turned, Kate flung the net down over her. She gave a shuddering cry, and pushed out with her arms, dropped both pistol and torch to claw with her fingers at the hampering silk. Her fingers caught in the meshes. Kate, leaping to the ground, drew the net tight around her towards the back. The torch on the floor brilliantly illuminated the dropped pistol, the crack between two flags and the yellow wood-dust covering the floor under an old lowboy.

Kate's chief concern was to prevent the woman from calling for help. She clapped a hand over her mouth, clasping her tightly with an arm hooked round her neck, and so forced a sort of temporary grunting, struggling silence on her. But Kate had only two hands, and while one was thus engaged, the other could not fasten the net securely round her victim. And it was only a matter of time before Douglas Morrison, whom Kate could now remotely hear going up the attic stairs, would complete his search. Kate could at least, perhaps, with a struggle, secure the dropped automatic.

She tugged and stooped, and her left hand was straining down towards it, when she became suddenly aware of a third person close to them. Another hand was stretching down for that pistol. The shock of this gave an extra spurt to Kate's strength, so that she succeeded, sobbing, in snatching the weapon up from the ground, prepared, if this were Morrison, to sell her liberty dear. But the other person made no attempt either to forestall her or to wrest the weapon away from her. His hand, instead, picked up the torch and set it on the lowboy. He was taking off his scarf. It was Colin.

"Oh, Colin!" uttered Kate faintly, and for a second, far from feeling overjoyed, she felt as faint and weak as Sidney Brentwood himself, with relief. She was saved. She would relinquish her hold on Ellida Morrison. She would relinquish everything. Colin would see to everything. She would sit down; preferably, on the floor.

"Hold on, Kate!" muttered Colin urgently. He was tying his scarf around Mrs. Morrison's mouth. Thank Heaven, Kate need not clasp her round the neck and intimately smell her hair and talcum powder any longer!

"Oh, Colin! Oh, Colin!"

"All right, Katy! Now we'll put her behind the wall. That'll keep her quiet for a bit."

"You know about it?"

"How do you think I got here?"

"Oh, Colin, was it you I was running away from down that tunnel? Oh, if only I'd known!"

"Where's Morrison?"

"Upstairs! He'll be down in a minute, though."

A space of fifteen inches or so is wider than it looks, and even a portly human body is smaller. Kate held the timber, while Colin assisted the groaning Ellida through. She went quite meekly. Perhaps the tunnel seemed to offer to her at least a dim prospect of at least temporary escape.

"Now you and I, Kate, quick!"

Kate stared at Colin.

"What, through there? No!"

"But, of course! You've no *idea* of the danger here!"

"I can't go off and leave the kids!"

"What kids? '

"Ronnie and Sidney. I found him! I found him! I told you I would! They're out in the yard, hidden in a bracken-cart."

"My God, Kate, what did you think you were going to do here, single-handed, with two kids?"

"I didn't know I was coming here! I was looking for Sidney! Never mind that now! What shall we do?"

"Where are the others?"

"Rosaleen went to get the car out and fetch somebody called Joe. I don't know where Maud is."

"Could we stop Rosaleen?"

"I don't know. I haven't heard the car, but then I've been listening to other things."

"Can you keep out of Morrison's way, if I go and see?"

"I should think so. He can't see me without a light, and if he puts his on I can see him first. Thank God there are two staircases in this house!"

"Take this," said Colin, handing her Mrs. Morrison's automatic. It was a small but wicked-looking thing. Kate had never before held a loaded pistol in her hand. She looked at it with aversion and distrust.

"What about you?"

But Colin gave a faint, grim smile.

"I've got one of my own, my dear."

Chapter Twenty-One

It was most unlike Colin to be going about with a pistol of his own, and at any other moment Kate would have been considerably surprised. But there was no time now to pursue hidden tracks of speculation into the oddities of one's friends' characters and habits. Kate could hear Morrison coming down the attic stairs. Evidently he had satisfied himself that she was not lurking in that dusty wilderness of posts and tie-beams. Her heart beat fast, but now that Colin's arrival had momentarily tipped the odds in her favour, worry about the children, rather than alarm about her own situation, obsessed her mind. She could dodge Morrison. Colin and she together could outmanoeuvre the whole gang: but they could not leave the Veault while the children remained in hiding there, and they could not hope, so far as Kate could see, to get the children away without being discovered.

Kate regretted now that she had allowed Ronnie to choose such a damned silly place to hide in—a place out in the open, a place from which they could not quickly extricate themselves, a place in which they were, should suspicion light there, utterly trapped, defenceless. The fact was, Kate had become weak at the knees for a moment, and had submitted to the judgment, not, as her weakness allowed her to imagine, inspired, but merely reckless, of a child. No good to blame herself now. But, if any harm should come to those two kids—

These useless and agitated reflections which flickered about Kate's mind while she stood tensely on the alert listening to get the direction of Morrison's approach, were brought to an end by the sudden realisation that she and Colin had taken no precaution against Mrs. Morrison returning, once she had worked her hands free of the net they had tied behind her, to the contest. There was no sound from that quarter, and the timber upright stood massive and motionless as if it were indeed the framework it appeared to be: but they could not rely on their prisoner remaining in her safe seclusion.

Kate was, in the circumstances, very much averse from making a noise: for Morrison must by now be beginning to feel apprehensive of the possible failure of his cornering stratagem, and Kate would have preferred to keep him in ignorance of her whereabouts as well as of his wife's. But even more important than to keep Morrison in ignorance, was to prevent the re-emergence of Ellida.

Kate cast the light of her torch quickly round the room. In the wide ingle-nook stood a small iron coffer, much nailed and banded, with large iron handles at the sides and an immense lock. This stood not more than eighteen inches in height, and yet its weight should serve to prevent an, movement of the hinged wall-timber. Gosh, though, what a noise it would make being dragged over the stone floor!

Gosh, what a noise it did make! Kate had to force herself to finish the job when she heard that grating and squeaking. The coffer was satisfactorily heavy, though. She heard footsteps on the landing overhead. Jamming the coffer against the wall and switching off her torch, she fled, lightly and quickly as she could go on her stockinged feet, out of the room and into the kitchen, where she stood listening.

The back stairs led up from the passage the other side of the kitchen. Thank God that Rosaleen had shown her round the house!

One of the kitchen windows was uncurtained, and allowed Kate to find her way around the table without knocking anything over. A grandfather clock—Kate could see its big white face like a dim moon on the dark wall near the window— clacked loudly in the silence. Kate switched on her torch for a second, and the white painted face, blooming momentarily into a spray of roses and the picture of a ship, announced that it was ten minutes to five. The beginning of daylight was not so very, very far away, but much too far to be relied on to bring help. Ronnie would not be missed from his bed for an hour-and-a-half yet, probably. Aminta was already up. It was strange to think that Aminta was placidly at her milking while Kate, in peril of her own and others' lives, stood in the darkness here, less than a half-a-mile away, and clutched an automatic pistol—

But where was that pistol? Kate's hand, unused to clutching such things as pistols, had not missed it till now. Oh, she had put it down when she moved the iron coffer, and had not picked it up again! Should she go back to the hall for it? No, most definitely not! Footsteps were descending the staircase. A light went on. Morrison's voice said urgently and softly:

"Ellida! Ellida!"

Kate held herself tense for flight. The back door still stood open. There was a good chance that Morrison would believe that Kate and Ellida had gone out again into the open, and that he would follow. But Kate did not welcome this chance. She could not bear the thought of that defenceless bracken cart being approached again by this desperate and ruthless man, while she hid in temporary security in the house. As his foot-step fell on the hall flags, she deliberately gave a push to the kitchen table. Its legs squeaked on the stone floor. She fled through to the back stairs and bounded up them.

"Ellida, is that you?" hoarsely whispered Morrison, and, as no answer came, followed.

It was Kate's intention to go straight through the long gallery, or the string of four little bedrooms that lay behind it, and down the front stairs again. If Morrison followed, she would repeat the performance. If he did not, she would wait below for a sign from him. So long as she kept well ahead and out of the light of Morrison's torch and the line of fire of his pistol, she did not see why she should not go on playing this simple kind of hide-and-seek with him until Colin returned to the house.

As she passed up the narrow oaken staircase where, on a previous occasion, she had seen a tool-bag lying, she thought of Gwyn Lupton, and wondered that that craftsman, with his opportunities, should have remained in ignorance of the existence of the secret passage.

The long-gallery door seemed to be locked, so she tried the door of the bedroom behind it. But that also was fastened. The latch would not rise. She struggled with it a moment, and tried the long-gallery door again. But both were locked. Her heart gave a nasty little thump, and she fled on up to the second flight. Morrison was already coming up the first. On the second landing the ceiling was lower, and no gleam came through the tiny window or reflected up from the floorboards. Kate flung herself eagerly at the nearest door. It was locked! It was locked! And the farther door was locked!

For a moment, heart thumping, trying to ward off terror, Kate stood with her thumb on the latch. Morrison, as he came through, had locked these doors. Was there no escape? The window? No, impossible! It was tiny, it was two storeys up, it did not look as if it even opened. Once more, only the stairs remained, the stairs to the attic this time, and Kate ran on up, in her mind the cold desperate dismay of one whose plan has failed and who now has no plan and can fix on none. Should she attempt to break a window in the attic—if there were a window—and escape? Should she seize up a weapon from among the lumber and attack Morrison over the well of the stairs as he came up? Should she put on her torch so that she could see him? Or creep about in the dark, hoping he would not see her? Oh, Colin, Colin! Kate found herself whimpering. Should she shout to Colin for help? Or should she rely on silence to gain a little time? Oh, what a fool she had been to put down Ellida's pistol!

But as she emerged into the vast long attic where a coppice of great timber uprights, grey with dust and age, supported the high-angled roof, a square of light sky broke on her eyes, and with a renewed jump of hope she saw that the brick wall by the back chimney-stack was still out. She remembered that there was scaffolding around the chimney outside. This was her chance, her only one. That pale grey square of sky was her one hope.

Kate scarcely noticed the violent bump she gave to the back of her head as she ducked, carelessly, under a cross-beam. The glow from Morrison's torch already illuminated the cobwebs of the stairhead rail.

Kate's knee was already on the oak frame, the blessed moon shone, tranquil and reassuring as a goddess, upon her face, when a voice from behind her said quite pleasantly:

"If you move, you'll sure get a bullet in your back. If you *don't* move, lady, you might not."

Had Morrison spoken threateningly, Kate would probably have risked a scramble out. But his voice, gentle, sub-humorous, with a flattering, teasing intonation, arrested her almost against her will. It was the voice of the detached and humorous American family-man who had come down the hall-stairs to make her acquaintance on that first sunny afternoon. For a second it even made her feel that there was some fantastic misunderstanding, and that a word or two between them might put it right: so utterly divorced from the meaning of the words it uttered was that voice.

Kate paused, and it was too late to attempt flight. She moved, but only to slip down to the floor again, to turn and face him. She was conscious of his broad, sallow face wearing a smile that curiously tightened the nostrils, the lock of grey hair falling across one eyebrow, the thick, creased collarless neck, the whole burly formidable body. But what focussed and held her eyes was the muzzle of the pistol he held in his right hand. The torch in his left dazzled her, and he politely lowered it.

"Now, Miss Mayhew, calm yourself! I'm real sorry if I've scared you, but I'm scared myself. I'm scared for myself, I don't mind admitting, but also I'm scared for those two kids. They gotter be found and brought to safety. There's things going on around here you don't know about, Miss Mayhew—"

Kate interrupted, with the courage of despair, for she did not see why Mr. Morrison should have a monopoly of words as well as of weapons:

"So I'd guessed!"

He wagged his head sympathetically. His features were good, with something of the cut about them of a Red Indian run to fat. He looked no more ruthless, no more cruel, no more likely to shoot a defenceless fellow-creature in cold blood, than any other man. Kate had, with a sort of incredulity, to remind herself that he was desperate, afraid for his own life, and that he truly intended to shoot both the children and herself.

"Things," he went on, "that make it very, very unsafe for li'l kids to be out in the fields in the dark."

"Safer than they would be here, by a long way!"

"Now, Miss Mayhew, it's this gun of mine makes you say that, I know. You think I'm a desperate character, and so, sure enough, I am. But I ain't so desperate I can think of two li'l kids running into terrible danger without wanting to help them. We're on opposite sides of the fence in some ways, sure enough, Miss Mayhew, you and me. But where those kids are concerned we're on the same side. We both want their safety. You let me know where they are, so's I can give orders they come to no harm."

"Oh yes?"

"Miss Mayhew, what can you do for them, as things are?"

"I can hope they get safely away to Llanhalo," said Kate, bluffing. Where was Colin? Would he ever find her here?

"You know as well's I do one of those kids is sick. You want to help him, and I want to help him. Why can't we co-operate?"

"Well, what do you want me to do?" asked Kate slowly, playing for time.

"That's more reasonable! I want you just to take me to those kids, so's we can co-operate to see they're put in a safe place. You've guessed it, young lady. We're not on your side in this war, and it looks to me as if we've come to a pretty sticky jam, thanks partly to you. But we're not fighting kids. We must get the kids safe before Joe comes back, or he'll put a bullet through them soon's look at them."

"If he can find them, whoever he is."

"Oh, you've hidden them somewhere, have you? Let's go find them while there's still a chance."

Nothing was going to induce Kate to go out into the open at the point of Mr. Morrison's pistol. She did not trust that flimsy bracken cart not to shout its secret in the moonlight. She did not trust Ronnie's capacity to lie hidden through all temptations. Leaning against the open frame of the panel, that beckoning but hopeless exit to freedom, the moon above the chimney reminding her of many, many romantic, peaceful and lovely night scenes, Kate folded her arms and shook her head. Oh Colin, Colin, how will you know that I am here?

"You think I wish the kids harm?" said Mr. Morrison, and for the first time there was a hastier, grating undertone in his smooth, reasonable voice. "You don't trust me?"

"Right in one."

"Now, would I have kept that kid Sidney here all this while if I hadn't meant well by him? Wouldn't I have put him out of the way if I'd been the monster you think me?"

"It was Ellida's mother-complex stopped you," said Kate in a dry, daring voice.

For the first time an angry and dangerous look came over the man's smooth broad face.

"What?"

"It's no use your talking like Dr. Barnardo to *me*, Mr. Morrison. I heard all you said when you came into the house just now. And I haven't any intention of telling you where the boys are!" Kate felt cold, but her cheeks were burning. As she spoke she thought she heard a cautious footstep below in the courtyard. Colin! Would he look up? Would he see the light in the attic, if he did? Or did the scaffolding and chimney hide the opening in the wall-frame?

"Now see here," said Morrison, approaching slowly closer to her, and as he slowly approached, his eyes seemed to become slowly narrower, his lips thinner, his nostrils turned into white slits, and curious lines to develop at each side of the bridge of his broad jutting nose, so that his face seemed simplified into a stage mask. Kate drew back, flattened herself against the wall. Would she have spoken so bravely, had she foreseen the result of her speech? She was, for a moment, terror-stricken at the change in the man's face, and could have screamed for help, had her voice remained with her. With parted lips and constricted chest-wall, like one in a dreadful dream whose effortful cries emerge as faint, stifled moans, she stared at him.

"Now see here. You waste my time."

He was so close to her now that the scents that hung about him were as real to her as the sight of him and terrifying, at such a moment, in their commonplaceness, the scents of strong tobacco, soap, menthol, and warm human breath. He made a sudden quick movement and she felt the hard barrel of the pistol against her ribs.

"You take me to where those kids are. Make a move! Or I shoot you dead before you can count twenty. I'm not bluffing lady, don't you bank on it. I'm at that crisis in my history where it'd mean nothing to me to stretch out a dozen like you. Now!"

Oddly enough, the feeling of the hard pistol against her side braced Kate. This was reality, no kind of nightmare, and terrifying as was Morrison's hate-filled aspect, she knew that he was more terrified than she.

"All right," said Kate. "I'll show you."

"Ah!"

"No need to go down, though. I can show you from here, if you'll let me use my torch."

She saw a look, first doubtful, as though he perceived a trap, then thoughtful, cross Morrison's face.

"It'd be quicker," said Kate, with false carelessness. To flash a light from the open panel was her one hope of attracting Colin's attention. "I don't suppose the A.R.P. wardens will notice it, at this hour."

"Okay," said Morrison slowly.

"And then you'll let me go?"

"Sure, I'll let you go—when I've got the kids," said Morrison at her shoulder. Kate already had her torch on and directed over the cross-beam into the night and was moving it about as though to find her bearings, praying that Colin was within sight.

"And you'd better not try to fool me."

"I shouldn't be so silly," said Kate lightly, with a hammering heart.

"No? I reckon I won't risk much on your sagacity, just the same, Where are they?"

"You see that gate in the field?"

"Well alongside it, just up the slope behind the barns, there's a kind of dingle," said Kate, who had noticed this as she drove away yesterday in Major Humphries's car. "They're there…" She spoke slowly, drawing time out. Sister Ann, Sister Ann, do you see anyone coming? No one coming, nothing coming, not even the morning.

The light of Kate's torch did not really reach to the dingle she was romancing about. She wondered that Morrison did not draw his own conclusion from this, and ask why she needed a torch to tell him the children were in the dingle, but he did not. He leant by her shoulder and let her move the feeble yellow light here and there, now illuminating sharply a patch of lichen on the stone chimney-stack so close to the wall and the pale coarse rope that fastened together an angle of the scaffolding around it, now flitting ineffectually across the weather-boarded barns beyond the farmyard, now vanishing to a little haze in the far field, now flashing past a farm cart loaded with bracken that stood with supine shafts resting on the ground, while Kate listened with all her ears for even the tiniest sound in the house to show that Colin was on his way to her: but nothing came, not even the creak of a stair under a stealing foot.

"Half-a-minute!" said Morrison at her ear. "This bird's-eye view of the premises you're giving me has put an idea into my head, young lady. What's in that demure-looking bracken cart out there—besides bracken?"

He had turned his own torch on as he spoke, but used it not to augment the light of Kate's but to study at close hand the change in her face. Her face did change—she knew it, she could not help it. A sort of stony indifferent look fell upon it which was not the true look of surprise. But something seemed to have hit her hard in the centre of her being, and she was not an experienced enough actress to show no sign of it.

"Aha!" said Morrison softly, switching off his torch and turning from the window. "I thought if I let you have your way, your torch would show me what you wanted to hide. It was as good as a lie-detector, lady, the way it jumped away whenever it got near that bracken cart. Thought you'd send me off on a chase down the dingle, didn't you? It was a good idea, but not such a good one."

He stood and faced her with a tight and narrowed smile of triumph on his face. Kate brought her torch in and turned it on him. Had she really ever thought that face a friendly and a pleasant one? She looked at it with a thoughtful and solemn air, but she was not really thinking now. There was nothing left for her to think about. Was this then really the end of the adventure upon which she had so recklessly set out? And nothing she could do to avert the end? Nothing, except say brokenly and uselessly:

"Don't hurt the kids. What harm can they do you?"

The man's grin tightened. His nostrils went white as if he were angry.

"Think again, girl! They got tongues, haven't they? What would *you* do, if I let you go?"

What was the good of trying to placate this devil?

"Go to the police."

"Or the Home Guard, eh? Wouldn't our friend Humphries just sparkle in the part of the man who puts his country before his love. Well, I'm not going to let you go, sweetheart! So what?"

"I might try to de-materialise." Why reply at all to words which were only taunts? Well, because time, such little poor trickle of time as there was, was on Kate's side, not Morrison's.

"You might, indeed, but it would be a long study, and I ain't going to allow time for it," said Morrison. "Good-bye, Donna Quixote de la Mancha! You haven't made such a great success of your own plans. But you've sure thrown the whole tool-box into the works of mine, so let that be your comfort—"

Kate tried not to shut her eyes. But the explosion banged them shut. Had he missed? Surely one does not hear and have time to speculate about, the explosion from the pistol which is aimed at one's own heart? Thought flies quickly, but not so quickly as this. There was a small crash on the floor.

Morrison's pistol was on the floor. Morrison's torch was on the floor, directing a bright beam at the toe of his brown canvas shoe, which was twisting slowly round, as though for some reason he had risen on his toes and were performing a right-about turn on them. Morrison himself, with an expression of strange, remote and glassy surprise upon his face, his hands clutched at his chest, was falling forwards, was on the floor. The posts and tie-beams, in the light of Kate's limply-swinging torch, seemed to sway and dip crazily, then, as her fingers tightened, righted themselves. A little darker piece of darkness detached itself from the rafters and went looping and swooping over the floor, appearing and disappearing. Dust rose slowly around the figure of Morrison extended quite still upon the dusty boards.

Chapter Twenty-Two

A smell like fireworks was in Kate's nose and throat. Colin, behind her at the open frame, said close to her ear:

"That was a near thing!"

At his voice, breathless and shaken, but so fresh and light in quality after the grating nasal tones of the man Morrison, the scene lost its nightmare quality for Kate. That was only a frightened bat, poor creature, not a swooping emanation of evil and the darkness. The queen-posts stood as rigid and upright as they had stood for centuries. She gave a little relieving sob.

"Poor Kate, I oughtn't to have left you alone, said Colin, climbing in. "It was all for nothing, too. The car's gone."

"Oh Colin, the doors were all locked! And I left the pistol behind!"

"Take this one," said Colin, nodding towards the weapon that lay on the floor out of reach of Morrison's outstretched, unmoving hand. Kate picked it up.

"Colin, he's not dead?"

"Indeed, he is," said Colin gravely. "And we won't waste tears on him."

"It seems so sudden and so ordinary. He was there, he was terrifying and now—"

"People of Baum's kind don't often die to slow music in their beds, I fancy."

"Baum?"

"That was the name he went by in Rio. And it was his real name, I believe. He was a dealer in works of art, then, or posing as one. His real activities were those of a Nazi agent."

"A German?"

"Yes, mostly. American-born."

"Did you know him, Colin?"

"No, but I saw him several times in Rio, when I was there eighteen months ago."

Colin, to Kate's impatience, went on his knees beside the dead man and started turning out his pockets.

"Oh, *must* you do that now, Colin?"

"Yes, I must. It's what I'm here for, apart from looking after you... In Rio, I thought spies and all that sort of thing were a great joke. But when I came across this chap in London almost as soon as I got home, calling himself Morrison and playing the philanthropist, he didn't seem a joke at all. I was almost sure it was Baum, but I wasn't quite sure until I tracked him up here and saw his wife. If I'd been sure, I'd've put the police on his track, of course. But he'd worked up a good disguise as the humorous American family-man, and I couldn't be sure enough."

Colin examined the contents of an envelope he had taken from the dead man's pocket, and slipped it into his own.

"I've got something here he didn't intend to part with... I'm sorry if I've seemed a bit secretive, Kate. But I'd only just arrived here when you came on the scene, and I didn't want to drag you into danger, if there was going to be any. I didn't know you were going to dive straight in on your own account."

"I didn't dive in, I crawled. Looking for Sidney. And what's going on here I still don't know, and don't care much. All I care about is getting those two kids safely out of this... Oh, listen, Colin! Isn't that a car?"

She looked out. The dimmed-down headlights of a motor car, like luminous antennae, were feeling their way down over the field.

'Oh Colin! And those children! We're too late!"

'We'll stay here for the moment," said Colin softly, putting out the light. "Leave the first move to them. We've got them covered."

Kate gripped Morrison's pistol, getting used to the cold, lifeless feeling of the thing in her hand. The car drew up outside the courtyard gate, not three yards from the bracken cart. The door slammed, and Rosaleen, an overcoat slung over her shoulders, got out and came into the cobbled court. A man of medium height followed her, a man in light trousers and dark jacket, wearing a dark felt hat at a rakish angle.

"I suppose that's the man I saw at Hymn's Bank," breathed Kate.

The two stood a moment at the gate, then quietly crossed the yard.

"No light in the house," said the man softly at the back door. "Can't see a crack of it. We'd better go carefully, Rosa, till we're sure things are O.K. There may be a frame-up."

"Frame-up!" said Rosaleen scornfully. "The girl hadn't a gun, and she was alone! She came prancing in like a kitten asking for milk! If Doug and Ellida haven't managed to settle her, well—"

"All the same, go easy, Rosa. Subdue that temperament of yours. Let's go in quiet, and see what's going on."

His voice died away as the two came into the house.

"Yes, that's the voice I heard at Hymns Bank," whispered Kate. "Only—why do I think it sounds like a woman's voice, now? At Hymns Bank, I didn't think that. Oh! Colin! Is that—is he—?"

"The children's nurse," murmured Colin. "She was a tall, deep-voiced sort of girl, wasn't she? Not a difficult make-up for a man, with that stiff collar and white muslin thing to hide his neck and ears."

"A more difficult part to play than Major Humphries," murmured Kate.

"Major Humphries? What's he got to do with it?"

"Nothing at all. I miscast this man, that's all," whispered Kate, talking for the comfort it gave her, a little feverishly, and shivering, feeling both hot and cold with apprehension.

"Be ready," whispered Colin. "I think they're coming upstairs."

"Who the *hades* locked all these doors?" they heard Rosaleen's muffled voice cry excitably below. "Joe!"

A door was violently opened, and the voices rang clearer and hollow up the stairs.

"Shut up, Rosa," said the man calmly. "We're searching the house, not playing question-and-answer. Up the next flight. Keep with me. There's something wrong here."

Footsteps echoed woodenly in the unfurnished rooms below. "Come," whispered Colin, his knee upon the frame of the open panel. "Follow me. Put the safety catch on your pistol."

Kate's hands trembled.

"Which—where? Oh, I see!"

She slipped the little catch over. In a moment they were standing on the scaffolding platform outside: none too soon, for already footsteps were on the attic stairs.

"Go up, not down."

"Up! On the roof?"

Colin nodded.

It seemed to Kate that the friendly moon encouraged her as she hauled herself up on to the planks above. She was in the angle now between the chimney-stack and gable-end. The glazed ridge-tiles glistened, the big sparse leaves that still hung on the ash tree and fingered the roof looked inky black against the thinly-clouded sky. She got a knee in the lead gutter that lined the angle between the gables, and dragged herself up on to the roof. These stone tiles gave a good grip to stockinged feet.

But as she kicked off from the scaffolding, her foot touched something that rocked and fell. She had noticed on the platform a mortar-board left there by some careless workman; and as soon as her foot touched that shifting object, long, it seemed, before she heard the crash on the scullery roof below, she knew what she had done.

"Oh, Colin!"

Her sob of warning, and the crash of the mortar-board coincided. Colin, whom some sixth sense seemed to have warned, was up beside her in a flash, holding her hand tight as if to restrain further sound or movement. At the same moment the empty frame in the gable-end showed a shifty light. There were footsteps on boards, a silence and then a cry:

"My God! It's Doug!"

"Rosa, did you hear that noise?"

"*Doug!*"

"It was outside. Go and look out."

"But *Doug!* Joe, that girl hadn't a gun! She can't have—"

"Well, she's got Doug's gun now!" said the man's voice grimly. "Do as I say, Rosa. Be careful, though. She's still about."

Through the frame, the pale blur of Rosaleen's face showed, leaning cautiously out and scanning the cobbled yard below.

"I can't see anything!"

She withdrew.

"Where's Ellida? Has she got Ellida too" There was a sort of fascinated horror in Rosaleen's voice.

"Probably. Some kitten, Rosa, that of yours! She told me she was an actress, blast her! I wish I'd wrung her neck at the post last night. Still, the pleasure's before me."

Rosaleen said in a voice that shook:

"Hadn't we better get away, Joe? I—I don't like this."

"I don't like it either. But if we lose our nerve, Rosa, we'll land in something we like less. We've got to get the girl and the kids before we make a bolt."

"For the love of Mike, what's the use *now*?"

"A lot o' use. To stop them talking. See here, Rosa. If we make a bolt for it now, leaving them behind, we'll have all the cops in the country on our trail in less than half-an-hour. But if we settle the girl and the kids first, it may be half-a-day, with luck, before anyone smells out anything wrong here. Jefferson and Mary'll be coming up from the cottage about midday. They'll soon find the game's up, and tidy the place and scoot. We'll all have a fair start, that way. We'll make for the wilds. If we can hold out till the day after to-morrow, remember, and things go according to plan, there'll be plenty of muddles then for us to get lost in for a bit before we make contact with friends! The police'll be too busy to spare much time tracking us. It's our one chance, believe me. We must stop the girl and the kids."

"But, Joe, it'll be daylight in less than an hour!"

"Now, Rosa, it isn't like you to go pappy. If you wanted safety, you ought to a stuck to knitting socks this war! I in going to get those papers Doug was taking care of, out of the case. You go out, take your torch, look for the girl. She's not far off. She must a made that noise we heard. And it'll be a headache to her to get those kids away, with one of them sick! Be thorough. There won't be anyone around here for hours yet, remember. I'll bring everything to the car. And then I'll help you. And, Rosa," finished he grimly, "don't try to make a get-away without me. I've got the car-key."

"Well you needn't a said *that*, Joe!"

"Thought perhaps you'd be bolting to throw yourself on Humphries's manly bosom."

"Aw, don't be silly!"

Their footsteps descended the stairs. Kate and Colin were alone on the gable slant.

Colin said grimly:

"If the papers Doug was taking care of, were those he was carrying in his breast-pocket, our friend's going to be unlucky.

"Shall we go down?"

"No. Better stay here and keep watch for the moment."

Kate had thought the night quiet, but now wished it quieter, so that she could the better listen. An owl hooted a long melancholy note from not far away. And there was already a sleepy jack-jacking from one of the buildings as though some daws there felt in their feathers the not-far-off coming of the morning. Rosaleen came around the house, walking lightly a cat. She stood a moment in the court and examined with torch every inch of it, up the path at the back of the stables, along under the scullery wall, and then, as if perhaps inspired by the soft hoot of the owl that came again just then, up the scaffolding. Kate flattened herself, holding Colin's hand, shrinking against the slope of the roof. It frightened her to see that light swinging from bough to bough of the ash tree so near at hand. She could hear Rosaleen's unsteady breathing, and the soft swish of her corduroy trouser-legs rubbing together, as she turned away and went quickly across the court into the farmyard and round by the stable out of sight. The bracken cart was safe for the moment, but for how long?

Rosaleen was searching the stable now. Kate could hear the stamping movement of the horse.

"Colin, why did I let the boys hide in that bracken cart?"

Her voice trembled with despair, and Colin's hand gripped hers tightly.

"Steady, Kate. It's not a bad hiding-place. At least, we've got it in view."

"In view! What use'll that be, if she finds the boys?"

"She won't hurt them—at first. She'll try to make them say where you are."

"And then?"

"Well, we're both armed, Kate. We'll have to do the best we can."

"Oh, hadn't we better go down?"

Colin shook his head.

"We've got the advantage for the moment. We must keep it till we're forced to give it up."

"But—"

Kate had never before this night held in her hand a weapon loaded with anything more lethal than caps. Yet her hand instinctively tightened on Morrison's pistol, and she raised it to the ready. Somebody *was* coming across the farmyard, in the shadowless light of the high moon in the thinly clouded sky. Somebody was moving nearer and nearer to the bracken cart. It was not Rosaleen, for Rosaleen was searching the stable. It was somebody taller than Rosaleen, walking softly and silently in gumboots. The figure passed the bracken cart, and the muscles of Kate's right hand relaxed a little. With the figure's approach came a soft clinking sound which even at this moment brought to the back door of Kate's mind mirage-like images of comfort, and the morning, and new-lit fires. Somebody crossed the cobbled court and put something softly down near the back door. Somebody fumbled in a pocket, and after what seemed an age to Kate as she peered down from the roof, lit a match. It was Aminta. Aminta, in her stained old milking-mackintosh, lighting a cigarette. Two tall cans stood on the flags by the back door.

"Aminta," breathed Kate. "*Aminta.*"

Aminta looked sharply up. Her match went out.

"I'm Kate, Don't speak."

"*What?*"

"No one must know I'm here."

"Where are you?" breathed Aminta, her blurred face turned vaguely towards the upper windows.

"*Danger*. Aminta! Do one thing to help. Drive the bracken cart away."

"Horse isn't in!"

"Put it in! Drive to Llanhalo! Don't tell *anyone* why!"

"But—"

"Go on, you fool! Quick! Quick!"

Aminta's mind moved slowly, but since she blessedly lacked both curiosity and apprehensiveness, it moved surely, once in train. Kate sensed rather than saw the shrug with which her friend registered her willingness to humour, within reason, any that Kate might be afflicted with. She stumped softly away in her gum-boots, back to the courtyard gate, where she stopped and leisurely lit the oil-lantern she had brought with her, whistling.

"Good, Kate," said Colin gently. "If it comes off, good. If it doesn't, well, we'll go down and fight it out."

Kate, all her chest stiff with apprehension, saw Rosaleen appear quickly from the farmyard. At sight of Aminta she stopped as if shot. There was a moment's pause. Then she approached, and Kate heard her say with a cracked lightness:

"Aminta! Is it *that* late?"

"Late! I'm early this morning. We're threshing. Got a full day in front of us."

Aminta spoke, thank Heaven, in her usual leisurely and cheerful fashion. Kate's ears could not detect the slightest note of constraint that might have put Rosaleen on her guard. Blessed, obtuse Aminta, incapable of curiosity, almost incapable of surprise! Swinging her lantern in the centre of its wide circle of light, she moved towards the stable.

"One of the cows is sick," Kate heard her inventing in her loud, cheerful voice, "and we've got to have some fresh litter up, so I might as well take this last load. I've finished cutting, anyway."

The lantern light disappeared with the two girls. After a moment with a jingling of harness and a plodding of hoofs, they reappeared.

"Can I help you put the gee in?" said Rosaleen, still with that brittle, cracked imitation of liveliness in her voice.

"You can hold the lantern while I do up the buckles."

The two girls' figures converged upon the shaft, as though the precise doing-up of a harness buckle were the chief, the only care in both their minds. Aminta stood easily on her planted feet. But Rosaleen's little tense figure was all curved with impatience, from her feet to her stooped, stiffly-held head.

"Old Gid's in a foul temper this morning," said Aminta cheerfully, taking the reins and swinging herself up on to the cart. "That young man who's drawing the ruins and seems to be a friend of Kate's, broke into the cellar in the night looking for an underground passage, the silly ass, and broke the lock of the cellar door, and took a grating out of the cellar-wall, and heaven knows what and all. Gid is just gibbering with wrath, and Sister Maisie and I tremble and bolt when we hear him coming."

"What?" said Rosaleen in a cracked, hard voice. "Who? Colin Kemp? How do you know?"

"Well, because all the doors were open, for one thing. You know, Rosa, there's some silly legend about the entrance to a secret passage at Llanhalo, just rot, of course, and old Gid won't hear of it and I don't blame him, but these archaeologists will believe anything it seems to me, with apologies to your learned uncle—"

"But how do you know it was Colin Kemp broke in?" asked Rosaleen, in a voice that shook with harsh impatience.

"He left his gloves behind in the dairy. The cat's got in and licked the butter and drank the cream. Archaeology's all very well, but—"

The rest of Aminta's discourse was drowned in the creaking of wheels and axles as she turned her horse. Then:

"Good-bye, Rosa!" she called.

"Good-bye! Good-bye!" cried Rosaleen at the courtyard gate, in a strange, loud, empty tone. The cart disappeared behind the stable buildings. As soon as it had gone, Rosaleen jumped into activity and hurried towards the house. Before she could enter the door, however, the man Joe stopped her, coming hurriedly out.

"Rosa," he said, in a curt, stiff-lipped tone. "The papers are gone. That damned girl's got them. She must have taken them off Doug. Now, we *must* find her!"

It isn't the girl! Listen, Joe!" said Rosaleen, clutching the man's arm and speaking very quickly. "It isn't the girl! It's that blasted Kemp! He's been here!"

"What? How do—"

"Never mind how I know! I do! He's been here, and he knows everything, and *he's* got the papers, if anyone has! He's working for the Government, I believe, and the girl's working in with him. We ought to've jumped to it from the first. We've been had for suckers, all of us! Kemp's a dick, and he's been here all along, as well as the girl! The whole thing's a plant, if you ask me! We can't tackle him as well as the girl and the kids, even if he's still here! We must get out of this, quick!"

There was a short pause. Then the man said abruptly: "You're right, Rosa. We'd better bolt. I'll change the number plate. You get her started up."

"We'll make for the wilds, like you said. There's a chance, after all!"

"That's more like you, Rosa! Never say die!"

"I guess we can die without saying it, if we have to," said Rosaleen harshly.

The car lights went on. The soft throbbing of the engine drowned any further exchange of words. The door slammed. The car backed and turned, sending probing beams of light now here, now there, about the abandoned Veault, then with a long whining purr made its way up the field track towards the road. Kate held her breath and listened. But after the sound of the car had died away, she could still hear the distant, homely rumble of Aminta's wheels carrying the children back to safety.

She drew a long breath. She felt, listening to the receding rumble of those wheels, as she had felt sometimes at the end of a performance which had not been long enough in rehearsal, for which the stage was too large, in which she had had to act a leading part as well as make the most of the props and stage-manage the show, and which had yet, more by luck than management, arrived at a triumphant curtain-fall. Over the woods to the east a thin greenish light was stealing up into the sky. Kate's long, long breath without warning shook itself into three short ones, and to her surprise tears poured down her face.

As stage-manager and general factotum of a small repertory company, Kate was more accustomed to drying other people's happy or despondent tears than to shedding them herself. It was an agreeable sensation, for once, to be the object of somebody else's tender consolations.

Chapter Twenty-Three

"Old Gid's decided to forgive you," said Aminta to Colin. "He says he won't have archaeologists crawling about under his house, but he doesn't mind rat-catchers, that's only plain common-sense!"

Colin laughed. They were on their way to Sunnybank, where Sidney, already getting restless in the part of petted invalid, had prevailed on Mrs. Howells to let him come downstairs to tea and see some company. Kate was carrying Sidney's net, which she had been over to the Veault to retrieve from the police. Aminta had a small basket of duck eggs, for which Sidney's returning appetite had shown a wistful yearning, and Colin, who had just come back from London where he had been to interview an official at the Home Office, was carrying a partridge in a paper bag, an offering from Davis Pentrewer.

"Does Gid realise how he let Morrison exploit him, though?" asked Colin. "If your Gid hadn't hated archaeologists, Morrison would never have been able to clear out that bolt-hole for himself in the secret passage! Atkins himself could be trusted from the beginning not to make awkward investigations at his end of the passage. And by the time Morrison had finished working him up against archaeologists, he could be trusted to prevent anybody else investigating, either! So Morrison and his friends could clear a way from their end, and loosen the grating at the Llanhalo end, at their leisure, relying on our friend Atkins and his hatred of archaeologists to protect them from interference."

"That's not how *he* looks at it, I can tell you! He says he always knew archaeologists were a fishy lot and now everybody else knows it too."

"Don't tell him, but I thought he was the fishy one," said Kate. "I thought all that fuss about hating archaeologists and not letting anybody go into the cellar was very fishy indeed. I also thought he was in league with Major Humphries."

"Good Lord, Kate, if there's anything Gid hates worse than archaeologists, it's fox hunters."

"I know. But I thought, you see, that that was rather fishy, too. And they were both such character-parts! I suppose," added Kate, "it was the man called then, who stuck that piece of green tinfoil on to the door of Major Humphries car that afternoon. He'd just been quarrelling with Humphries, and no doubt it appealed to his sense of humour to send me off on that particular false scent. I suppose he took it off the door at Hymns Bank that night—I gave myself away rather when I saw it, and he must have realised what had startled me."

"Was it Sidney who stuck it there?"

"Yes. He says that when he realised the danger, and that they weren't going to let him go, he wanted to write something on a piece of paper and drop it, in the hope somebody would be able to track him. But he hadn't a pencil, and this piece of sticky toffee-paper in his pocket, was all he could think of. And that reminds me, Colin, I've been wondering all the time you've been away, what made you follow me to Llanhalo that night? *I* didn't leave even a bit of tinfoil for anybody to track me by!"

"Well, Kate, you remember Gwyn Lupton invited me down that night to see the putty mould he'd taken of the silver penny of Ceowulf?"

"Yes, and a Bible with pictures in it, and a thorn tree root not quite in the shape of a weasel."

"It was the silver penny of Ceowulf that put me on the track. I'd planned to go up to Hymns Bank late that night, so I had plenty of time to fill in, and I went to Gwyn Lupton's as late as I dared without risking finding him in bed. He'd just taken his boots off when I arrived, but was very pleased to see me, as Mrs. Gwyn had retired to bed early in a depressed state, with tooth-ache, and Gwyn, as he put it, 'felt the need to listen to the voice of a friend.' I needn't tell you it was I who did most of the listening! We sat by the fire and drank homebrewed cider out of a cask Gwyn had behind the door, and he discoursed about all sorts of things, and finally showed me his collection of curios. It was housed for safety under one of those enormous old-fashioned cheese-covers, which was a bit of a curio itself, according to Gwyn, having belonged once to Miss Gilliam's great-aunt at the Cefn, who used it in the old days for blanching rhubarb. Well, the little illustrated Bible, and the thorn-tree root, almost, but not quite, in the shape of a weasel, about fulfilled my expectations. But the putty mould didn't."

"Wasn't it clear?"

"Oh, as clear as the coin it was taken from, no doubt, which isn't saying much. But it just wasn't the mould of a silver penny of Ceowulf. It wasn't the mould of a Saxon coin at all. It was the mould of an English florin of William the Fourth, much defaced and corroded.

"Oh, poor, poor Gwyn!"

Colin protested:

"Poor Gwyn, indeed! Why poor Gwyn? He'd had five pounds given him for what was only worth the melting price of the silver! Lucky Gwyn! It puzzled me awfully, though. Morrison must have known perfectly well what the coin was. Why did he give Lupton five pounds for it? He couldn't possibly have wanted the coin. And what on earth made him tell you it was a silver penny of Ceowulf? I couldn't see any sense in it. Gwyn Lupton was obviously as pleased as Punch with his treasure and his acumen in taking it to the antiquary gentleman at the Veault, *he* had no doubt of its value. Well, I had a fairly long seance with Gwyn, who treated me once again to his views on the folly and wickedness of digging in tumuli, and afterwards I went up to Hymns Bank, where I had to wait about in hiding for a long time before our friend turned up. I think it was to be the last night at Hymns Bank, by the way, Kate. He was packing up and clearing everything away. Obviously your visit the night before had shaken their confidence in the isolation of Hymns Bank, and they weren't going to risk using that post any more. When I'd seen enough, I went back to Pentrewer. The matter of Gwyn Lupton's coin had gone right out of my head, but when I got back and saw the tumulus, I remembered it again. What the dickens was Morrison's game with that coin, I kept asking myself. It was only a little puzzle, but it nagged at me, somehow. What had buying this absurd coin to do with the treason going on at the Veault? *Had* it anything to do with it? What on earth made Morrison, who knew a reasonable amount about such things, first pay five pounds for an utterly worthless old coin, and then invent a yarn for your benefit about it being a silver penny of Ceowulf? Well, obviously, it seemed to me, he invented the yarn because he didn't want you to know that he had paid five pounds for a worthless coin. But why did he pay the five pounds?"

"Why, of course!" cried Kate, stopped by a sudden memory of her first meeting with Gwyn Lupton. "The skeleton in the cupboard!"

"I'd got back to Pentrewer, Mr. and Mrs. Davis had been in bed for hours, the fire was out, and I wanted a warm-up to think things over by. The kindling-wood's kept in the cupboard beside the fireplace. As I opened the cupboard door I remembered what you'd said about Gwyn Lupton being a carpenter and knowing all about the skeletons in the local cupboards. A carpenter, I thought, and a cupboard at the Veault with a skeleton in it. Something at the Veault that a carpenter who'd been working there might have discovered, and that Morrison might want kept quiet. Something in a cupboard, something behind a door or a wall, something secret, a secret storeroom—staircase-passage—Well, after all, there was supposed to be a secret passage at Llanhalo, not a quarter-of-a-mile away! Suppose there was a secret passage at the Veault, too—even the other end of the same passage? Suppose the inquisitive Gwyn Lupton in the course of his repairs at the Veault had come across something unusual in the structure of the house—a sliding panel, or a dropping stair, or a cavity in a wall? And suppose Morrison knew of this old secret place, and were using it for purposes of his own? Mightn't Morrison have shut Gwyn Lupton's mouth in the obvious way? I give you five pounds for your old coin, and live pounds each for as many more as you can find: you keep quiet about this tricky piece of carpentry in my house, there's a good chap: I don't want a lot of curious visitors disturbing us here, this is a creche, not a showplace: and anyway, it's only some old priest's hidey-hole, lots of old houses have them! I could easily imagine Morrison flattering Gwyn Lupton into silence and clinching the bargain by buying his corroded florin off him for some staggering sum. And then, of course, as soon as I thought of the Llanhalo passage, I thought of you, Kate."

"Why of me?"

"I knew you'd made up your mind to look for the secret passage, and I knew my warning words hadn't made any impression on you. I hadn't worried much as long as I felt pretty sure there wasn't any secret passage to speak of—I thought you were in for an unpleasant scene with our friend Atkins, but nothing worse. But now that I was beginning to there *was* a secret passage, after all, and that it might lead straight into the arms of Morrison and Company—well, Katy, you can imagine my feelings!"

Kate said, all the more lightly because the seriousness of Colin's tone had touched her heart:

"Imagine mine when I had heard you turning the handle of the cellar door, and thought you were the enemy close on my heels! Ah, but it made up for it, Colin, when you suddenly materialised out of space beside me when I was struggling with Ellida! I was never so glad to see anyone in all my life, as I was to see Colin then! Unless it was to see *you*, Aminta, a little later on—the one person in the world who could be useful at that moment, the one person in the world who could be trusted not to ask questions and not to be surprised!"

Aminta protested:

"It's not much use asking questions when a person hisses 'Don't speak!' at you as soon as you open your mouth. And I *was* a bit surprised, as a matter of fact, when Rosaleen suddenly came towards me flourishing a pistol."

"But did she—"

"Yes. She whisked it away again as soon as she saw who I was. But I'd seen it. I thought then there must be *something* up," said Aminta.

Kate turned and looked at her friend with a new respect.

"Do you mean to say that when you went through that piece with Rosaleen about wanting litter for a sick cow, and about Colin breaking into the cellar, you knew she'd got a pistol in her hand?"

"It was in her pocket, then," said the literal-minded Aminta.

"And you didn't so much as stammer or flick an eyelash?"

"Why should I?"

"Aminta, I'd no idea you were such an actress!"

Aminta looked vague, as if she had no idea she was, either, and changed the subject, for it bored her to talk about herself.

"It was queer how I liked Rosaleen... You liked her, too, Kate."

"Not queer at all. *She* was an actress, if you like! You liked the act she put on, you didn't like her."

"I'm glad she was caught, anyway. I wonder what'll happen to her, Kate, and to Mrs. Morrison and Joe?"

It was Colin who answered gravely:

"I doubt if you'll know, for certain, until after the war is over. There may be a little paragraph in the papers—'Three spies were executed in such and such a prison on such and such a date... But spies aren't tried in public in wartime."

A little grim silence fell. Aminta broke it on a more practical note:

"Fancy having all those repairs done at the Veault, and all that decorating, all those workmen about for months putting in baths and lavatories and things, for children who all the time never existed!"

"The children existed all right," said Colin, "though, of course, there was never any intention that they should exist at the Veault! But the Morrisons were actually in touch with the W.V.S. about real evacuee babies. They'd decided to paint themselves as rich American philanthropists, and they did it thoroughly and used the best paint. And remember, too, those builders and their repairs were very useful. They made a great excuse for delay."

"Yes, where there's babies there has to be plumbing," quoted Kate. "And if our dilatory English builders took a long while to put it in, so much the better, I suppose."

"The Morrisons had calculated our dilatory builders, and their own dilatory orders, would hold up the plumbing until Hitler's troop-carrying planes landed on Radnor Forest, among other places," said Colin. "By then, they calculated, evacuation schemes wouldn't be what they were and needn't trouble them! In fact, they expected to be busy before now evacuating themselves to wherever fifth-columnists could be most useful. But something went wrong with the programme, and the expected invasion was postponed. Its latest postponement, by the way, which was Rosaleen's and Joe's last forlorn hope, was until the day before yesterday."

"I didn't notice anything then," said Aminta. "Did you, Kate?"

"The day before yesterday passed quite peacefully in Hastry," agreed Kate. "A telegram miles long from Sidney's great-aunt in London was our only excitement. She wired to explain that she couldn't possibly leave London at the moment, because Pixie— that's another of her precious cats—has followed Bobbie's example and run away from home, and she's distracted, and wants Sidney to return to London as soon as he's fit to travel. The wire was reply-paid, and Sidney wired back: *'Staying here till Dad comes, good luck to Pixie'*: We haven't had an answer to that yet."

"And I suppose, Kate," said Colin, as they went up the steep steps of Mrs. Howells's front garden, "you feel an urgent call now to go back to London and look for the old lady's cats for her?"

"No, I *don't!*" protested Kate. "They're probably having the time of their lives in the wide open space-of Bayswater, posing as poor bombed cats on every charitable window-sill. I shan't be going back to London for a long while, I expect, Colin. I've got a job."

"Good for you, Kate! What sort of job?"

"I've been offered the lead in a piece called 'Till the Cows Come Home'."

"Where's it coming on?"

"Oh, round about here. I've joined the Radnorshire branch of the Women's Land Army."

"Good!" said Aminta gladly. "I *knew* my letters'd fetch you, Kate!"

She spoke with the satisfaction of a recruiting-sergeant who has done a good bit of work, and Kate was almost moved to retort that, on the contrary, her letters had nearly sent Kate flying into the A.T.S. But since Aminta liked her own simple explanations, and since Kate liked Aminta, she contented herself with saying:

"It wasn't only your letters, Aminta. I think the way your milk cans clinked across the yard in the dark the other morning had something to do with it, too. There's more drama in country life than I thought."

"But no more rescue-dramas, please, Kate," said Colin, "because I'm joining up, and I shan't be here to rescue the rescuer."

"No, this is going to be a simple comedy of rural life. And I'm afraid," said Kate, a little ruefully, "it's going to have rather a long run!"

THE END